CONVOCO ! EDITION 2010

CORINNE MICHAELA FLICK (HRSG.)

STAATSFINANZIERUNG UND WIRTSCHAFTS-FINANZIERUNG AM SCHEIDEWEG

CONVOCO ! EDITION

1. Auflage 2010

Umschlagmotiv: Camao AG, München
Gesamtherstellung: Laura J Gerlach, Frankfurt
Satz: psb, Berlin
Druck und Bindung: CPI – Ebner & Spiegel, Ulm
Printed in Germany
Vertrieb durch die Frankfurter Verlagsanstalt GmbH
ISBN: 978-3-627-10001-8

INHALT

RESÜMEE

DR. CORINNE MICHAELA FLICK

EINFÜHRUNG

Liebe Convoco-Freunde,

zu unserem diesjährigen Thema »Staatsfinanzierung und Wirtschaftsfinanzierung am Scheideweg« möchte ich Ihnen mit der nachfolgenden kurzen Darstellung der einzelnen Gedanken und Ansätze eine Karte an die Hand geben, wie Sie mit den Texten umgehen können, wo Sie Ihren persönlichen Ansatzpunkt finden.

In unserer immer komplexer werdenden Welt wird dieses »Mapping« jeden Tag wichtiger, denn es geht nicht nur um das Wissen an sich, sondern um eine Orientierung, wie man mit dem Wissen umgeht, wo man es findet und, ganz wichtig: wie man es zu einem logischen Ganzen zusammenfügt.

Convoco (lat.) heißt »ich rufe zusammen«. Der Ruf gilt dem gemeinsamen Nachdenken. Er gilt aber auch der Forderung, gemeinsam Lösungen zu erarbeiten und auch Lösungsansätzen Gehör zu verleihen. Gleichzeitig versucht Convoco, ein Thema aus verschiedenen Perspektiven zu beleuchten und zu »kartographieren«.

Die Ereignisse der letzten Jahre haben gezeigt, wie sehr unsere vernetzte Welt ein gemeinsames Schicksal teilt. Heute steht eindeutig fest: In einer globalisierten Welt müssen alle lernen, die Perspektive der anderen mit einzubeziehen. Das *bonum commune* Ciceros und Cäsars ist auch für das Zusammenleben von Staaten unabdingbar. Thomas Jeffersons *pursuit of happiness* führt nur dann zum Glück, wenn es das Wohlergehen der Anderen – auch der anderen Staaten – mit einschließt. Die Verantwortung für die Gemeinschaft kommt ebenfalls im Gedanken des englischen Commonwealth, des Gemeinwohls zum Ausdruck. Und an dieser Verantwortung, denke ich, hat es in den Jahren vor der Krise gemangelt.

Der Zusammenbruch des Marktes für problematische Hypotheken (»subprime mortgages«) löste eine Finanzmarktkrise aus, die schließlich die ganze westliche Welt erfasste. Das Kollabieren einzelner Institute bzw. die Gefahr des möglichen Kollabierens führte auch zu negativen Folgen in der Realwirtschaft, obwohl diese selbst gesund war und sich nicht in Bedrängnis befand. Der Grund war eine Kreditunterversorgung. Man kann also sagen, dass das so genannte systemische Risiko zu einer Krise in Finanz und Wirtschaft führte.

Prof. Otmar Issing legt dar, wie es so weit kommen konnte und schlägt gleichzeitig Lösungen für die Zukunft vor. So möchte er eine effektive ex-ante-Abgabe einführen mit zwei Zielen: Erstens die sozialen Kosten, die durch systemische

Risiken entstehen, auf der Ebene individueller Finanzinstitute zu internalisieren und zweitens, ausreichend Mittel zu sammeln, damit die Aufsichtsbehörden im Falle von Finanzkrisen Stützungsmaßnahmen durchführen können.

Prof. Roland Berger gibt in sieben Thesen aktuelle wirtschaftliche Aspekte zum Thema Staatsverschuldung und Staatsinsolvenz. Um zu verhindern, dass unsere Staaten sich in Zukunft weiterhin in zu hohem Maße verschulden, fordert Prof. Berger eine koordinierte Wirtschafts- und Fiskalpolitik innerhalb der europäischen Staatengemeinschaft und auch einen neu gefassten Stabilitätspakt innerhalb der Eurozone.

Auch Sir Howard Davies glaubt, dass die EWU ohne Strukturveränderungen nicht überleben kann. Europas Wirtschafts- und Währungsunion – »unfinished business?«, dieser Frage geht er in seinem Beitrag nach. Streng betrachtet stehen die Länder der Eurozone vor der Alternative einer Vertiefung der europäischen Zusammenarbeit oder der Preisgabe des Euro. Die Asymmetrie zwischen der vollständigen ökonomischen und der unvollständigen politischen Einigung Europas führt zu unerwünschten Folgen, wie wir sie erlebt haben und erleben.

Prof. Stefan Korioth richtet sein Augenmerk darauf, ob es auf Dauer einen stabilen Währungsverbund ohne Ausgleichsmechanismen zwischen den Mitgliedstaaten geben kann, und überlegt dann die Frage, ob die Euro-Rettungsschirme überhaupt rechtmäßig sind. Er kommt zu dem Schluss, dass sie nicht von der verfassungsrechtlich gebilligten Übertragung von Hoheitsrechten, wie sie in den geltenden Verträgen niedergelegt ist, abgedeckt sind.

Die Ursachen für das Versagen des Stabilitäts- und Wachstumspakts in Europa sieht Prof. Kai Konrad nicht in den Regeln des Paktes selbst, sondern in Schwächen des privaten Finanzmarktsystems. In seinem Aufsatz deutet er die Ist-Situation der Bankenwelt. Für ihn liegt hier das Problem und damit gleichzeitig der Ansatz zu seiner Lösung. Er fordert Reformen auf den Finanzmärkten und nicht die Reform des Stabilitäts-und Wachstumspakts.

Dass Staaten pleite gehen können, hat die Geschichte gezeigt, wenn es hier auch einen gravierenden Unterschied zur Insolvenz von Unternehmen gibt: Anders als finanziell in Not geratene Unternehmen existieren Staaten weiter. Prof. Christoph Paulus entwickelt für den Staatsbankrott ein rechtliches Instrument. Er plädiert für ein *Resolvenzrecht* im Falle der Insolvenz. Ein solches geordnetes Verfahren ist in seinen Augen möglich, sinnvoll und letztendlich unumgänglich: Insolvenzrecht als Hilfestellung zur Rettung. In der Entwicklung eines solchen könnte Europa Vorreiter sein.

Nach der Frage der Ursachen der Finanzmarktkrise und nach der Überlegung, wo Europa in seiner Entwicklung steht, geht es um den Umgang mit zu hohen Staatsschulden.

Staatsentschuldung durch Wirtschaftswachstum propagiert Prof. Burkhard Schwenker. Seine Sicht auf Europa und Deutschland ist positiv. Die industrielle Kompetenz Europas erkennt er als entscheidend, um Wirtschaftswachstum zu erreichen. Dieses ist für ihn immer noch der beste Weg aus der Krise. Als ausschlaggebend beurteilt er auch das Management in Europa, das sich grundsätzlich von dem amerikanischen unterscheidet. Die spezifisch europäische Komponente in der Führung von Unternehmen ergibt sich aus der Tatsache, dass Europa durch eine Handwerkskultur geprägt ist, die den Wunsch hat, etwas Dauerhaftes, Bleibendes zu schaffen. In dieser langfristigen Orientierung, die den kulturellen Unterschied zu Amerika, das durch eine Kaufmannskultur geprägt ist, ausmacht, sieht Burkhard Schwenker die große Chance für Europa.

Und zur Rückbesinnung auf die Freiheit vom Staat als Grundlage moderner Staatlichkeit ermahnt Prof. Paul Kirchhof. Denn darin liegt das Wesen unserer Demokratie. Diese Freiheit sollten wir nicht leichtfertig aufs Spiel setzen. Sie macht unser Leben in unserem Staat aus. Denken wir an Thomas Jefferson, der sagte: »A government big enough to give you everything you want, is also strong enough to take everything from you.« In dem Maß, wie der Bürger vom Staat nimmt, in dem Maß gibt er einen Teil seiner Freiheitsrechte ab. Wir sollten unsere Freiheitsrechte nicht zu gering achten, sondern sie verteidigen.

Convoco will anregen, Verantwortung zu übernehmen. Dass wir an einem Scheideweg stehen, ist nicht zu übersehen.

Unsere Welt wird immer globaler. Das ist wahrscheinlich unsere größte Herausforderung. Der Begriff »global« existiert erst seit gut 25 Jahren, steht aber heute bei jährlich 700 Veröffentlichungen im Titel. Die globale Welt – was wie eine Tautologie klingt – war immer da, aber sie war nicht präsent. Nun ist sie es. Am Beispiel der Finanzkrise ist uns diese Präsenz in unangenehmer Weise auch bewusst geworden. Es ist notwendig, Entscheidungen zu treffen. Jetzt besteht dazu die Chance. Mit diesen Entscheidungen stellen wir die Weichen für die nachfolgenden Generationen. Ihnen sollte die Freiheit der Gestaltung erhalten bleiben. Diese Freiheit ist Voraussetzung für Kreativität, für neue Ideen und Lösungen. Darauf hat jede einzelne Generation einen Anspruch. Wir haben nicht das Recht, diesen Gestaltungsfreiraum zu beschneiden. Henning Ritter* formuliert es so: »Denn in der Geschichte haften Kinder für ihre Eltern.«

Es macht mich froh, mit meiner Initiative einen Beitrag leisten zu können, unseren Kindern diese Freiheit zu erhalten. Ich danke allen Teilnehmern und Autoren für ihre Unterstützung, für ihre Gedanken, Meinungen und Beiträge. In diesem Zusammenwirken liegt die Kraft zu initiieren, zu

* Henning Ritter, Notizhefte. Berlin Verlag, Berlin 2010

verändern und zu bewegen. Mein Dank gilt auch allen, die als Zuhörer und Zuschauer kritisch die Gedanken aufnehmen, weitertragen und fortführen.

Mit dieser Veröffentlichung liegt der dritte Band der Convoco Edition vor: *Die Erneuerung des Finanzstaats* (2008) – *Der demographische Wandel* (2009) – und nun *Staats- und Wirtschaftsfinanzierung am Scheideweg* (2010) bilden die Reihe.

Ich freue mich, dass es Convoco gelungen ist, wichtige Themen zum richtigen Zeitpunkt behandelt und dadurch transparent gemacht zu haben. Aus dem Zusammenkommen der einzelnen Aspekte ergibt sich das Bild unserer heutigen vielschichtigen Welt – nicht mehr vergleichbar mit dem eindeutigen *imago mundi*. Dieser Komplexität möchte Convoco Rechnung tragen. Darin liegt die Herausforderung unserer Zeit.

Corinne Flick

Dr. Corinne Michaela Flick, im Oktober 2010

LECTURES

SIR HOWARD DAVIES

ECONOMIC AND MONETARY UNION IN EUROPE: UNFINISHED BUSINESS

My title this evening is taken from a statement by Joaquin Almunia, then European Commissioner for Economic and Monetary Affairs, in October 2008 at a conference in Washington to celebrate the Euro's 10th birthday. He said then »the tenth anniversary of the introduction of the Euro is characterised by deep crisis. The European Commission's argument that we need to do more work on the single currency is now evident. EMU is not finished. It is unfinished business. It needs to be further developed«.[1]

The truth of that contention has been amply demonstrated in the last few weeks, as the Greek debt crisis has played out. This has not, to put matters as delicately as I can, been Europe's finest hour. Although the nature of the problem was well understood, and the market risks were identified, it has proved extraordinarily difficult to reach any agreement which would be useful to the Greeks or others. What has been agreed was settled at five minutes to midnight. There has been much criticism, as a result, of Greek governments, both past and present, of German politicians, of the leadership at the European Central Bank, and indeed of the lack of leadership of the European Union as a whole.

The episode has generated much adverse publicity for Europe around the world. In the last month I have been to

China, Hong Kong, India, Singapore and the United States and everywhere I have been asked, with some puzzlement, about why the nettle was not grasped earlier. The episode has been used to demonstrate that, once again, Europe cannot solve its own problems. The attitude was well summarised in a headline in the *New York Times* two weeks ago: »As Greek drama plays out, where is Europe?«.

It is not my aim this evening to offer a blow-by-blow analysis of the crisis, or to take part in this blame game in relation to individuals. All of the people concerned are well qualified for, and well rehearsed in, the parts they play. They have all been attempting to resolve the problem, and to succeed in a way which maintains the integrity of the monetary union. The fact that they have found it difficult to do so powerfully suggests that there is a flaw in the structures within which they operate. It seems obvious, therefore, that if the Greek crisis is not to spread to the other countries we unflatteringly call the PIGS we need to analyse these structural flaws quite carefully and seek a solution for them. This is a more useful endeavour than trying to blame the rating agencies, who in this case, I believe, have simply been – possibly rather late – crystallising a general view of the unsustainability of Greek finances without some external intervention.

But is it appropriate at all for an Englishman to comment on these matters? We are on the sidelines, and highly likely to remain so. Indeed *The Economist*, in an amusing redrawing of the map of Europe, has repositioned us alongside Portugal, disappearing off into the mid-Atlantic.

Certainly, we can say that there is little or no chance of the UK seeking to become a member of the Euro area in the foreseeable future, whatever the outcome of the current crisis. I am as certain as I can be that we will not be members in my lifetime – and I am feeling quite well. Indeed, our membership has become even less likely as a result of the Greek tragedy. Our Liberal Democrat party was in theory supportive of UK membership of the Euro, but they rapidly changed that position when challenged in the election campaign.

I am one of very few people in the UK who has been prepared to say in public that he is in favour of Euro membership, which in London is »the love that dare not speak its name«. Even I have begun to entertain some doubts in the light of recent events, but I speak as a commentator who wishes this project to succeed. I also speak against the background of some research I have carried out over the last two years on central banking, and particularly on the construction and constitution of the European system of central banks. That has just been published – indeed the publication date is Wednesday of this week – in a book called »Banking on the Future: The Fall and Rise of Central Banking«.

The big question I will attempt to answer this evening is »can EMU survive without structural changes and, if not, what should those changes be?«

Taking a step back first, we should recall that there are those who have always maintained that the monetary union was ill designed. One disinterested observer said at the start »I believe that the European single currency is bound to fail, economically, politically, and indeed socially, although the timing, occasion and full consequences are all necessarily unclear«. That was Margaret Thatcher.[2]

But we might also recall that in 1991 Helmut Kohl said »It cannot be repeated often enough. Political union is the indispensable counterpart to economic and monetary union. Recent history, and not just that of Germany, teaches us that the idea of sustaining economic and monetary union over time without political union is a fallacy«.[3]

It is striking that many commentators on recent events have tended to see in them confirmation of positions they have long held. So we have heard many commentators in the UK produce various versions of »I told you so«, explaining that the Greek problem was a crisis waiting to happen, and that a »one size fits all« monetary policy could never possibly work for such a diverse economic area. This is called ›Schadenfreude‹, I understand, though we don't have a word for such a disgraceful emotion in English. There has been much self congratulation about our decision to stay outside. Indeed in the last days of the campaign Gordon Brown attempted to turn that into a strong point in his favour.

It is not only British commentators who have found their prejudices confirmed. The French have for some time argued that there needs to be an economic government in Europe as a counterweight to the European monetary authority in the ECB – an argument which has not typically held much appeal for German leaders. Dominique Strauss-Khan has once again said »I know of no country that has a currency, but with no finance minister in charge of that currency … we have a very strong central bank but in front of that no real person in charge of the economy … it is very difficult to make decisions without a centralised power«.[4]

A more typical German view – I recognise that there has not been simply one German view in this crisis – came from Otmar Issing. His call has been for a return to the rules, which were an essential element in the construction of EMU at the outset. »Lax monitoring and compromises when it comes to observing implementation of rules have to stop. EMU is a club of states with firm rules accepted by entrants. These rules must not be changed ex post«.[5]

Those firm injunctions appeared in the *Financial Times* under the headline »Europe cannot afford to rescue Greece«. We know, of course, that many Germans, and indeed other economies around Europe, believed that the rules were bent at the outset to admit Greece, and indeed other countries like Italy and Belgium.

I could recall that the Stability and Growth Pact was abandoned when Germany failed to meet its strict conditions, and that on its 2009 performance Germany would not qualify for entry to EMU itself. I am speaking in Germany so I will not make those points.

The crisis has been an opportunity for the restatement of long held views. But it has also been a moment when some interesting rethinking has been underway, in an attempt to identify ways in which the construction of the monetary union might be made more robust. In an attempt to make these arguments easier to follow, I suggest there are six different areas on which we might focus our attention. Some of them are relatively uncontroversial, though that does not necessarily mean they are easy. Others take us into far more disputed territory. I begin with fiscal discipline.

1. Fiscal discipline

There is little doubt that tighter fiscal discipline within the Eurozone, and more effective monitoring of fiscal positions, is going to be needed in future, at the very minimum. We cannot possibly imagine a repeat of the experience of the last few years during which Greece reported deficits to the

European Commission which turned out to be significantly understated.

It is clear that the European Commission needs much stronger auditing powers, as indeed it has itself proposed.[6] The Commission proposal envisages in depth methodological visits to member states by Eurostat, which go beyond the mere checking of compliance with statistical standards. Eurostat would have access to far more raw data than has been the case in the past.

That is now rather uncontroversial, in the light of the Greek experience, though it has been resisted in the past. But it will not be effective unless there is a renewed commitment to a new Stability and Growth Pact (SGP). As we know, that pact was sidelined in 2003. It needs to be reinstated in some form. Of course the terms of the old pact are extremely difficult for countries to meet at present. As I have pointed out, even Germany does not do so. We remain in a post crisis situation, so that is not unexpected. But the question of how quickly countries should return to the terms of the pact, and indeed whether those terms need to be revised in the light of experience, is an open one. There is understandable nervousness about fiscal tightening at a time when the recovery is hardly assured in many places. The numbers involved for some EU countries are enormous, with the UK in as serious a position as anyone. Tightening is now unavoidable where debt is unaffordable, as in Greece, but may be unwise elsewhere. So there is a big task ahead for Europe's finance ministers, which they did not resolve over the week-end. What we now have is a series of specific conditional packages, but no new SGP.

But will it be enough just to reinstate the pact? Otmar Issing thinks so. He has argued that »the Stability and Growth Pact contains the rules that are necessary for monetary union to function. There is no need for co-ordination of macroeconomic policy to go any further than this«.[7] Others disagree, and think there are more fundamental problems to address. The most important one is competition. That was not dealt with at all yesterday, though arguably it is what the problem is all about.

2. Competitiveness

One remarkable, and perhaps surprising feature of the evolution of the Euro area over its first decade has been the changes in real exchange rates and competitiveness. Germany, which may have joined at an overvalued exchange rate, has improved its relative labour unit costs year on year. Italy, Spain and Portugal have done the reverse, failing to control domestic costs or to enhance productivity. With hindsight, it seems that they regarded Euro membership as a excuse no longer to worry about external competitiveness. These changes have produced predictable consequences in very different relative export performance, country by country.

One can see that declining competitiveness and poor export performance go hand in hand. In the case of Greece, competitiveness has declined by 5 % or so. So arguably the Greek problem is largely a fiscal policy issue, rather than one of competitiveness. But in the case of Spain, Italy and Portugal the position is really rather different. In an interesting Bruegel policy brief paper recently, Marzinotto, Pisani-Ferry and Sapir point out that there are significant differences between Greece and Spain. Their paper »Two Crises, Two Responses«[8] argues that Spain's problem originated in a domestic credit boom. So while it was assumed when the Euro was constructed that the main threats would come from undisciplined fiscal policy, we can see that there are other potential issues too. Spain could well have remained in compliance with the Stability and Growth Pact but still had a problem.

What is the answer to that, apart from exhortation? Issing's view is that the solution lies in »creating the necessary flexibility in markets, above all the labour market«. The theory may be correct, but there has so far been little sign that Spain is prepared to follow that prescription. So what does the EU do in response, apart from hoping and praying?

Sebastian Dullien and Daniela Schwarzer believe that excessive external imbalances also pose a serious danger to the stability of the European Monetary Union, and think these deficits also need to be monitored at the European level to mitigate risks as early as possible. When the EMU was constructed, it was generally assumed that the only deficit that then mattered was the external deficit of the Euro area as a whole. Dullien and Schwarzer argue that that is not correct and that the EMU needs an »external stability pact« to complement the existing agreements.[9] On this analysis there should be agreed thresholds for external balances. They recommend that the Pact would need to stipulate that no Eurozone country may have a current account imbalance of more than 3 % of GDP, either as a deficit or as a surplus. Exceeding either threshold would initially result in a warning, followed by the determination of appropriate measures to bring the imbalance down.

I can understand the logic behind this proposal. A similar argument, though one which does not quite reach the same conclusion, has been advanced by Daniel Gros and Thomas Mayer.[10] They point out that the vulnerability of different euro area countries can come from different sources. One of those sources will be the external balance, in particular what they describe as »the need for external finance and the competitive position as an indicator of the ability to service external debt«. So they have devised a Euro-area vulnerability index. You can see from their calculation that Greece scores highest, largely driven by its fiscal position. Portugal, second in this inverted league table, finds itself vulnerable largely because of its current account and net national savings position. So external balances and competitiveness are very significant indicators. But I have to wonder whether an external stability pact is feasible. Is Germany ready to be told by the European Commission to reduce its trade surplus? German politicians reacted rather sharply to suggestions along these lines from Christine Lagarde of France.

More importantly, is this not a rather heavy-handed attempt to manipulate the location of economic activity across Europe? Within an economic area as diverse as the EMU, there will be significant changes in relative competitiveness and I cannot see that the European Commission is powerful enough to resist them. That said, one crucial lesson of the last decade is that the countries who see a continued, relentless decline in their competitiveness will pay the price one day. It is for national governments, in my view, to respond, although the Commission, and perhaps the ECB, could be more forthright and outspoken in their commentary on these trends.

So the focus of this week-end amendments was on fiscal problems, but they are not the fundamental issues for Spain and Portugal.

3. European Monetary Fund

Gros and Mayer, who note that vulnerability can arise either from fiscal indiscipline or from a decline in competitiveness, argued for a European Monetary Fund (cf. Ref 10) in a paper published in February of this year. Their views were echoed in an article in the *Financial Times* by Wolfgang Schäuble called »Why Europe's monetary union faces its biggest crisis«.[11] Schäuble's argument was that emergency liquidity assistance might be made available from a European Monetary Fund »in the case of emergencies that present a threat to the financial stability of the whole Euro area«.

Gros and Mayer argue the case slightly differently. They note that when imbalances, whether fiscal or external, arise, countries may well need to undergo painful adjustments if their public debt position is to become sustainable again. But given the intense pressures from financial markets, and we have seen a vivid illustration of that recently, »it is likely that in some cases a tough fiscal adjustment programme ... might not be enough to avoid a ›sudden stop‹ of necessary external funding of the public sector«. That is clearly what happened to Greece two weeks ago. They discuss whether it should be for the EU or the IMF to handle the problem. That discussion clearly went on, perhaps in a dysfunctional way, within the Chancelleries of Europe, over the winter. Gros and Mayer describe the dilemma well, and think it could be avoided by creating an EMF. They acknowledge that some may object to the scheme, on the grounds that it violates the no-bailout provision of the Maastricht Treaty. »However, we would argue that our proposal is actually the only way to make the no bail-out rule credible ... The drafters of the Maastricht Treaty had failed to appreciate that, in a context of fragile financial markets, the real danger of a financial meltdown makes a ›pure‹ no-bail-out response unrealistic«.

Willem Buiter, formerly of the LSE and now at Citigroup, has sketched out some more details of how a European Monetary Fund might be set up.[12] He thinks it would not require a Treaty amendment and could be set up under the Enhanced Cooperation provisions in the Treaty of Lisbon. Subscriptions to the fund would be in proportion to member states' equity stakes in the ECB. The amount committed would have to be significant, he estimates – 2 trillion, but the amount paid in could be much smaller than that, perhaps 10 %, as long as the body managing the fund have the power to call committed money on demand. The Board would consist of representatives of member states, of the Commission and of the ECB. Germany would provide more than a quarter of the needed finance.

Have we now got this? Not really. The Stabilisation Fund is a Special Purpose Vehicle for 3 years, not a permanent feature. I think it will be necessary to make it permanent.

Another proposal, which has also been debated recently, is that the Euro area should issue bonds backed by all its governments. There is some element of that in what was agreed. Jacques Delpla and Jakob von Weizsäcker for the Bruegel Institute issued a paper last week proposing an ingenious scheme whereby EU countries might pool their obligations and issue so-called ›Blue Bonds‹ which would be collectively backed. Each member would be entitled to issue Blue Bonds up to the value of 60 percent of GDP. If they wished to borrow more, they would issue ›Red Bonds‹ which would be junior, nationally backed debt.[13]

I say this is ingenious, but it may be too ingenious for its own good. I doubt if it would reduce overall borrowing costs, as the authors suggest. Different countries are in different historical debt positions. Then there is the politiclal difficulty of persuading tax payers to back bonds in other countries. I doubt if the idea will find favour.

But there are other areas where it may be that enhanced European machinery is necessary. That is particularly true in relation to the Financial System. The broader financial crisis has demonstrated weaknesses in the way Europe's single financial market operates, weaknesses which need attention. Here we are talking about issues which could affect the UK directly, although the arguments apply with particular force within the Euro-zone.

This is perhaps less urgent than the Stabilisation Fund. But we know that the fiscal problem can quickly bounce back to the Bank. And some of them are still fragile.

4. Financial Regulation

The Icelandic banking problem, in particular, demonstrated a flaw at the heart of the single financial market. Icelandic banks – and the European Economic Area, rather than the Euro area is the relevant jurisdiction here – were supervised by the Icelandic authorities, and used the provisions of the Single Market to establish branches and take deposits in other member states. In those member states neither the liquidity nor the solvency of the branches was under the authority of the local regulators. When the branches collapsed, it became clear that the Icelandic authorities were unable to back them effectively, and taxpayers in the Netherlands and in the UK had to step in. The eventual cost-sharing arrangements between the host countries and the home country have yet to be resolved, and of course have become matters of high politics in Iceland.

This problem, and others, were put in the hands of Jacques de Larosière, always a good place to go when you have an intractable issue to resolve. De Larosière produced a report[14] which made a number of important recommendations, most of which have been broadly accepted by the Council of Ministers – albeit with some reluctance in the case of the UK. De Larosière recommended a new European Financial Stability Board, chaired by the President of the ECB, which should map well into the strengthened Global Financial Stability Board under the G20. He also recommended that the old Committee of Regulators should become authorities, with their own staff etc. These authorities, however, would be set up within the existing legal framework, and it may be argued that they are hardly authorities in the proper sense of the term. Their ability to direct national regulators is very limited indeed.

This was an artful construction, and may well have been the best that could have been done in the political circumstances of the time. There remains little appetite for new constitutional measures in Europe, given the difficulty of getting the Lisbon Treaty through. But is it enough? My own answer to that question is no, and that in due course we will need to move to a more centralised European regulatory system, with a European Financial Authority to oversee and stand behind pan – European banks, in particular. But how effective would that regulator be if it was not linked to any mechanism to recapitalise or provide financial support to banks in difficulty? Here again the Greek case is relevant. It is clear that at present Greek banks may only secure funding from the ECB. And if there were to be any kind of haircut on Greek debt, an outcome which can be by no means excluded, they may well find themselves insolvent. For that reason, Buiter argues that in addition to a European monetary fund we need central funds to recapitalise systemically important cross-border financial institutions, either to allow them to continue operating or to wind up or liquidate them without unnecessary social costs (cf. Ref 12)

Buiter calls this a Financial Institution Recapitalisation Fund. It differs from the ECB in that it effectively has a call on tax payers, which the ECB does not. Buiter thinks that the EMF and the FIRF could be separate institutions or could be merged, and that this is ›the minimal fiscal Europe‹ which is politically and economically necessary. The Bruegel group has proposed something similar. They have termed it a European Resolution Fund, on the model of the authority which is currently under discussion in the US in the financial regulatory reform bill now in Congress.

This idea also raises very significant political questions. It opens up the possibility that taxpayers in country A are supporting banks in country B. But perhaps, in the unusual circumstances of a financial crisis which we are currently living through, that is a better option than any of the available alternatives. Certainly there is a strong collective interest in Europe in maintaining the integrity of the Economic and Monetary Union, and that may be the price that has to be paid. I believe, therefore, that some kind of European resolution authority ought also to be on the Council of Ministers' agenda.

5. Fiscal Transfers

Some would argue, though, that even this is not enough, and that the real lesson of the crisis is that Europe needs a much more centralised fiscal policy, and the ability to generate significant fiscal transfers from one member state to another. How powerful is that argument?

The idea that a single currency would need a coordinated fiscal policy is not a new one. Indeed the MacDougall report in 1977 argued that in the context of a monetary union a budget of up to 25 percent of European Union GDP would be needed at the centre to cope with stabilisation, and to offset economic differentials between countries. But in the intervening 30 years there has been little political appetite for a move in that direction, and the EU budget remains at only around 1.5 percent of GDP.

Some economists have continued to argue that if autonomy over monetary policy is conceded to a central institution, alternative adjustment mechanisms to cope with asymmetric shocks are necessary. The experience of the first decade of monetary union has shown that the alternative of greater economic flexibility, in the form of labour mobility or wage adjustments, has not been working effectively. Indeed, as we have seen, wage flexibility in Germany has delivered changes in relative hourly labour costs and competitiveness which are an important part of the reason for the crisis we are in.

This has led some economists to argue that if the eurozone is to survive, there will be a need for more central funds to promote economic stabilisation. One proposition is that there should be some degree of basic unemployment insurance funded at European level. That would assist the adjustment mechanisms of countries whose competitiveness has declined, as in Spain, and where unemployment is very high – 20 percent – and putting enormous pressure on domestic budgets. There are arguments, too, for more centralized corporation taxes.

Issing strongly disagrees with these arguments. In his view, the Stability and Growth Pact is all that is necessary to make the EMU work well. And it is perhaps the existence of these grander schemes of European fiscal integration which creates suspicion of the motives of those who argue for some form of European economic governance to match the central monetary policy. After all, it is fairly clear in which direction these fiscal transfers would go. From here, they would travel South-West and South-East, and the Alps would be an ineffective barrier. So for the moment I regard these as ideas in the realm of theory, not practice. But they are canvassed in an interesting way in a forthcoming paper by Dullien and Schwarzer called »Bringing Macroeconomics into the EU Budget Debate: Why and How?«.[15]

6. Euro System Reform

Finally, there is another possible agenda of change which may emerge on the horizon. We hear less of it in Germany, and almost nothing in the UK. But there are those in France, particularly, who are concerned about the structure of the ECB, its independence, its accountability and its decision-making processes. President Sarkozy has often criticized it for taking too rigorous a line. I suspect these debates may achieve some greater prominence as the question of the succession to Jean-Claude Trichet in Frankfurt begins to be discussed. Trichet steps down at the end of his un-repeatable 8-year term during 2011.

There has been great pressure on the ECB in recent years. Governments have wanted it to intervene in the bond market. It was finally agreed, though clearly the Governing Council was not unanimous.

And there is another reason why the issue might arise. For the moment, the possibility of rising European interest rates seems very remote. The whole of the European economy remains in a delicate condition, as doctors would put it. But it is quite evident that the prospects for the next two or three years are very different in different countries. Greece is likely to remain in recession, if the required budget adjustment process is carried forward. The prospects for Spain and Portugal look poor, too, while Northern members may well recover more quickly. Setting the monetary dial appropriately in these circumstances will be a challenge. There is no ducking that challenge: there can only be one short-term interest rate in a monetary union. It will be essential for the ECB to maintain its independence and legitimacy, in the face of inevitable protests – from one group of countries or another.

By international standards, the ECB is a highly independent institution. There are various competing measures of independence in the academic literature, but on all of them the ECB is the most independent central bank among the major developed countries, and the Bank of Japan the least. The ECB has a price stability mandate enshrined in the Maastricht Treaty and is able to determine its own definition of it. The Bank of England has a target set by government, which can in principle be changed by politicians, while the Fed must also aim at maximum employment. The ECB can ignore employment if it wishes, and can take no instructions from the Council of Ministers.

The ECB is also less accountable than other Central Banks, in terms of its obligations to explain and justify its decisions. One study[16] shows it to be the most independent and the least accountable Central Bank in the world.

These characteristics stem from its Bundesbank ancestry, on the one hand, and the unusual political framework within which it operates: as Strauss-Kahn points out, there is no finance ministry to act as interlocutor, and the European Parliament is a far weaker legislator than the US Congress.

There is one other unusual feature of the ECB. It is very high as the index of what we might call ›unrepresentativeness‹. One feature of that is obvious. The ECB was set up as a ›one vote per country‹ system. Germany is the major sufferer, if we look at voting weights in relation to GDP.[17]

There is an alternative, more sophisticated, construction which looks at the balance between the centre and the regions. This will be especially significant in a situation in which there are major divergences in growth performance. In Europe the ratio of regional votes to central votes is much larger than in the Federal Reserve System. In other words, the number of appointees at the Bank itself, who are there precisely to take a Europe-view, is small. In an EMU of 15 members it is 2.5 regional votes to one central vote. In the case of the Federal Reserve it is 0.7 of a regional vote to each central vote. There are seven governors and five voting regional Fed presidents. For comparison the old Bundesbank operated with a ratio of 1.1 to 1.

This ratio would become even more marked with new members. The ECB has begun to think about rotation, and in future not all members would always have a vote. But its current proposals will do little or nothing to correct the imbalance I have noted. They only prevent it moving further towards the regions.

There is a further point to note about the ECB. Its decision-making processes are far less transparent than those of the Federal Reserve or the Bank of England. Both of them have voting procedures (somewhat different in each case) which highlight the balance of views. The minutes of their meetings are published, with a delay. We know much less about the balance of views in the Governing Council.

This is complex territory. In our book on the future of central banking published this week, David Green and I explore the arguments in some depth. All these features are strengths, in one way. But in difficult economic circumstances the risk is that they become weaknesses, and attract political criticism.

Our conclusions are that it will be important to strengthen the accountability mechanisms of the ECB. Its processes should become more transparent, and the ›misrepresentation index‹ should, at the very least, not be allowed to increase. We say this not because we wish to diminish the ECB independence, but because we want to preserve it. We see a risk that in difficult times there will be pressure for more political control of the ECB, which is dangerous. To head that off, the ECB should be prepared to open up its processes now, to give more confidence to those affected by its decisions. We also note that if the ECB has more influence over financial stability matters, as is envisaged, that would put further pressure on its accountability. Quite different mechanisms are required for regulatory decisions.

Conclusions

There is, therefore, a lengthy agenda of change ahead in EMU, if it is to be refurbished in the light of the experience of the first decade, and especially in the light of the current crisis. I do not know if this is quite what Commissioner

Almunia had in mind when he referred to ›unfinished business‹, but it is my own suggested menu.

Overall, we have to recognise that the early years of monetary union was relatively calm. As we say in »Banking on the Future«: »In retrospect it can be seen that the euro's first decade was a propitious one for the launch of an untried experiment … It remains to be seen whether the euro area will remain as comfortable, and the ECB's policies as well accepted, with the ending of the period of unprecedented economic calm«.

At a ceremony in Strasbourg in July 2009 to celebrate the euro's tenth birthday, Jean-Claude Trichet said »the financial crisis is demonstrating that in turbulent financial waters it is better to be on a large, solid and steady ship rather than on a small vessel«. He went on to say that »together we have shown that Europe is capable of taking decisions, even in the most difficult circumstances«.

I am the proud owner of a small (10 metre) elderly vessel. We keep it in Greece, as it happens. Sometimes I am tempted to think that it is safer than some of the huge cruise ships I see in the Corfu channel, struggling to manoeuvre. I do not mean to imply that the Greeks would be better off relaunching the SS Drachma. But those on the bridge of the mother ship Euro need to acknowledge that merely asserting the value of size, and dwelling on past successes, will not suffice. There is an overhaul task ahead, or some of the passengers may choose to man the lifeboats. My aim this evening has been to suggest a few areas in which maintenance work is most needed.

The changes agreed over the week-end are a start, but do not go far enough. They do not address competitiveness. They do not set up a permanent fund. I fear this won't be the last word, for Europe or for Greece. I would be surprised if Greece avoids a restructuring, unless the economy picks up very fast. This debt to GDP ratio rises to 150 % even with currently agreed budget cuts, so the structure remains flawed, and EMU is still unfinished. Europe's leaders may have bought themselves some time, but they will need to use it well.

The Convoco Lecture held by Sir Howard Davies took place on 10th May 2010 in Munich.

References

1 Joaquin Almunia, The European Economy as Home to the Next Global Currency. »The Euro at 10« conference, Peterson Institute for International Economics, Washington, 10 October 2008.

2 Margaret Thatcher, Statecraft, HarperCollins, 2002.

3 Helmut Kohl, Government Statement to the Bundestag, 6 November 1991, www.bundestag.de

4 Answer from Dominique Strauss-Kahn to a question from the public, »The Euro at 10« conference, Peterson Institute for International Economics, Washington, 10 October 2008.

5 Otmar Issing, Europe cannot afford to rescue Greece, The Financial Times, 15 February 2010, www.ft.com

6 EMU@10: successes and challenges after 10 years of Economic and Monetary Union. DG for Economic and Financial Affairs. European Commission, 2008, http://ec.europa.eu

7 Otmar Issing, The Euro – A Currency Without a State, CFS Working Paper No. 2008/51, December 2008, www.ifk-cfs.de

8 Jean Pisani-Ferry, André Sapir and Benedicta Marzinotto, Two crises, two responses, Bruegel Policy Brief 2010/01, 22 March 2010.

9 Sebastian Dullien and Daniela Schwarzer, The Euro Zone Needs an External Stability Pact, SWP Comments 9, July 2009, www.swp-berlin.org

10 Daniel Gros and Thomas Mayer, Towards a Euro(pean) Monetary Fund, Economic Policy CEPS Policy Brief No. 202, February 2010.

11 Wolfgang Schäuble, Why Europe's monetary union faces its biggest crisis, The Financial Times, 11 March 2010, www.ft.com

12 Willem Buiter, Global Economics View: Sovereign Debt Problems in Advanced Countries, Citigroup, 26 April 2010.

13 Jacques Delpla and Jakob von Weizsäcker, The Blue Bond Proposal, Bruegel Policy Brief 2010/03, May 2010.

14 High-Level Group on Financial Supervision in the EU, chaired by Jacques de Larosière, February 2009, http://ec.europa.eu

15 Sebastian Dullien and Daniela Schwarzer, Bringing Macroeconomics into the EU Budget Debate: Why and How?, Journal of Common Market Studies Vol. 47 No. 1, 2009.

16 Andrew Hughes Hallett and Jan Libich, Central Bank Independence, Accountability and Transparency: Complements or Strategic Substitutes?, CEPR Discussion Papers 5470, January 2006.

17 Helge Berger, Optimal Central Bank Design: Benchmarks for the ECB, CESifo Working Paper No. 1697, March 2006.

SIR HOWARD DAVIES

WIRTSCHAFTS- UND WÄHRUNGSUNION IN EUROPA: UNVOLLENDETE AUFGABE

Mein Titel heute Abend stammt von einem Ausspruch Joaquin Almunias, den er als damaliger Europäischer Kommissar für Wirtschaft und Währung im Oktober 2008 bei einer Konferenz in Washington anlässlich des 10. Geburtstages des Euros machte. Er sagte damals, dass »der zehnjährige Geburtstag der Einführung des Euros von einer tiefen Krise geprägt« sei. »Das Argument der Europäischen Kommission, dass wir mehr für die Einheitswährung tun müssen, ist nun offenkundig. Die EWU ist nicht vollendet. Sie ist eine unvollendete Aufgabe. Sie muss noch weiterentwickelt werden.«[1]

Die Wahrheit dieser Behauptung wurde in den letzten Wochen weitreichend aufgezeigt, als die griechische Schuldenkrise ins Rollen kam. Es handelte sich dabei nicht – ich formuliere so behutsam wie möglich – um Europas Sternstunde. Obgleich das Wesen des Problems sehr wohl verstanden und die Marktrisiken identifiziert worden waren, stellte es sich als außerordentlich schwierig heraus, zu irgendeiner Übereinkunft zu kommen, die den Griechen oder anderen nützlich wäre. Das, worauf man sich einigte, wurde fünf Minuten vor Mitternacht besiegelt, mit dem Ergebnis, dass griechische Regierungen – frühere sowie die aktuelle –, deutsche Politiker, die Führungsriege der Europäischen Zentralbank, beziehungsweise der Mangel an Führungskompetenz der Europäischen Union insgesamt stark kritisiert wurden.

Dieser Fall hat Europa überall in der Welt viel schlechte Presse eingebracht. Letzten Monat war ich in China, Hong Kong, Indien, Singapur und in den Vereinigten Staaten, und überall wurde ich mit einiger Verwunderung gefragt, warum man nicht früher Initiativen ergriffen habe. Der Fall wurde herangezogen, um von Neuem zu zeigen, dass Europa nicht in der Lage sei, seine eigenen Probleme zu lösen. Die Stimmung wurde vor zwei Wochen in einer Schlagzeile der *New York Times* gut zusammengefasst: »Wo ist Europa, während sich das griechische Drama zuspitzt?«

Es ist heute Abend nicht mein Ziel, eine minutiöse Krisenanalyse vorzulegen, auch nicht, mich den Schuldzuweisungen in Bezug auf Individuen anzuschließen. All die Betroffenen sind sehr wohl qualifiziert und geübt in den Rollen, die sie verkörpern. Sie haben alle versucht, das Problem zu lösen und es auf eine Art zu schaffen, die die Integrität der Währungsunion aufrechterhalten sollte. Die Tatsache, dass es ihnen schwerfiel, dies umzusetzen, deutet stark darauf hin, dass es eine Schwachstelle in den Strukturen gibt, innerhalb derer sie aktiv sind. Es scheint daher offensichtlich, dass wenn die griechische Krise sich nicht auf die wenig schmeichelhaft von uns PIGS genannten Länder ausbreitet, wir diese strukturellen Mängel mit höchster Sorgfalt analysieren und nach einer Lösung für sie suchen sollten. Dies ist ein nützlicheres Bestreben als der Versuch, die Ratingagenturen zu beschuldigen, die meines Erachtens in diesem Fall ganz einfach – und womöglich eher spät – eine allgemeine Vorstellung der fehlenden Nachhaltigkeit griechischer Finanzen ohne eine Form von äußerer Intervention haben.

Aber ist es für einen Engländer überhaupt angebracht, diese Angelegenheiten zu kommentieren? Wir befinden uns auf den Außenbahnen, und es ist höchst wahrscheinlich, dass dies auch so bleiben wird. In der Tat hat uns der *Economist* in einer erheiternden Neugestaltung der Europa-Karte neben Portugal gesetzt, im Mittelatlantik verschwindend.

Sicherlich können wir sagen, dass es in absehbarer Zeit nur eine geringe, oder eben gar keine Chance gibt, dass das Vereinigte Königreich um eine Mitgliedschaft in der Euro-Zone ersucht, wie auch immer der Ausgang der augenblicklichen Krise ausfallen mag. Ich bin so sicher, wie ich nur sein kann, dass wir zu meinen Lebzeiten nicht Mitglied werden – und ich fühle mich ganz gut. Und tatsächlich ist unsere Mitgliedschaft wegen der griechischen Tragödie noch unwahrscheinlicher geworden. Unsere Partei der Liberaldemokraten war theoretisch Befürworterin einer Euro-Mitgliedschaft des Vereinten Königreichs, aber sie haben diese Position rasch gewechselt, als sie während des Wahlkampfs auf die Probe gestellt wurden.

Ich bin einer der wenigen Menschen im Vereinigten Königreich, der dafür gewappnet war, sich in der Öffentlichkeit für eine Euro-Mitgliedschaft auszusprechen, was in London verstanden wird als »Die Liebe, die nicht wagt, sich selbst beim Namen zu nennen«. Ich selber habe begonnen, im

Angesicht der jüngsten Ereignisse einige Zweifel zu hegen, jedoch spreche ich als Kommentator, der diesem Projekt Erfolg wünscht. Ich spreche auch vor dem Hintergrund einiger Forschungen, die ich im Laufe der letzten beiden Jahre über zentrales Bankenwesen, und dabei insbesondere über die Errichtung und Konstitution eines europäischen Systems von Zentralbanken betrieben habe. Die Forschungsergebnisse wurden vor kurzem publiziert – genauer gesagt ist das Veröffentlichungsdatum Mittwoch dieser Woche –, und zwar in einem Buch namens »Banking on the Future: The Fall and Rise of Central Banking«.

Die große Frage, die ich heute Abend zu beantworten versuche, lautet: »Kann die EWU ohne Strukturveränderungen überleben, und wenn nicht, wie sollten diese Veränderungen aussehen?«

Zuerst sollten wir einen Schritt zurückgehen und uns ins Gedächtnis rufen, dass es Stimmen gibt, die die Währungsunion stets für schlecht geplant hielten. Eine objektive Beobachterin sagte zu Beginn: »Ich glaube, dass die europäische Einheitswährung zum Scheitern verurteilt ist, wirtschaftlich, politisch, und nicht zuletzt sozial, obwohl das Timing, der Anlass und das ganze Ausmaß der Konsequenzen durchaus unklar sind«. Es war Margaret Thatcher.[2]

Wir könnten uns auch daran erinnern, was Helmut Kohl 1991 sagte: »Man kann dies nicht oft genug sagen. Die Politische Union ist das unerlässliche Gegenstück zur Wirtschafts- und Währungsunion. Die jüngere Geschichte, und zwar nicht nur die Deutschlands, lehrt uns, dass die Vorstellung, man könne eine Wirtschafts- und Währungsunion ohne Politische Union auf Dauer erhalten, abwegig ist.«[3]

Es ist frappierend, dass viele Kommentatoren bezüglich der jüngsten Ereignisse dahin tendierten, in ihnen eine Bestätigung ihrer bereits lange vertretenen Positionen zu sehen. Auf diese Weise konnten wir vernehmen, wie viele Kommentatoren im Vereinten Königreich verschiedene Versionen des »Hab' ich doch gesagt« hervorbrachten. Sie erklärten, dass das griechische Problem einer Krise gleichkam, die früher oder später eintreten musste, und dass eine auf »Einheitsgröße« basierende Währungspolitik in Anbetracht der vielfältigen Wirtschaftsregionen niemals aufgehen konnte. Das nennt man ›Schadenfreude‹ – auf Englisch haben wir für solch ein infames Gefühl keinen Begriff. Es grassierte viel Eigenlob bezüglich unserer Entscheidung, außen vor zu bleiben. In den letzten Tagen seiner Kampagne bemühte sich Gordon Brown, zu seinen Gunsten daraus Kapital zu schlagen.

Nicht nur die britischen Kommentatoren sahen sich in ihren Vorurteilen bestätigt. Einige Zeit lang argumentierten die Franzosen, dass es in Europa eines wirtschaftlichen Gegengewichts zur europäischen Währungsautorität der EZB bedürfe – ein Argument, das bei deutschen Kommentatoren nicht sonderlich viel Anklang fand. Dominique Strauss-Kahn hat erneut gesagt: »Mir ist kein Land bekannt, das eine Währung hat, aber keinen Finanzminister, der für diese Währung zuständig ist ... wir haben eine sehr starke Zentralbank, aber an der Spitze keine reale Person, die für die Wirtschaft zuständig ist ... ohne zentralisierte Kraft ist es sehr schwierig, Entscheidungen zu treffen.«[4]

Eine mehr typisch deutsche Sichtweise – ich gebe zu, dass es in dieser Krise nicht bloß einen deutschen Standpunkt gab – liefert uns Otmar Issing. Seine Forderung zielt auf eine Rückkehr zu Regeln, die ein grundlegendes Element zu Beginn der Erschaffung der EWU waren. »Bei der Überwachung von der Umsetzung von Regeln muss Schluss sein mit laxem Monitoring und Kompromissen. Die EWU ist eine Staatengemeinschaft mit festen Regeln, die von jedem neuen Mitglied akzeptiert wurden. Diese Regeln können nicht nachträglich verändert werden«.[5]

Diese festen Vorschriften erschienen in der *Financial Times* unter der Schlagzeile »Europa kann es sich nicht leisten, Griechenland zu retten«. Natürlich wissen wir, dass viele Deutsche, und gewiss auch andere Staaten in Europa glaubten, dass man zu Beginn die Regeln etwas freier ausgelegt hat, um Griechenland zuzulassen, und auch andere Länder wie Italien und Belgien.

Ich könnte daran erinnern, dass man vom Stabilitäts- und Wachstumspakt abkam, als es Deutschland nicht gelang, die strengen Kriterien einzuhalten, und dass es mit seiner Quote aus dem Jahr 2009 nicht zur Aufnahme in die EWU befähigt gewesen wäre. Ich spreche hier in Deutschland, deswegen führe ich diese Punkte nicht weiter aus.

Die Krise gab Gelegenheit zur Neuformulierung von lange vertretenen Standpunkten. Zugleich kommt es bereits seit einiger Zeit zu einem interessanten Umdenken, und zwar in einem Versuch, Wege auszumachen, die der Beschaffenheit der Währungsunion zur mehr Stabilität verhelfen würden. Um diesen Argumenten leichter folgen zu können, schlage ich vor, dass wir unseren Blick auf sechs verschiedene Bereiche lenken. Einige von ihnen sind vergleichsweise wenig umstritten, was aber nicht unbedingt bedeutet, dass sie einfach sind. Bei anderen bewegen wir uns auf weit strittigerem Terrain. Ich beginne mit der Finanzdisziplin.

1. Finanzdisziplin

Es wird kaum Zweifel geben, dass eine höhere Finanzdisziplin innerhalb der Eurozone und ein effektiveres Monitoring von Haushaltslagen in Zukunft notwendig sein werden, als absolute Mindestvoraussetzung. Es wäre undenkbar, die Erfahrungen der letzten Jahre noch einmal durchzumachen, als Griechenland der Europäischen Kommission Defizite angab, und sich später herausstellte, dass deutlich zu niedrig beziffert worden war.

Es ist eindeutig, dass die Europäische Kommission viel stärkere Prüfungsinstanzen benötigt, und in der Tat kam der diesbezügliche Vorschlag auch von innen.[6] Der Vorschlag der Kommission sieht bei Mitgliedstaaten vertiefte methodologische Visiten durch Eurostat vor, was über das bloße Überprüfen der Einhaltung statistischer Standards hinausgeht. Eurostat bekäme Zugang zu weit mehr Rohdaten, als dies in der Vergangenheit der Fall gewesen ist.

Dies ist nun eher unumstritten, angesichts der griechischen Erfahrung, obgleich es in der Vergangenheit auf Widerstand stieß. Aber es wird nicht wirksam, außer man lässt ein Bekenntnis zu einem neuen Stabilitäts- und Wachstumspakt (SWP) wieder aufleben. Es ist bekannt, dass der Pakt 2003 aufs Abstellgleis geschoben wurde. Er muss in irgendeiner Form wieder in Kraft treten. Natürlich sind heute für viele Länder die Bedingungen des alten Paktes extrem schwer einzuhalten. Wie ich bereits erwähnte, tut nicht einmal Deutschland dies. Wir verbleiben in einer post-Krisensituation, deswegen kommt es nicht ganz unerwartet. Die Frage jedoch, wie rasch die Länder zu den Bedingungen des Paktes zurückkehren sollten, und ob diese Bedingungen angesichts der Erfahrungen überarbeitet werden sollten, bleibt offen. Es besteht ein nachvollziehbares Unbehagen über eine steuerliche Verschärfung zu einer Zeit, in der eine Erholung vielerorts noch nicht gesichert ist. Die damit für einige EU-Länder verbundenen Beträge sind enorm, und das Vereinigte Königreich befindet sich in einer genauso ernsten Position wie alle anderen auch. Eine Verschärfung ist momentan dort unvermeidbar, wo man sich Schulden nicht leisten kann, wie etwa in Griechenland, aber es könnte anderswo nicht ratsam sein. Insofern haben Europas Finanzminister eine große Aufgabe vor sich, die sie nicht einfach so über das Wochenende lösen konnten. Was im Augenblick vorliegt, ist eine Reihe von Paketen mit spezifischen Bedingungen, jedoch kein neuer SWP.

Aber wird das ausreichen, um den Pakt wieder in Kraft zu setzen? Für Otmar Issing schon. Er führt an, »der Stabilitäts- und Wachstumspakt enthält die Regeln, die für das Funktionieren der Währungsunion notwendig sind. Es besteht kein Anlass, die volkswirtschaftliche Politik dahingehend zu koordinieren, über das jetzige Stadium hinauszugehen«.[7] Andere widersprechen dem, und halten grundlegendere Probleme für erörterungswürdig. Das wichtigste davon ist der Wettbewerb. Darum ging es gestern gar nicht, obgleich dies das ganze Problem ausmacht.

2. Wettbewerbsfähigkeit

Eine bemerkenswerte und vielleicht überraschende Eigenschaft der Entwicklung der Eurozone in ihrem ersten Jahrzehnt waren die Veränderungen in den tatsächlichen Wechselkursen und die Wettbewerbsfähigkeit. Deutschland, das zu einem überschätzten Umtauschkurs beigetreten sein mag, hat seine relativen Lohnstückkosten Jahr für Jahr verbessert. Bei Italien, Spanien und Portugal war es der umgekehrte Fall, es gelang ihnen nicht, die inländischen Kosten zu kontrollieren oder die Produktivität zu steigern. Im

Nachhinein scheint es, als hätten sie die Euro-Mitgliedschaft als eine Entschuldigung gesehen, sich ihrer Sorgen um eine äußere Wettbewerbsfähigkeit zu entledigen. Diese Veränderungen haben Land für Land zu vorhersehbaren Konsequenzen in sehr unterschiedlichen relativen Exportleistungen geführt.

Man sieht, dass zwischen abnehmender Wettbewerbsfähigkeit und schwacher Exportleistung ein Zusammenhang besteht. Im Fall Griechenlands ging die Wettbewerbsfähigkeit um etwa 5 % zurück. Das macht das griechische Problem wohl weitgehend zu einem Thema der Steuerpolitik, und weniger der Wettbewerbsfähigkeit. Im Fall Spaniens, Italiens und Portugals jedoch ist die Lage eher anders. In einem jüngst veröffentlichten, interessanten Strategiepapier von Bruegel haben Marzinotto, Pisani-Ferry und Sapir auf signifikante Unterschiede zwischen Griechenland und Spanien hingewiesen. Ihr Paper »Two Crises, Two Responses«[8] argumentiert, dass Spaniens Problem seinen Ursprung in einem inländischen Kreditboom hatte. Und als zur Zeit der Euro-Konstruktion angenommen wurde, dass Haupt-Schwachstelle eine undisziplinierte Steuerpolitik sei, sehen wir nun, dass es auch andere potentielle Probleme gibt. Spanien hätte sehr wohl die Kriterien des Stabilitäts- und Wachstumspaktes einhalten können, und würde immer noch ein Problem haben.

Wie könnte die Antwort darauf aussehen, abgesehen von einer Ermahnung? Laut Issing besteht die Lösung darin, die »nötige Flexibilität in Märkten zu schaffen, vor allem beim Arbeitsmarkt«. Diese Theorie mag stimmen, aber bislang gab es noch keinen Hinweis, dass Spanien bereit sei, dieser Vorschrift zu folgen. Wie fällt also die Reaktion der EU darauf aus, abgesehen von Hoffen und Beten?

Sebastian Dullien und Daniela Schwarzer glauben, dass exzessive externe Ungleichgewichte ebenfalls eine ernsthafte Gefahr für die Stabilität der Europäischen Währungsunion darstellen. Sie denken, dass diese Defizite auch auf europäischem Niveau überwacht werden sollten, um Risiken so früh wie möglich zu entschärfen. Als die EWU geschaffen wurde, hat man allgemein angenommen, dass das einzige ausschlaggebende Defizit das externe Defizit der Eurozone als Ganzes sei. Dullien und Schwarzer stimmen dem nicht zu, ihrer Meinung nach braucht die EWU einen »externen Stabilitätspakt«, um die existierenden Übereinkünfte zu ergänzen.[9] Basierend auf dieser Analyse sollte es abgestimmte Grenzbereiche für externe Gleichgewichte geben. Sie empfehlen, dass der Pakt festlegen sollte, dass kein Land der Eurozone ein Ungleichgewicht in der Leistungsbilanz von mehr als 3 % des Bruttoinlandsprodukts (BIP) aufweisen sollte, weder als Defizit noch als Überschuss. Ein Überschreiten jedweden Grenzbereiches zöge eine Verwarnung nach sich, gefolgt von der Bereitschaft, zu angemessenen Maßnahmen zu greifen, um das Ungleichgewicht zu reduzieren.

Ich kann die Logik hinter diesem Vorschlag verstehen. Eine vergleichbare Argumentationsweise, obwohl sie nicht ganz zu derselben Lösung führt, verfolgen Daniel Gros und Thomas Mayer.[10] Sie verweisen darauf, dass die Anfälligkeit verschiedener Länder des Eurogebietes unterschiedlichen Ursprungs sein kann. Einer davon ist externes Gleichgewicht, insbesondere was sie als »die Notwendigkeit von Außenfinanzierung und einer wettbewerbsfähigen Position als Nachweis der Befähigung, Auslandsschulden nachkommen zu können« bezeichnen. Daher haben sie einen Anfälligkeitsindex für das Euro-Gebiet aufgestellt. Man kann anhand ihrer Berechnung erkennen, dass Griechenland Höchstwerte erzielt, was vor allem durch seine steuerlichen Tatbestände bedingt ist. Portugal, Zweiter in dieser umgekehrten Ligatabelle, ist besonders wegen seiner aktuellen Bilanz und wegen der Position seiner reinen gesamtwirtschaftlichen Ersparnis anfällig. Folglich sind externes Gleichgewicht und Wettbewerbsfähigkeit äußerst bedeutsame Indikatoren. Aber ich frage mich, ob ein externer Stabilitätspakt machbar ist. Ist Deutschland bereit, sich von der Europäischen Kommission sagen zu lassen, es müsse seinen Handelsüberschuss reduzieren? Deutsche Politiker haben eher scharf auf solcherart Vorschläge von Christine Lagarde aus Frankreich reagiert.

Wichtiger noch, ist dies nicht eher ein unbeholfener Versuch, die Lage wirtschaftlicher Aktivität in Europa zu manipulieren? Innerhalb eines Wirtschaftsgebietes, das so vielfältig ist wie die EWU, wird es einschneidende Veränderungen in relativer Wettbewerbsfähigkeit geben, und ich kann mir nicht vorstellen, dass die Europäische Kommission genug Macht hat, dem zu widerstehen. Nichtsdestoweniger besteht eine wichtige Lehre des vergangenen Jahrzehnts darin, dass die Länder, die einen kontinuierlichen, unnachgiebigen Abfall in ihrer Wettbewerbsfähigkeit durchmachen, eines Tages den Preis dafür zu entrichten haben. Es liegt meiner Ansicht nach nicht an nationalen Regierungen, darauf zu reagieren, obwohl die Kommission, und vielleicht die EZB, in ihren Kommentaren zu diesen Trends offener und direkter sein könnte.

Folglich galt das Hauptaugenmerk dieser Ergänzungen vom Wochenende Steuerproblemen, aber sie sind nicht die grundlegende Schwierigkeit für Spanien und Portugal.

3. Europäischer Wirtschaftsfonds

Gros und Mayer, die erwähnen, dass Anfälligkeit entweder aus steuerlicher Undiszipliniertheit oder aus einem Abfall in Wettbewerbsfähigkeit entstehen kann, sprachen sich in einem im Februar diesen Jahres veröffentlichten Paper für einen Europäischen Wirtschaftsfonds aus (vgl. Anm. 10). Ihre Ansichten stießen bei Wolfgang Schäuble auf Resonanz, wie sein Artikel in der *Financial Times* bezeugt: »Why Europe's monetary union faces its biggest crisis«.[11] Schäubles Argument bestand darin, dass Notfall-Liquiditätshilfe durch einen Europäischen Währungsfonds »im Notfall, der eine Bedrohung für die finanzielle Stabilität des gesamten Euro-Gebietes darstellt«, verfügbar gemacht werden könnte.

Gros und Mayer räsonieren etwas anders. Für sie gilt, dass wenn Ungleichgewichte, egal ob nun finanzpolitisch oder extern, eintreten, Länder gegebenenfalls schmerzhafte Anpassungen durchlaufen müssen, wenn ihre öffentliche Schuldenlage wieder tragfähig gemacht werden soll. Aber angesichts des immensen Drucks von Seiten finanzieller Märkte, und wir waren unlängst Zeuge einer lebhaften Veranschaulichung, »ist es wahrscheinlich, dass in einigen Fällen ein strenges finanzielles Anpassungsprogramm … nicht ausreichen wird, um einen ›plötzlichen Stopp‹ der notwendigen externen Finanzierung des öffentlichen Sektors zu verhindern«. Genau dies ist Griechenland vor zwei Wochen passiert. Sie diskutieren, ob es an der EU oder dem IWF liegt, das Problem anzugehen. Diese Diskussion hielt den Winter über sichtbar an, wahrscheinlich auf gestörte Weise, innerhalb der Kanzleien Europas. Gros und Mayer liefern eine gute Beschreibung des Dilemmas, und denken, dass dieses Dilemma durch die Schaffung eines EWF verhindert werden könnte. Sie gestehen ein, Einige könnten Vorbehalte gegenüber diesem Schema haben, weil es gegen die No Bail-out-Bestimmung des Maastrichter Vertrags verstößt. »Dennoch möchten wir darlegen, dass unser Vorschlag eigentlich der einzige Weg ist, um die No Bail-out-Regel glaubhaft zu machen … Die Verfasser des Maastrichter Vertrages hatten es versäumt einzusehen, dass in einem Zusammenhang brüchiger Finanzmärkte die wahre Gefahr eines Finanzkollaps eine ›reine‹ No Bail-out-Antwort unrealistisch macht.«

Willem Buiter, einst an der LSE und jetzt bei der Citigroup, hat weitere Details umrissen, wie ein Europäischer Währungsfonds aufgebaut sein könnte.[12] Er ist der Meinung, ein Vertragszusatz sei nicht vonnöten und könnte unter den verstärkten Zusammenarbeits-Provisionen aus dem Lissabonner Vertrag aufgesetzt werden. Bezüge aus dem Fonds stünden in Proportion zur Kapitalbeteiligung der Mitgliedstaaten in der EZB. Das anvertraute Geld wäre bedeutsam, er schätzt 2 Billionen Euro. Der bezahlte Betrag könnte viel kleiner ausfallen, vielleicht 10 %, solange das Organ, das den Fonds verwaltet, die Befugnis hat, über das anvertraute Geld auf Abruf zu verfügen. Der Vorstand würde sich aus Repräsentanten der Mitgliedstaaten, der Kommission und der EZB zusammensetzen. Deutschland würde für mehr als ein Viertel der benötigten Finanzen aufkommen.

Liegt dies nun vor? Nicht wirklich. Der Stabilisationsfonds ist eine Zweckgesellschaft für drei Jahre, keine ständige Einrichtung. Ich denke, dass es notwendig sein wird, ihn dauerhaft einzurichten.

Ein weiterer Vorschlag, der jüngst debattiert wurde, sieht vor, dass das Euro-Gebiet Wertpapiere ausgeben sollte, für die alle Regierungen bürgen würden. Ein gewisses Element davon findet sich in dem wieder, worauf man sich geeinigt hatte. Letzte Woche haben Jacques Delpla und Jakob von Weizsäcker für das Bruegel-Institut ein Paper herausgegeben, in dem sie ein kluges Prinzip vorschlagen. Demnach sollen EU-Länder ihre Pflichten bündeln und so genannte ›Blue Bonds‹ ausgeben, für die kollektiv gebürgt wird. Jedes Mitglied hätte das Recht, Blue Bonds auszugeben bis zu einem Wert von 60 % des BIP. Bei einer höheren Kreditaufnahme würden ›Red Bonds‹ in Junior-Tranchen ausgegeben, als Schulden, für die der Einzelstaat verantwortlich ist.[13]

Ich halte dies für eine intelligente Lösung, aber vielleicht ist sie zum eigenen Besten auch etwas zu geistreich. Ich bezweifle, dass es allumfassende Kreditkosten reduzieren kann, wie es die Autoren suggerieren. Verschiedene Länder befinden sich in unterschiedlichen historischen Schulden-Positionen. Und dann ist da auch noch die politische Schwierigkeit, Steuerzahler davon zu überzeugen, Wertpapiere in anderen Ländern zu unterstützen. Ich bezweifle, dass diese Idee Zustimmung finden wird.

Aber es gibt andere Bereiche, wo eine verstärkte europäische Maschinerie möglicherweise notwendig ist. Das gilt insbesondere im Zusammenhang mit dem Finanzsystem. Die ausgedehnte Finanzkrise hat Schwächen in Europas Binnenfinanzmarkt aufgezeigt – Schwächen, auf die man achten sollte. Hier sprechen wir vorrangig über Probleme, die das Vereinigte Königreich direkt betreffen könnten, dennoch beziehen sich die Argumente auch besonders auf die Eurozone.

Dies ist vielleicht weniger dringend als der Stabilisationsfonds. Aber wir wissen, dass das Steuerproblem schnell auf die Bank zurückfallen kann. Und einige von ihnen sind noch nicht wieder gefestigt.

4. Finanzregulierung

Das isländische Bankenproblem hat vornehmlich gezeigt, dass es eine Schwachstelle im Herzen des Binnenfinanzmarktes gibt. Isländische Banken – der Europäische Wirtschaftsraum ist hierbei eher als die Eurozone der Zuständigkeitsbereich – wurden von isländischen Behörden überwacht. Sie machten von den Vorschriften des Binnenmarktes Gebrauch, um Zweigstellen zu eröffnen und Einlagen in anderen Mitgliedstaaten zu tätigen. In diesen Mitgliedstaaten stand weder die Liquidität noch die Solvenz der Filialen unter der Amtsbefugnis der lokalen Regulierungsbehörden. Als die Zweigstellen kollabierten, wurde offensichtlich, dass die isländischen Behörden nicht in der Lage waren, für sie wirksam zu bürgen, und dass Steuerzahler in den Niederlanden und im Vereinigten Königreich dafür aufkommen mussten. Die letztlichen Selbstbeteiligungs-Arrangements zwischen den Gastgeberländern und dem Heimatland müssen noch beschlossen werden, und natürlich zur Angelegenheit der hohen Politik in Island werden.

Dieses und andere Probleme wurden in die Obhut von Jacques de Larosière gegeben. Er ist immer eine gute Anlaufstelle, wenn es darum geht, eine Lösung für ein heikles Thema zu finden. De Larosière legte einen Bericht[14] vor, der eine Anzahl von wichtigen Empfehlungen enthielt. Die meisten davon wurden weitestgehend vom Ministerrat akzeptiert – wenn auch mit einigem Widerwillen im Fall des Vereinten Königreiches. De Larosière empfahl einen neuen europäischen Finanzstabilitäts-Vorstand, mit dem Präsidenten der EZB als dessen Vorsitzendem, was gut mit dem gestärkten globalen Finanzstabilitäts-Vorstand unter den G20 vereinbar sein sollte. Er empfahl ebenfalls, dass der alte Ausschuss der Regulierungsbehörden eine Behörde werden sollte, mit eigenem Personal usw. Diese Behörde jedoch wäre innerhalb des bereits existierenden Regelwerkes einzurichten. Man kann einwenden, dass dies kaum Behörden im engen Sinne des Wortes sind. Ihre Handlungsmöglichkeit, nationale Regulierungen zu steuern, ist relativ gering. Dies war eine raffinierte Konstruktion. Sie mag die beste gewesen sein, die angesichts der politischen Umstände jener Zeit hervorgebracht wurde. Es ist nur noch wenig Lust für neue Verfassungsmaßnahmen in Europa übrig, in Anbetracht der Schwierigkeiten, den Lissabon-Vertrag durchzusetzen. Aber reicht sie aus? Meine persönliche Antwort auf diese Frage lautet nein. Ich denke dennoch, dass wir zu gegebener Zeit einen Schritt in Richtung eines zentralisierteren europäischen Regulationssystems machen müssen, mit einer europäischen Finanzbehörde, die vor allem pan-europäische Banken betreut und hinter ihnen steht. Die Frage ist aber, wie wirksam diese Regel wäre, wenn es mit keinem Mechanismus zusammenhinge, der Banken in Schwierigkeiten rekapitalisiert oder finanziell unterstützt? Erneut ist hier der griechische Fall relevant. Es ist klar, dass griechische Banken gegenwärtig nur von der EZB Geldmittel einholen können. Gäbe es irgendeinen Bewertungsabschlag auf die griechischen Schulden, eine Folge, die keineswegs ausgeschlossen werden kann, wären sie am Ende vielleicht sogar insolvent. Aus diesem Grund plädiert Buiter für einen Zentralfonds zusätzlich zu einem europäischen Währungsfonds, um systematisch wichtige grenzübergreifende Finanzinstitutionen zu rekapitalisieren. Entweder um ihnen zu gestatten, ihren Betrieb weiter aufrecht zu erhalten, oder um sie abzuwickeln oder zu liquidieren, ohne unnötige soziale Ausgaben (vgl. Anm. 12).

Buiter nennt dies einen Finanzinstitutions-Rekapitalisierungsfonds. Er unterscheidet sich dadurch von der EZB, dass er tatsächlich den Steuerzahler in Anspruch nimmt, was die EZB nicht tut. Buiter glaubt, dass die EZB und der FIRF sowohl getrennte Institutionen sein als auch fusionieren können, und dass dies ›das minimale Finanz-Europa‹ ist, das politisch und wirtschaftlich notwendig ist. Die Bruegel-Gruppe hat etwas Ähnliches vorgeschlagen. Sie haben es einen Europäischen Resolutionsfonds genannt, basierend auf dem Instanzenmodell, das aktuell in den USA im Finanzregulierungs-Reformentwurf im Kongress diskutiert wird.

Diese Idee wirft auch sehr bedeutsame politische Fragen auf. Sie eröffnet die Möglichkeit, dass Steuerzahler im Land A Banken im Land B unterstützen. Aber vielleicht, unter den ungewöhnlichen Umständen einer Finanzkrise, wie wir sie derzeit erleben, ist dies eine bessere Option als jedwede andere verfügbare. Sicherlich gibt es ein starkes kollektives Interesse in Europa, die Integrität der Wirtschafts- und Währungsunion aufrechtzuerhalten, und so mag dies der Preis sein, den man dafür zu zahlen hat. Ich glaube deswegen, dass eine Art Europäische Beschlussbehörde auch auf der Agenda des Ministerrats stehen sollte.

5. Finanztransfers

Einige könnten einwenden, dies sei nicht genug und die wahre Lektion der Lehre aus der Krise bestehe darin, dass Europa eine weitaus zentralisiertere Finanzpolitik braucht, ebenso wie die Fähigkeit, bedeutsame Finanztransfers von einem Mitgliedstaat zum anderen vorzunehmen. Wie leistungsfähig ist dieses Argument?

Die Idee, dass man für eine Einheitswährung eine koordinierte Finanzpolitik braucht, ist nicht neu. Tatsächlich hat der McDougall-Bericht 1977 argumentiert, dass im Rahmen einer Währungsunion im Mittel ein Budget von bis zu 25 % vom BIP der Europäischen Union benötigt wird, um mit einer Stabilisierung zurecht zu kommen und um ökonomische Unterschiede zwischen Ländern auszugleichen. In den verstrichenen 30 Jahren gab es jedoch wenig politisches Bestreben, den Weg in diese Richtung einzuschlagen. Das EU-Budget verbleibt bei nur ca. 1,5 % des BIP.

Einige Ökonomen haben nicht von der Meinung abgelassen, dass wenn einer zentralen Institution Autonomie gegenüber einer Währungspolitik gewährt wird, alternative Anpassungsmechanismen notwendig werden, um asymmetrische Schocks bewältigen zu können. Die Erfahrung der ersten Dekade mit einer Währungsunion hat gezeigt, dass die Alternative mit größerer ökonomischer Flexibilität, in Form von Arbeitsmobilität oder Lohnausgleich, nicht wirkungsvoll funktioniert hat. In der Tat haben wir gesehen, dass in Deutschland die Lohn-Flexibilität für Veränderungen in den relativen Arbeitskosten pro Stunde und in der Wettbewerbsfähigkeit gesorgt hat, was ein wichtiger Grund für die Krise ist, in der wir uns befinden.

Dies veranlasste einige Ökonomen zu der Äußerung, dass wenn die Eurozone überleben soll, es die Notwendigkeit zentralerer Fonds geben wird, um eine wirtschaftliche Stabilisierung zu fördern. Ein Vorschlag ist, dass es eine gewisse Stufe grundsätzlicher Versicherung gegen Arbeitslosigkeit geben sollte, die auf europäischem Niveau mit Mitteln versehen wird. Dies käme den Veränderungsmechanismen von Ländern mit zurückgegangener Wettbewerbsfähigkeit zugute, wie zum Beispiel Spanien, und dort, wo die Arbeitslosigkeit sehr hoch ist – 20 % –, und für enormen Druck auf Haushaltsbudgets sorgt. Auch für eine zentralisiertere Körperschaftssteuer gibt es Argumente.

Issing widerspricht diesen Argumenten vehement. Seiner Ansicht nach braucht man nichts anderes als den Stabilitäts- und Wachstumspakt, um die EWU gut funktionieren zu lassen. Vielleicht ist es ja das Vorhandensein dieser größeren Szenarien von europäischer Finanzintegration, die für Verdacht bezüglich derer sorgen, die sich für eine Art europäischer Wirtschaftssteuerung einsetzen, um mit der zentralen Währungspolitik gleichzuziehen. Schließlich ist es ziemlich offensichtlich, in welche Richtung diese Finanztransfers gehen würden. Von hier aus würden sie gen Südwesten und Südosten wandern. Die Alpen wären eine wirkungslose Barriere. Deswegen ordne ich diese Ideen im Moment dem Reich der Theorie zu, nicht der Praxis. Zumindest sind sie auf interessante Weise eingefügt in ein bald erscheinendes Paper von Dullien und Schwarzer namens »Bringing Macroeconomics into the EU Budget Debate: Why and How?«[15]

6. Euro-Systemreform

Schließlich gibt es noch eine weitere Agenda des Wandels, die am Horizont auftreten könnte. Wir hören davon weniger in Deutschland, und fast gar nichts im Vereinigten Königreich. Aber es gibt besonders in Frankreich Stimmen, die Besorgnis über die Struktur der EZB, ihre Unabhängigkeit, ihre Rechenschaftspflicht und ihre Prozesse der Entscheidungsfindung äußern.

Präsident Sarkozy hat sie oft für ihre zu rigorose Linie kritisiert. Ich vermute, dass diese Debatten größere Wichtigkeit erlangen, da man nun beginnt, die Frage der Nachfolge Jean-Claude Trichets in Frankfurt zu diskutieren. Trichet wird im Laufe des Jahres 2011 nach Erfüllung seiner achtjährigen Amtszeit zurücktreten; eine Wiederwahl ist ausgeschlossen.

In den letzten Jahren wurde viel Druck auf die EZB ausgeübt. Regierungen wollten, dass sie in den Aktienmarkt eingreife. Letztlich einigte man sich darauf, obgleich von Seiten des EZB-Rates eindeutig nicht einstimmig.

Und es gibt einen weiteren Grund, warum dieses Thema auftreten könnte. Im Moment scheint die Möglichkeit eines Anstiegs der europäischen Zinsraten sehr fern zu sein. Die Gesamtheit der europäischen Wirtschaft verharrt in einem kritischen Zustand, wie Ärzte es formulieren würden. Aber es ist ganz offensichtlich, dass die Aussichten für die nächsten zwei bis drei Jahre je nach Land höchst unterschiedlich sind. Griechenland wird voraussichtlich in einer Rezession bleiben, wenn der erforderte Prozess der Haushaltsanpassung vorangetrieben wird. Die Aussichten für Spanien und Portugal sind ebenfalls düster, wohingegen die nördlichen Mitgliedstaaten sich eher schnell erholen könnten. Den Währungszeiger angemessen zu stellen wird unter diesen Umständen eine Herausforderung sein. Man kann sich vor dieser Herausforderung nicht drücken: Es kann nur eine kurzfristige Zinsrate in einer Währungsunion geben. Es wird für die EZB grundlegend sein, ihre Unabhängigkeit und Legitimität zu bewahren, angesichts unvermeidbarer Proteste – von der einen oder anderen Ländergruppe.

Gemäß internationaler Standards handelt es sich bei der EZB um eine höchst unabhängige Institution. In der Forschungsliteratur gibt es verschiedene konkurrierende Unabhängigkeits-Maßstäbe, aber allen zufolge ist die EZB die unabhängigste Zentralbank unter den großen Industrienationen, wohingegen die Bank of Japan die am wenigsten unabhängige ist. Die EZB hat ein im Maastrichter Vertrag verankertes Preisstabilitätsmandat und ist in der Lage, dieses selber definieren zu können. Die Bank of England bekommt ihre Zielsetzung von der Regierung, welche prinzipiell von Politikern abgeändert werden kann, während die Fed maximale Beschäftigung anstreben muss. Wenn es der EZB beliebt, kann sie die Beschäftigung ignorieren und muss auch keine Anweisungen des Ministerrates befolgen.

Die EZB ist weniger rechenschaftspflichtig als andere Zentralbanken, wenn es darum geht, ihre Verpflichtungen zu erklären und ihre Entscheidungen zu rechtfertigen. Eine Studie[16] führt sie als die unabhängigste und am wenigsten rechenschaftspflichtige Zentralbank der Welt.

Diese Charakteristika stammen einerseits von ihrer Bundesbank-Herkunft, und andererseits von dem ungewöhnlichen politischen Rahmen, innerhalb dessen sie operiert: Strauss-Kahn betont, dass es kein Finanzministerium gibt, das als Gesprächspartner auftreten kann, und das Europäische Parlament ist ein weitaus schwächerer Gesetzgeber als der US-Kongress.

Und noch ein weiteres ungewöhnliches Merkmal weist die EZB auf. Es rangiert sehr hoch als der Index dessen, was wir die ›Nicht-Repräsentativität‹ nennen könnten. Ein Merkmal davon ist offensichtlich. Die EZB wurde mit einem ›Eine Stimme pro Land‹-System errichtet. Deutschland leidet darunter am meisten, wenn man die Stimmgewichte in ein Verhältnis mit dem BIP stellt.[17]

Es gibt ein alternatives, durchdachteres Konstrukt, das das Gleichgewicht zwischen dem Zentrum und den Regionen betrachtet. Dies wird dann besonders bedeutsam, wenn große Abweichungen in der Wachstumsleistung auftreten. In Europa ist der Verhältniswert von Regionalstimmen zu Zentralstimmen viel größer als im Zentralbanksystem der Vereinigten Staaten. Mit anderen Worten ist bei der Bank selber die Zahl der Angestellten, die eben gerade dafür da sind, eine europäische Perspektive zu vertreten, klein. In einer EWU mit 15 Mitgliedern bedeutet das 2,5 Regionalstimmen gegenüber einer Zentralstimme. Im Fall der US-Zentralbank sind es 0,7 Regionalstimmen gegenüber einer Zentralstimme. Es gibt sieben Governors und fünf stimmberechtigte regionale Fed-Präsidenten. Zum Vergleich: Bei der alten Bundesbank galt das Verhältnis 1,1 zu 1.

Dieses Verhältnis wurde immer ausgeprägter mit neuen Mitgliedern. Die EZB hat begonnen, Rotation in Erwägung zu ziehen, und in Zukunft hätten nicht alle Mitglieder permanentes Stimmrecht. Die aktuellen Vorschläge werden jedoch wenig bis gar nichts an dem von mir erwähnten Ungleichgewicht ändern. Sie verhindern bloß ein weiteres Abdriften in die Regionen.

Ein weiterer Punkt bezüglich der EZB verdient Beachtung. Ihre Prozesse der Entscheidungsfindung sind weit weniger transparent als die der US-Zentralbank oder der Bank of England. Beide haben Stimmverfahren (im einzelnen etwas unterschiedlich gestaltet), die das Gleichgewicht der Ansichten hervorheben. Die Protokolle ihrer Meetings werden mit Verzögerung veröffentlicht. Über das Gleichgewicht der Ansichten im Direktorium der EZB wissen wir weitaus weniger.

Dies ist komplexes Terrain. In unserem Buch über die Zukunft von Zentralbanken, das diese Woche veröffentlicht wird, betrachten David Green und ich die Argumente etwas genauer. Einerseits sind alle diese Merkmale Stärken. Aber in schwierigen Zeiten besteht das Risiko, dass sie zu Schwächen werden und politische Kritik nach sich ziehen.

Unsere Schlussfolgerungen sind, dass es wichtig sein wird, die Mechanismen der Rechenschaftspflicht der EZB zu stärken. Die Vorgänge sollten transparenter werden, und der ›Index der fehlerhaften Anzeige‹ sollte zumindest nicht weiter ansteigen dürfen. Wir sagen dies nicht, weil wir die Unabhängigkeit der EZB verringern möchten, sondern gerade weil wir sie erhalten möchten. Wir sehen ein Risiko darin, dass in schwierigen Zeiten Druck auf die EZB nach mehr politischer Kontrolle ausgeübt werden könnte, was gefährlich ist. Um dem entgegenzuwirken, sollte die EZB bereit sein, ihre Vorgänge jetzt offenzulegen, um denen, die von ihren Entscheidungen betroffen sind, mehr Vertrauen zu vermitteln. Wir halten ebenfalls fest, dass wenn die EZB über mehr Einfluss bezüglich Angelegenheiten der Finanzstabilität verfügt – wie auch vorgesehen ist – würde dies zu weiterem Druck auf ihre Rechenschaftspflicht führen. Recht unterschiedliche Mechanismen sind also für regulierende Entscheidungen vonnöten.

Schlussfolgerungen

Der EWU steht deswegen eine umfangreiche Agenda des Wandels bevor, wenn sie nach den Erfahrungen des ersten Jahrzehnts, und speziell nach denen der aktuellen Krise, neu geordnet werden soll. Ich weiß nicht, ob dies die Absichten von Kommissar Almunia waren, als er von ›unvollendeter Aufgabe‹ sprach, jedenfalls ist das mein Vorschlag.

Insgesamt müssen wir uns bewusst machen, dass die ersten Jahre der Währungsunion relativ ruhig verliefen. Wie wir in »Banking on the Future« sagen: »Rückblickend kann man feststellen, dass das erste Euro-Jahrzehnt günstig für die Lancierung eines unerprobten Experiments war ... Man wird sehen, ob das Euro-Gebiet so komfortabel bleibt, und die Verfahrensweisen der EZB gleichermaßen so akzeptiert, nun, da eine noch nie dagewesene Periode wirtschaftlicher Ruhe ein Ende hat«.

Bei einer Feierstunde im Juli 2009 in Straßburg zum zehnten Geburtstag des Euros sagte Jean-Claude Trichet: »Die Finanzkrise demonstriert, dass es in bewegten finanziellen Gewässern besser ist, sich auf einem großen, soliden und verlässlichen Schiff als auf einem kleinen Boot zu befinden.« Er fuhr fort: »Gemeinsam haben wir bewiesen, dass Europa Entscheidungen treffen kann, selbst unter schwierigsten Umständen.«

Ich bin der stolze Besitzer eines kleinen (10 m), älteren Bootes. Zufällig liegt es in Griechenland vor Anker. Manchmal bin ich geneigt zu glauben, es sei sicherer als einige der großen Kreuzfahrtschiffe, die ich im Korfu-Kanal mit ihren Manövern ringen sehe. Ich möchte nicht den Eindruck erwecken, dass die Griechen besser daran täten, das Drachme-Dampfschiff wieder zu aktivieren. Aber diejenigen, die auf der Brücke des Euro-Mutterschiffs stehen, sollten eingestehen, dass das bloße Geltendmachen eines Größenwerts und das Verweilen bei vergangenen Erfolgen nicht ausreicht. Eine gründliche Überholung steht noch aus, sonst werden es einige Passagiere vorziehen, die Rettungsboote zu besteigen. Mein Ziel heute Abend war es, einige Bereiche aufzuzeigen, wo Wartungsarbeiten am notwendigsten sind.

Die Veränderungen, auf die man sich am Wochenende geeinigt hat, sind ein Anfang, aber gehen noch nicht weit genug. Sie machen Wettbewerbsfähigkeit nicht zum Thema. Sie schaffen keinen permanenten Fonds. Ich befürchte, dass dies nicht das letzte Wort gewesen sein wird, weder für Europa, noch für Griechenland. Ich wäre überrascht, falls Griechenland einer Restrukturierung ausweicht, außer wenn die Wirtschaft schnell wieder in Fahrt kommt. Dieses Schulden-BIP-Verhältnis steigt auf 150 % an, selbst mit aktuell abgestimmten Budgeteinschnitten, insofern bleibt die Struktur mit Mängeln behaftet, und die EWU ist immer noch unvollendet. Europas Führungskräfte haben vielleicht ein bisschen Zeit gewonnen, aber sie müssen sie dann auch gut zu nutzen wissen.

Übersetzung: Richard Pfennig

Der Text beruht auf dem Vortrag, den Sir Howard Davies im Rahmen der Convoco Lectures am 10. Mai 2010 in München gehalten hat.

Anmerkungen

1 Joaquin Almunia, The European Economy as Home to the Next Global Currency. »The Euro at 10« conference (Die Europäische

Wirtschaft als Zuhause der nächsten Globalen Wirtschaft, »Dem Euro zum 10.«-Konferenz), Peterson Institute for International Economics, Washington, 10. Oktober 2008.

2 Margaret Thatcher, Statecraft (Staatsführung), HarperCollins, 2002.

3 Helmut Kohl, Regierungserklärung vor dem Bundestag, 6. November 1991, www.bundestag.de

4 Antwort von Dominique Strauss-Kahn auf eine Frage aus dem Publikum, »The Euro at 10« conference (»Dem Euro zum 10.«-Konferenz), Peterson Institute for International Economics, Washington, 10. Oktober 2008.

5 Otmar Issing, Europe cannot afford to rescue Greece (Europa kann es sich nicht leisten, Griechenland zu retten), The Financial Times, 15. Februar 2010, www.ft.com

6 EMU@10: successes and challenges after 10 years of Economic and Monetary Union. DG for Economic and Financial Affairs. European Commission (EWU@10: Erfolge und Herausforderungen nach 10 Jahren Wirtschafts- und Währungsunion. GD für Wirtschafts- und Finanzangelegenheiten. Europäische Kommission), 2008, http://ec.europa.eu

7 Otmar Issing, The Euro – A Currency Without a State (Der Euro – Eine Währung ohne Staat), CFS Working Paper Nr. 2008/51, Dezember 2008, www.ifk-cfs.de

8 Jean Pisani-Ferry, André Sapir und Benedicta Marzinotto, Two crises, two responses (Zwei Krisen, zwei Antworten), Bruegel Policy Brief 2010/01, 22. März 2010.

9 Sebastian Dullien und Daniela Schwarzer, The Euro Zone Needs an External Stability Pact (Die Eurozone braucht einen externen Stabilitätspakt), SWP Comments 9, Juli 2009, www.swp-berlin.org

10 Daniel Gros und Thomas Mayer, Towards a Euro(pean) Monetary Fund (In Richtung eines Euro(päischen) Währungsfonds), Economic Policy CEPS Policy Brief Nr. 202, Februar 2010.

11 Wolfgang Schäuble, Why Europe's monetary union faces its biggest crisis (Warum Europas Währungsunion vor ihrer größten Krise steht), The Financial Times, 11. März 2010, www.ft.com

[12] Willem Buiter, Global Economics View: Sovereign Debt Problems in Advanced Countries (Globale Wirtschaftsansicht: Probleme der Staatsschulden in Industrieländern), Citigroup, 26. April 2010.

[13] Jacques Delpla und Jakob von Weizsäcker, The Blue Bond Proposal (Der Blue Bond-Vorschlag), Bruegel Policy Brief 2010/03, Mai 2010.

[14] High-Level Group on Financial Supervision in the EU, chaired by Jacques de Larosière (Spitzentreffen zur Finanzüberwachung in der EU, Vorsitz Jacques de Larosière), Februar 2009, http://ec.europa.eu

[15] Sebastian Dullien und Daniela Schwarzer, Bringing Macroeconomics into the EU Budget Debate: Why and How? (Über das Einbringen von Makroökonomie in die EU-Budgetdebatte: Warum und wie?), Journal of Common Market Studies Vol. 47 Nr. 1, 2009.

[16] Andrew Hughes Hallett und Jan Libich, Central Bank Independence, Accountability and Transparency: Complements or Strategic Substitutes? (Unabhängigkeit, Rechenschaftspflicht und Transparenz: Ergänzungen oder strategischer Ersatz?), CEPR Discussion Papers 5470, Januar 2006.

[17] Helge Berger, Optimal Central Bank Design: Benchmarks for the ECB (Optimales Zentralbank-Design: Maßstäbe für die EZB), CESifo Working Paper Nr. 1697, März 2006.

PROF. DR. H.C. ROLAND BERGER

SIEBEN THESEN ZUM THEMA STAATSVERSCHULDUNG UND STAATSINSOLVENZEN – AM BEISPIEL DER DERZEITIGEN PROBLEME DER EURO-ZONE UND DER EUROPÄISCHEN UNION

Die Rückführung der wachsenden Staatsverschuldung ist eines der drängendsten politischen und wirtschaftlichen Probleme unserer Zeit. Bereits 2010 werden alle Länder der Welt zusammen mit 48 Billionen Dollar verschuldet sein. Das sind etwa 80 % des globalen Bruttoinlandsprodukts.[1] Die Staatsverschuldung der Industrieländer liegt sogar bei über 100 %. Die Situation in Deutschland erscheint mit 75 % noch relativ stabil, doch auch auf jeden Deutschen kommen zur Zeit 21.025 Euro Schulden und jeden Tag werden es fünf Euro mehr.[2] Bis 2020 ist eine Verschuldung von 97 % des BIP zu erwarten.[3]

Zur Einführung und als mögliche Stichpunkte für unsere Diskussionen am heutigen Tag möchte ich sieben Thesen zu aktuellen wirtschaftlichen Aspekten zum Thema Staatsverschuldung und Staatsinsolvenzen darlegen und kurz erläutern:

These 1: Staatspleiten sind eine durchaus realistische Möglichkeit und nicht selten!

Richtig ist natürlich, dass Staaten anders als in finanzielle Not geratene Unternehmen nicht von der Landkarte verschwinden, wenn sie zahlungsunfähig sind. Es gibt auch – noch (!) – keine öffentliche Institution, die einen Staat offiziell für bankrott erklären kann. Aber »pleite gehen« können Staaten trotzdem. Eine Staatspleite liegt nach der gängigen Definition dann vor, wenn ein Land nicht mehr in der Lage ist, seine rechtlich unumstrittenen Schulden zurückzuzahlen.

Entgegen einer weitverbreiteten Meinung sind Staatsbankrotte keine Ausnahmeerscheinung. Ein Blick auf die Geschichte zeigt, dass praktisch alle Länder schon einmal pleite waren – viele sogar mehrfach. Seit dem Jahr 1800 gab es allein in Europa 59 Staatspleiten, davon auch sieben Staatsbankrotte Deutschlands.[4]

Eines der jüngeren Beispiele für die Zahlungsunfähigkeit von Staaten ist Argentinien: 2002 wollte niemand – weder institutionelle Investoren noch Privatpersonen und auch nicht einmal mehr der IWF – dem südamerikanischen Land Geld leihen. Die Regierung erklärte daraufhin ihre Zahlungsunfähigkeit und fror alle Bankguthaben ein, um einen Ansturm auf die Einlagen zu bremsen und weitere Kapitalflucht zu unterbinden. Tausende Argentinier zogen auf die Straßen, Banken verbarrikadierten sich, Bargeld wurde knapp. Die daraufhin folgende Rezession und das Chaos betraf vor allem die Ärmsten der Armen. Die Arbeitslosigkeit stieg auf 24 % und gegen Ende 2002 lebten 57 % des bis dahin mit am weitest entwickelten Landes Südamerikas unter der Armutsgrenze.[5]

These 2: Es gibt fünf Möglichkeiten, mit zu hohen Staatsschulden umzugehen

1. Staaten können die **Unabhängigkeit von Notenbanken aufheben und Geld drucken**, um die Schulden »wegzuinflationieren« – das geht in den einzelnen Ländern der Eurozone zum Glück nicht mehr. Doch für die gesamte Eurozone, wie für viele andere Länder der Welt, wäre das zumindest theoretisch eine Möglichkeit – solange eine unabhängige EZB nicht gegensteuert.
   Diese Möglichkeit wurde in der Vergangenheit oft gebraucht. Kaiser Nero war der erste, der versuchte Staatsschulden durch Geldentwertung zu vermindern. Die Römer verringerten schrittweise den Goldgehalt ihrer Münzen, bis Gewicht und Kaufkraft in etwa halbiert waren. Nachfolgende Herrscher setzten die Geldentwertung fort, so dass die Bevölkerung in den Jahren vor dem Untergang des Römischen Reiches in vielen Provinzen wieder zum Tauschhandel übergegangen war.
2. Die zweite Möglichkeit ist der **Staatsbankrott** mit allen negativen Konsequenzen für die Gläubiger und das eigene Land. Im Fall von Argentinien bedeutete das, dass die Gläubiger 75 % des Geldes, das sie diesem Staat geliehen hatten, abschreiben mussten.[6] Die staatsinternen gesellschaftlichen und wirtschaftlichen Folgen habe ich bereits erwähnt.
3. Die dritte Möglichkeit ist eine **geordnete Umschuldung** – begleitet z. B. vom IWF – meist unter strengen wirtschafts- und fiskalpolitischen Auflagen. Oftmals werden

Umschuldungen unterstützt durch weitere Geldzuflüsse von außen, in der Regel von interessierten Staaten und heute dem IWF.
Diese Möglichkeit hat allerdings in der Praxis dazu geführt, dass die Zahl der Staatspleiten zunahm, die Dauer der Zahlungsunfähigkeit von Staaten jedoch abnahm.

4. Am elegantesten ist natürlich eine **Entschuldung durch Wirtschaftswachstum**. So ermöglichte das Wirtschaftswachstum in der Nachkriegszeit den Amerikanern, ihre Staatsschulden deutlich zu reduzieren. Diese fielen in den Jahren 1945 bis 1975 von 116,0 % des BIP auf 32.5 %.[7]
5. Als fünfte Möglichkeit können Staaten mit einer **Politik des Sparens**, bei konsequenter Haushalts- und Steuerpolitik – d. h. der Rückführung von Ausgaben, meist verbunden mit einer Erhöhung der Einnahmen durch eine wachsende Belastung der Bürger – ihre Staatsfinanzen nachhaltig sanieren. Dies ist natürlich am erfolgreichsten in der Kombination mit einer stark wachsenden Wirtschaftsleistung.

Ein Blick in die Vergangenheit zeigt: Von 32 Schuldenkrisen nach 1930 wählten Staaten achtmal den Weg der Inflation, siebenmal gingen sie pleite, 16 Mal kamen sie durch Sparpolitik und externe Hilfen aus der Krise und nur einmal konnten die Schulden primär durch Wirtschaftswachstum abgebaut werden.[8]

Naturgemäß ist eine Kombination aus wachstumsorientierter Wirtschaftspolitik bei konsequenter Haushaltskonsolidierung – dann in der Regel mit externen finanziellen Überbrückungshilfen – der beste und einzige Weg, der nachhaltigen Erfolg verspricht. Die laufenden Defizite müssen zurückgefahren und idealerweise Haushaltsüberschüsse erzielt werden. Von zentraler Bedeutung für das langfristige Wirtschaftswachstum ist es, die jeweiligen Sparmaßnahmen auf ihre Wachstumsauswirkungen hin zu überprüfen. Es gilt, solche fiskalischen Maßnahmen zu ergreifen, die die Bedingungen für das Wirtschaftswachstum nicht verschlechtern, wie zum Beispiel Einsparungen im Bereich Bildung und Forschung dies tun würden.

Dass eine Kombination aus Sparmaßnahmen und Wirtschaftswachstum funktionieren kann, zeigte das Beispiel Irland vor der Krise: Von 1993 bis 2007 gelang es dem Land mit einer wachstumsorientierten Politik und zugleich einer Politik des Sparens seine Staatsverschuldung von 95 % auf 24 % seines BIP[9] zu reduzieren.[10] Ein weiteres Beispiel ist Dänemark, dessen BIP während der Konsolidierung von 1983 bis 1986 mit 3,7 % pro Jahr überdurchschnittlich gewachsen ist.[11]

These 3: Deutschland droht keine Staatspleite

Deutschland droht so schnell keine Staatspleite. Denn das Land ist strukturell und kulturell gut aufgestellt: Deutschlands Vorteile liegen in seiner starken Wirtschaftsleistung, seinem vergleichsweise hohen Kapitalstock, seinen Außenhandelsüberschüssen und auch in seiner ausgeprägten Stabilitäts-Kultur des Maßhaltens. Zum anderen hat sich das Land in die richtige wirtschafts- und fiskalpolitische Richtung entwickelt und Reformen angestoßen. Deutschland lebt nicht annähernd so sehr über seine Verhältnisse wie die PIIGS-Länder (Portugal, Italien, Irland, Griechenland, Spanien) oder z. B. Großbritannien. Zudem sind durch die mäßigen Tarifabschlüsse und das starke Produktivitätswachstum die deutschen Lohnstückkosten praktisch stabil geblieben (plus 2,7 % von 2000 bis 2008), während diese in den meisten anderen europäischen Staaten, vor allem in den PIIGS-Staaten um knapp 30 % gestiegen sind – mit allen positiven Folgen für die Wettbewerbsfähigkeit und die Leistungsbilanzüberschüsse Deutschlands.[12]

Abb. 1: Lohnstückkostenanstieg 2008 gegenüber 2000 (in %)

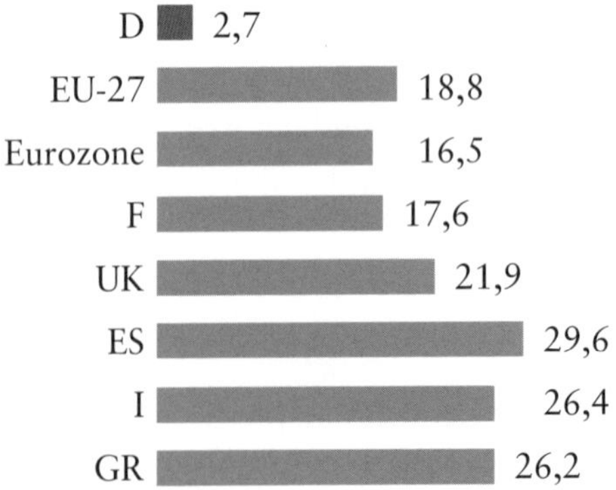

Quelle: Europäische Kommission

Ein weiteres Maß für das Insolvenzrisiko eines Staates ist die Zins-Steuer-Quote, also das Verhältnis der Zinszahlungen zu den Steuereinnahmen. Als kritisch gilt sie ab 30 %, bei 50 % ist der Staatshaushalt in der Regel am Ende. Deutschlands Zins-Steuer-Quote lag 2009 bei 10,1 %, 2010 wird sie voraussichtlich bei 11,5 % liegen.[13] Direkt betroffen von einer Staatsinsolvenz wird Deutschland also so schnell nicht sein. Das Land hat aber ein großes Interesse daran, dass zumindest innerhalb der Eurozone – idealerweise auch weltweit – Wege gefunden werden, mit exzessiver Staatsverschuldung und nicht an Währungs- und Haushaltsstabilität ausgerichteter Wirtschafts- und Fiskalpolitik umzugehen.

These 4: Die Eurozone ist labil – Es besteht eine reale Gefahr für den Euro

Griechenlands Wirtschaftsleistung hat an der EU zwar nur einen Anteil von gerade einmal 2,0 % und an der Eurozone von 2,7 % – das ist weniger als der Anteil der »notorischen Pleiteländer« Saarland und Bremen am deutschen Sozialprodukt, ohne dass die exzessive Verschuldung dieser Länder die frühere D-Mark je gefährdet hätte. Auch der US-Dollar ist durch den »bankrotten« Bundesstaat Kalifornien, der immerhin für 13 % der amerikanischen Wirtschaftsleistung verantwortlich zeichnet, nicht gefährdet. Die Reaktion der Märkte zeigt aber, dass die Lage beim Euro anders ist. Drei Gründe hierfür:

- Der vor neun Jahren real eingeführte Euro ist eine junge Währung, ganz im Gegensatz zum US-Dollar, der eine über 200 Jahre alte Tradition aufweisen kann, oder der D-Mark, die immerhin über ein halbes Jahrhundert als Synonym für Stabilität galt.

- Trotz Unabhängigkeit der Notenbank und bundesstaatlicher Verfassung haben die Vereinigten Staaten sowie Deutschland eine nationale Wirtschafts- und Fiskalpolitik, die auch für ihre Bundesstaaten bzw. Bundesländer bestimmend ist. Der Europäischen Union und der Eurozone fehlt es jedoch gänzlich an einer koordinierten Wirtschafts- und Fiskalpolitik.
- Zudem bestehen in den USA und in Deutschland klare Regeln für Bundesstaaten/Bundesländer, die finanziell in Schwierigkeiten geraten. In Deutschland haben wir den Länderfinanzausgleich. In den USA gibt es Restrukturierungs- bzw. Umschuldungsverfahren für Bundesstaaten – wie in New York 1975 erfolgreich durchgeführt – sowie klare Defizit- und Verschuldungsgrenzen. Im Euroraum dagegen gibt es im Lissabon-Vertrag die »no-bail-out clause«, die Rettungsaktionen zwischen den Mitgliedsländern untersagt – eine Klausel, die wohl de facto nicht durchsetzbar sein wird. Zur Überwindung der jetzigen Krise sind andere Wege einzuschlagen, bevor die Voraussetzungen für einen starken Euro und danach eine funktionierende Bail-out-Klausel gegeben sein werden.

In der EU erwirtschaftete Deutschland 2009 einen Außenhandelsüberschuss gegenüber den anderen 26 Mitgliedsländern von insgesamt 115.800 Millionen Euro (4,9 % des BIP), wovon 79.700 Millionen Euro (3,3 % des BIP) auf die Länder der Eurozone entfallen. Im Gegensatz dazu betrugen die Außenhandelsdefizite Spaniens –5,5 %, Griechenlands –11,2 % und Portugals –10,0 % des jeweiligen BIP.[14] Mit jedem Überschussjahr steigen die Forderungen der Überschussländer wie Deutschland gegenüber den Defizitländern. Laut einer Statistik der Bundesbank haben die Deutschen Ende 2009 ein Netto-Auslandsvermögen von 808,9 Milliarden Euro angesammelt. Im Jahr 2000 waren es erst 67 Milliarden Euro und damit weniger als ein Zehntel.[15] Dem entsprechend sind private und öffentliche Schulden in den Defizitländern weiter gewachsen. So werden die Budgetdefizite von Griechenland, Spanien und Portugal 2010 zwischen 8,5 und 12,5 % ihres BIP liegen und das von Frankreich bei ca. 8 %.[16]

These 5: Die hohe und wachsende Staatsverschuldung der Industrieländer und die niedrige und sinkende Staatsverschuldung der Schwellenländer wird das weltwirtschaftliche Gewicht der Schwellenländer noch schneller nach oben treiben

In der Vergangenheit fanden sich exzessive Staatsverschuldung und Staatsbankrotte vor allem in den Schwellenländern, wie z. B. in Argentinien, in Russland oder bei der Asienkrise.

Nun aber hat sich das Blatt gewendet. Die Welt wird sich in neue Gewinner und Verlierer aufteilen. Nach Berechnungen des Internationalen Währungsfonds wird die Staatsverschuldung der Industrieländer von durchschnittlich 78 % des BIP vor der Krise bis Ende 2010 auf über 100 % steigen.[17] Eine Studie der Deutschen Bank prognostiziert einen weiteren Anstieg auf 133 % im Jahr 2020. Die durchschnittliche Staatsverschuldung der Schwellenländer dagegen wird sich nach Erkenntnis der Deutschen Bank ohne größere fiskalische Korrekturen von heute 46 % des BIP auf etwa 35 % im Jahr 2020 reduzieren.[18]

Die vielbeachtete Studie »This Time is Different« der amerikanischen Ökonomen Carmen Reinhart und Kenneth Rogoff zeigt, dass Staatsverschuldung ab einer gewissen Höhe negativ mit Wirtschaftswachstum korreliert.[19] Vergangene Schuldenkrisen bestätigen, dass eine Schuldenquote von mehr als 90 % das Wirtschaftswachstum eines Landes spürbar belastet.[20] Die Industrieländer werden daher noch langsamer wachsen und die Schwellenländer werden noch schneller davonziehen.

Durch die unterschiedliche Verschuldung wird die Verschiebung der Wirtschaftsmacht in Richtung Schwellenländer also schneller geschehen, als uns das vor der Krise möglich erschien!

These 6: Die Eurozone braucht eine koordinierte Wirtschafts- und Fiskalpolitik

Die Krise der sogenannten PIIGS-Staaten legt nicht nur deren mangelnde Wettbewerbsfähigkeit offen, sondern verdeutlicht auch die Schwächen der gesamten Eurozone. Eine Währungsunion kann nur dann funktionieren, wenn klare Regeln für Fiskal- und Wirtschaftspolitik bestehen. Der bestehende Maastrichtvertrag kann jedoch offensichtlich keine dauerhafte Haushaltsdisziplin der Länder der Eurozone gewährleisten, ebenso wenig wie eine konsistente Entwicklung ihrer Wettbewerbsfähigkeit.

Bei Verletzungen des Stabilitätspaktes treten Sanktionen nicht automatisch ein. Und wenn eine größere Zahl von Ländern gleichzeitig die Defizitgrenze verletzt, dürfte sich kaum eine Mehrheit für die Anwendung von Strafmaßnahmen finden. Der Stabilitätspakt ist also eine Selbstverpflichtung, gegen die in Krisensituationen einfach verstoßen wird. Das zeigt die Tatsache, dass zur Zeit alle Länder der Eurozone die Maastricht-Kriterien überschreiten. Die Stabilität des Euro kann der Stabilitäts- und Wachstumspakt allein daher nicht sichern.

Die Eurokrise zeigt: Die Stabilität einer Währungsunion hängt nicht nur von der Geldpolitik der Europäischen Zentralbank ab. Auch die Fiskal- und Wirtschaftspolitik der einzelnen Mitgliedsländer spielen eine wichtige Rolle. Die Eurozone braucht deshalb künftig eine Institution, die die wirtschaftlichen und fiskalischen Prozesse verfolgt und wenn nötig steuert. Nur so können der notwendige Konsolidierungsprozess der PIIGS-Staaten wirksam überwacht, die Finanzlage der einzelnen Staaten besser präventiv und ex-post kontrolliert und Fehlentwicklungen wie die ökonomischen Ungleichgewichte zwischen einzelnen Mitgliedsstaaten rechtzeitig bekämpft werden.

Da einzelne Länder keine Möglichkeit mehr haben, ihre eigenen Währungen abzuwerten, um ihre Wettbewerbsfähigkeit wieder zu verbessern, gefährden die wachsenden makroökonomischen Asymmetrien und Ungleichgewichte die Stabilität der gemeinsamen Währung. Eine koordinierte Wirtschaftspolitik kann das verhindern und für eine abgestimmte Haushaltspolitik sorgen. Auch ein bewusstes Unterlaufen des Fiskal- und Stabilitätspakts oder die Angabe von falschen Zahlen, wie im Fall von Griechenland geschehen, könnte durch eine verantwortliche europäische Institution künftig verhindert bzw. zumindest erschwert werden.

These 7: Die Eurozone braucht einen neu gefassten Stabilitätspakt – das »Window of Opportunity« dafür besteht bis Ende 2010

Die Krise hat den Euro als »Schönwetterwährung« entlarvt. Der Stabilitäts- und Wachstumspakt von Maastricht aus dem Jahr 1992, der dies verhindern sollte, hat sich als

»zahnloser Tiger« erwiesen. Gelingt es den Euro in der jetzigen Krise durch gemeinsame Anstrengungen der Mitgliedsländer zu stabilisieren, dann ist zu dessen nachhaltiger Stabilität ein neuer Maastrichtvertrag unerlässlich. Sieben Grundsätze sollten darin festgeschrieben sein:

1. Obergrenze für Budgetdefizit in inverser Beziehung zur Schuldenquote
2. Koordinierte Wirtschafts- und Fiskalpolitik
3. Ex-ante-Budgetkontrolle durch eine dafür vorzusehende Instanz
4. Automatische Sanktionen
5. Geordnetes Insolvenzverfahren für Mitgliedsstaaten
6. Obergrenze für EU-Kredite an Mitgliedsländer
7. Verfahren zum Exit aus dem Euro

Gelingt es den Staaten der Eurozone und den Mitgliedsländern der EU, sich – in welcher Form auch immer – auf diese Spielregeln zu einigen und sie durchzusetzen, kann die gemeinsame Währung noch zum Erfolg werden. Damit wäre gleichzeitig eine wesentliche Grundlage für die weitere Prosperität und deren Wachstum in der EU sowie der Eurozone und den Mitgliedsländern gesichert.

Fazit

Bisher leben die meisten Industrieländer über ihre Verhältnisse – mit fatalen Folgen vor allem für künftige Generationen. Denn zusätzlich zu den expliziten Schulden droht auf lange Sicht eine weitere Gefahr: Die steigenden altersbedingten Ausgaben und Zahlungsverpflichtungen der Industrieländer. In Deutschland beträgt diese zusätzliche implizite Staatsschuld 6,2 Billionen Euro[21], die sich aus Pensionslasten und Ansprüchen an die Sozialversicherungen ergibt. Damit liegt die gesamte deutsche Schuldenquote bei 315 % des BIP.

Haushaltskonsolidierung ist also kein Selbstzweck, sondern eine Bedingung für Wirtschaftswachstum und eine Pflicht gegenüber kommenden Generationen. Ausgabenkürzung und strukturelle Reformen müssen jetzt angegangen werden! Schon 55 v. Chr. hat Cicero gesagt: »Das Budget sollte ausgeglichen sein, die öffentlichen Schulden sollten reduziert werden (...) und die Bürger sollten mehr arbeiten, statt sich auf die Gaben der Regierung zu verlassen!«

Der Text beruht auf dem Vortrag, den Prof. Dr. h.c. Roland Berger im Rahmen der Convoco Lectures am 13. April 2010 in München gehalten hat (noch vor dem Beschluss des Hilfspakets für Griechenland in Höhe von. € 110 Mrd. am 2. Mai 2010 und dem Rettungspaket für den Euro in Höhe von. € 750 Mrd. am 10. Mai 2010).

Anmerkungen

1 Kai A. Konrad/Holger Zschäpitz: Schulden ohne Sühne? Warum der Absturz der Staatsfinanzen uns alle trifft, München 2010.

2 Statistisches Bundesamt, Roland Berger Research.

3 DB Research: Staatsverschuldung in 2020. Eine Tragfähigkeitsanalyse für Industrie- und Schwellenländer, Frankfurt 2010.

4 Carmen M. Reinhart/Kenneth S. Rogoff: This Time is Different: Eight Centuries of Financial Folly, Princeton 2009.

5 EIU, IWF World Economic and Financial Surveys (2010): World Economic Outlook – Rebalancing Growth.

6 US Government: Historical Debt, US Treasury's measure of US National Debt.

7 Carmen M. Reinhart/Kenneth S. Rogoff: This Time is Different: Eight Centuries of Financial Folly, Princeton 2009.

8 Ebda.

9 EIU

10 Heute beträgt die Staatsverschuldung Irlands jedoch wieder 87 % des BIP. Die Erfolge Irlands bei der Haushaltskonsolidierung wurden in der Krise v. a. durch den hohen Kapitalbedarf der Banken zunichte gemacht. Alle großen Banken des Landes sind bereits teilverstaatlicht, faule Hypothekenkredite wurden von der Regierung abgenommen und die Banken mit frischem Kapital ausgestattet.

11 EIU

12 Europäische Kommission

13 Statistisches Bundesamt

14 Eurostat

15 Bundesbank

16 Eurostat

17 IWF World Economic and Financial Surveys (2010): World Economic Outlook – Rebalancing Growth.

18 DB Research: Staatsverschuldung in 2020. Eine Tragfähigkeitsanalyse für Industrie- und Schwellenländer, Frankfurt 2010.

19 Carmen M. Reinhart/Kenneth S. Rogoff: This Time is Different: Eight Centuries of Financial Folly, Princeton 2009.

20 Ebda.

21 Stiftung Marktwirtschaft: Bernd Raffelhüschen/Stefan Moog: Ehrbarer Staat? Die Generationenbilanz: Update 2009: Wirtschaftskrise trifft Tragfähigkeit, Argumente zu Marktwirtschaft und Politik, Nr. 108, Berlin 2009.

FORUM

DR. KAI ENGELBRECHT

PROTOKOLL DES CONVOCO FORUMS 2010: STAATSFINANZIERUNG UND WIRTSCHAFTS-FINANZIERUNG AM SCHEIDEWEG

Zum Convoco Forum 2010, das erstmals in Salzburg stattfand, folgten Professor Dr. h.c. Roland Berger, Professor Dr. Dr. h.c. mult. Otmar Issing, Professor Dr. Kai A. Konrad, Professor Dr. Christoph G. Paulus und Professor Dr. Dr. h.c. Wolfgang Schön der Einladung der Initiatoren Dr. Corinne M. Flick, Professor Dr. Dr. h.c. mult. Paul Kirchhof und Professor Dr. Stefan Korioth. Das diesjährige Thema – Staatsfinanzierung und Wirtschaftsfinanzierung am Scheideweg – war nicht nur infolge jüngster Entwicklungen von hoher Aktualität. Krisenhafte Zuspitzungen der Lage insbesondere an den Finanzmärkten mögen aus wirtschaftswissenschaftlicher Sicht erklärbar sein, illustrieren aber zugleich, dass sich das Recht in seiner Eigenschaft als Steuerungsinstrument bereits in einiger Distanz zum Ausnahmefall relativiert. Gleichwohl wies die Diskussion Wege des Umgangs mit neuartigen Anforderungen der ökonomischen Lebenswirklichkeit.

1. Gespräch (Freitag, 18. Juni 2010)

Die Gesprächsrunde am Freitagnachmittag eröffnete ein Einführungsreferat von Professor Dr. Dr. h.c. mult. Otmar Issing (Frankfurt).

Die gegenwärtige Finanz- und Wirtschaftskrise habe sich in drei Schritten entwickelt. Zunächst sei schon länger eine Abschwächung der Weltkonjunktur zu beobachten gewesen; hohen Überschüssen in einigen Ländern, wie zum Beispiel China, stünden Leistungsbilanzdefizite in anderen, etwa den USA, gegenüber. Bestimmte Industriezweige, so die Kfz-Industrie, hätten im Lauf der Zeit Überkapazitäten aufgebaut. In dieser Lage habe sich seit 2007 eine Finanzmarktkrise entwickelt. Der Geldmarkt und das Vertrauen der Banken untereinander sei ebenso gestört gewesen wie die Finanzierung der Märkte; in Teilen könne von einem »Marktverschwinden« gesprochen werden. Die Frage, ob diese Situation in einem Markt- oder einem Staatsversagen ihre Ursache habe, beantwortete Issing im Sinne einer Kombinationsthese. So sei die Hypothekenkrise am US-amerikanischen Immobilienmarkt darauf zurückzuführen, dass die finanzierenden Banken Kredite ohne hinreichenden Bedacht auf die Leistungsfähigkeit der Schuldner ausgegeben hätten. Zuvor seien aber Institute wie Fannie Mae und Freddie Mac mit dem Ziel gegründet worden, auch weniger solventen Bürgern eine Immobilienfinanzierung und damit ein eigenes Haus zu verschaffen. Im europäischen wie im nationalen Raum hätten sich Defizite bei der Bankenaufsicht gezeigt. Die Landesbanken verfügten mitunter nicht über ein Geschäftsmodell, das zu ihrem vergleichsweise hohen Eigenkapital passe. In der Europäischen Union seien hohe Lohnstückkosten und Leistungsbilanzdefizite festzustellen. Der Stabilitäts- und Wachstumspakt sei von den politischen Akteuren nicht in ausreichendem Maß ernst genommen und bei anstehenden Entscheidungen berücksichtigt worden. Schließlich habe sich in einem auch durch Interventionen herbeigeführten Ansteigen der staatlichen Verpflichtungen eine Schuldenkrise entwickelt. Unterdes seien notwendige neue Regeln bereits in Vorbereitung; wichtig seien etwa striktere Vorgaben betreffend das Eigenkapital der Banken.

Das Gespräch wandte sich zunächst der Frage zu, was die gegenwärtige Situation kennzeichne und welche Ursachen ihr zugrunde lägen.

Prof. Dr. Stefan Korioth (München) stimmte Issing in seinem Befund eines Zusammenspiels von Markt- und Staatsversagen zu. Auswege seien nicht leicht zu finden. Was ein Versagen von Marktregulierungen betreffe, sei insbesondere nach den Ursachen für strukturelle Entscheidungen zu suchen; vor dem Idealbild einer Selbststeuerung des Marktes sei das von Issing festgestellte Marktversagen eine Erscheinung, die es so »eigentlich« gar nicht geben dürfe.

Im Staatsversagen werde, so die Auffassung von Professor Dr. h.c. Roland Berger (München), eine Bereitschaft von Politikern offenbar, gesetzliche Regelungen zu schaffen, ohne sich an den wirtschaftlichen Folgen zu stören. Populistische Erklärungsmuster – »Schuld sind die Spekulanten« – stünden im Vordergrund. Anstehende politische Maßnahmen müssten sich gegen ein Überborden des Wohlfahrtsstaates richten, nicht hingegen auf eine Verteilung von Wohltaten, die von niemandem produziert werden könnten. Im Vergleich mit einem Hausbau müsse sich die staatliche Wirtschaftsweise eher am Prinzip des Ansparens orientieren als an der Bezahlung auf Kredit.

Issing bewertete die Gesamtlage weniger als düster denn als komplex. Was die USA betreffe, komme dem Staatsversagen gegenüber dem Marktversagen ein Übergewicht zu, allerdings spielten hier wohl auch selbstschädigende Geschäftsmodelle eine Rolle. Vor der Finanzmarktkrise seien die Renditeunterschiede bei Staatsanleihen marginal gewesen, dies habe selbst im Verhältnis von Deutschland und zweifelhaften Schuldnern gegolten. Renditeunterschiede müssten aber Differenzen im Risiko abbilden. Am Markt sei mittlerweile eine extreme Risikoscheu entstanden, die zurückgeführt werden müsse. Auch das systemische Risiko sei einzugrenzen. Die staatliche Aufsicht habe sich auf diese Aufgabe zu konzentrieren. Dabei sei auf eine höhere Kapitalisierung der Kreditinstitute zu achten; normativ seien Verfahren kontrollierter Abwicklung bereitzustellen. Dabei sei auch an das Modell eines »Bankenhospitals«[1] zu denken. Fremdkapitalelemente mit Eigenkapitalfunktion stellten ein wichtiges Stabilisierungselement dar. Dr. Corinne M. Flick gab die zwischenzeitlich signifikanten Unterschiede in den Renditen deutscher und griechischer Staatsbonds zu bedenken.

Professor Dr. Kai A. Konrad (München) bezeichnete als ein wesentliches Problem, dass die Marktakteure in weitem Umfang aus ihrer Verantwortung entlassen seien. Hafte der Einzelne im privaten Konkurs insofern beschränkt, als nachteilige Folgen des eigenen Handelns grundsätzlich weder generationenübergreifend noch in Bezug auf die persönliche Freiheit einträten – der »Schuldturm« sei eben abgeschafft –, zeige sich darin auch eine politische Leitlinie, dass dem Einzelnen eine umfassende Verantwortung nicht zugemutet werden könne.

Korioth hob die Prinzipien von Autonomie und Verantwortung hervor; präventive Eingriffe seitens des Staates setzten ausgleichsbedürftige Defizite voraus. Die Verhältnisse zeigten, dass Risiken erkannt, aus ihnen jedoch noch keine Folgerungen gezogen seien. Manche Marktakteure handelten in vorsätzlicher Gleichgültigkeit. Das von Konrad gewählte Bild, dass »Schulden ohne Sühne«[2] blieben, referiere auf eine theologische Begrifflichkeit. Konrad entgegnete, dass sich die Banken rational im Sinne ihrer Anteilseigner verhielten.

Berger erläuterte, dass infolge der Einführung des Euro eine Zinskonvergenz eingetreten sei, die im Vergleich zu früheren Zeiten etwa Spanien oder Griechenland eine Finanzierung ihrer Gemeinwesen, den Bürgern dieser Länder Investitionen wie für ein Haus zunächst erleichtert habe. Staatsversagen und Marktversagen seien getrennt zu würdigen.

Nach Auffassung Issings neigten viele Menschen zum Extrapolieren. In Bezug auf die Ausführungen Konrads mochte er eine unzureichende Bereitschaft vieler Marktteilnehmer erkennen, für die Folgen des eigenen Handelns einzustehen. Beispielhaft verwies er auf die Selbstverständlichkeit, mit welcher Entschädigungen für die Kunden der isländischen Kaupthing-Bank gefordert und gewährt worden seien. Die Haltung: »der Staat ist schuld und muss liefern« sei leider weit verbreitet wie auch einseitige Verantwortungszuschreibungen an »die Spekulanten«. Paulus befand, dass das Risiko für die Untauglichkeit eines Produkts mittlerweile geradezu grundsätzlich auf den Verkäufer übertragen worden sei; in einer solchen Risikoverteilung spiegele sich ein Verantwortungsdefizit.

Autonomie und Verantwortung bildeten, so Korioth, noch immer Kernprinzipien des modernen Rechtsdenkens. Allerdings würden die Einbruchstellen für andere Erwägungen zahlreicher. Dies sei auch auf Verschiebungen im Menschenbild zurückzuführen. Während Korioth einer »harten« Steuerung durch Verbote eine »weichere«, anders wirkende Regulierung gegenüberstellte, hob Issing hervor, dass auch diese eine »Höhendifferenz« zwischen regulierten und nicht regulierten Bereichen erzeuge. Daraus ergebe sich das Problem der Umgehungsgeschäfte.

Auf eine Frage von Frau Flick meinte Konrad, dass die gegenwärtige Krise bereits länger angelegt gewesen sei. Die Kapitalmärkte hätten allerdings zunächst nicht reagiert. Zwischen privater und öffentlicher Verschuldung bestehe ein wichtiger Unterschied: Einen Privaten treffe die Verpflichtung, aufgenommene Kredite zurückzuzahlen, in eigener Person; Politiker hingegen seien durch die Kürze der Wahlperioden in der Lage, Nachteile auf nachfolgende Politikergenerationen abzuwälzen. Zustimmend machte Berger bei politischen Funktionsträgern eine Tendenz zu drittschädigendem Verhalten aus. Dem sei durch geeignete Maßnahmen, etwa eine Schuldenbremse, entgegenzuwirken.

Mit Blick auf staatliche Aufgabenausweitungen fragte Korioth, warum keinem demokratischen Staat eine Schuldenbegrenzung gelinge, und zweifelte an der europarechtlichen Zulässigkeit eines von der Gemeinschaft aufgespannten »Rettungsschirms«. Issing hielt steuernde Eingriffe auf der Ebene der Rahmenbedingungen für möglich; allerdings ziele Politikberatung oftmals auf Maßnahmen, die ohnehin wahrscheinlich seien.

Schwerpunkt eines zweiten Abschnitts des Gesprächs war die Staatsverschuldung mit ihren ökonomischen und rechtlichen Implikationen. Berücksichtigung fand dabei auch die europäische Dimension.

In einigen einführenden Worten stellte Konrad die Staatsverschuldung in einen historischen Kontext. Im Jahr 2010 habe die Krise eine Zuspitzung erfahren. Die ökonomischen Ursachen seien unklar. Konrad wies einem Rudelverhalten von Gläubigern eine Schlüsselbedeutung zu: Solange alle annähmen, dass ein Land seine Schulden begleiche, entstehe kein Problem; gerate ein Land in Verzug oder stelle seine Zahlungen ein, komme es zu einem unkontrollierten Ansteigen von Renditedifferenzen zwischen den Staatsanleihen. Für die Zukunft rechnete Konrad mit zwei Szenarien: Zum einen könne sich eine europäische Wirtschaftsregierung etablieren, welche insbesondere die nationalen Haushalte vorab prüfe, um versteckte Schulden aufzuspüren. Eine solche Aufsicht sei kompliziert, da vielfältige haushaltstechnische Manipulationsmöglichkeiten bestünden und erkannt werden müssten. Dies sei nur um den Preis nachdrücklichen »Hineinregierens« in die nationale Sphäre möglich. Dennoch sei die europäische Wirtschaftsregierung ein realistisches Szenario. Die Alternative liege darin, die dreijährige Wirkungszeit des »Rettungsschirms« für eine Neuentdeckung des Stabilitäts- und Wachstumspakts zu nutzen. Besondere Bedeutung komme den Referenzkriterien sowie dem Gebot des No-Bailout[3] zu. Den Politikern müsse vermittelt werden, dass eine Umschuldung nichts Unnormales sei. Notwendige Umschuldungen seien vorzubereiten, auch um die Glaubwürdigkeit des No-Bailout zu wahren.

Während Korioth die Frage ansprach, welche der Alternativen aus rechtlicher Sicht wahrscheinlicher sei, hielt Berger auch eine Kombination beider Szenarien für möglich. Konrad machte Änderungsbedarf im Primärrecht aus und betonte die Notwendigkeit, die Portfolios institutioneller Anleger ausgewogen zu komponieren. Ein Zinsvorteil ohne realistisches Ausfallrisiko schaffe fragwürdige Anreize für den Erwerb unsolider Staatsbonds. Die Glaubwürdigkeit des No-Bailout war auch Issing ein wichtiges Anliegen.

Mit Blick auf das Berlin-Urteil[4] des Bundesverfassungsgerichts zu Finanzkrisen einzelner Länder des Bundes formulierte Korioth die Wertung: Wer Schulden eingehe, sei für diese auch selbst verantwortlich, als einen Grundgedanken der föderalen Finanzordnung. Die vom Bundesverfassungsgericht postulierte Ausnahme des bundesstaatlichen Notstands sei bewusst diffus gehalten. Im Länderfinanzausgleich komme das Kriterium gleichwertiger Lebensbedingungen nicht vor; entscheidender Vergleichsmaßstab seien die Steuereinnahmen eines Jahres. Auf der Ebene der Gemeinschaft werde die Frage nach den Rettungsobliegenheiten ihrer Mitglieder gegenüber anderen – entgegen dem Primärrecht – abweichend beantwortet. Die Berufung Griechenlands auf eine Notlage sei unzutreffend, weil die Schulden des Landes über einen langen Zeitraum bewusst aufgehäuft worden seien. Korioth erwartete für die Zukunft den situativen Einsatz der Gemeinschaft als »Feuerwehr«; die im Primärrecht klare Weichenstellung bei der Verantwortlichkeit werde im Tatsächlichen nicht beachtet. Ein Kläger sei hier aber nicht zu erkennen.

Issings Auffassung zufolge benötigt eine Wirtschafts- und Währungsunion politische Institutionen, diese müssten auch sicherstellen, dass notorischen Schuldenmachern die Mittel entzogen würden. Den Bürgern in Deutschland sei nicht zu vermitteln, dass sie Kürzungen zugunsten einer Konsolidierung des griechischen Staatshaushalts hinnehmen sollen. In Anbetracht der Einkommensunterschiede, die im Rahmen der Gemeinschaft erheblich stärker differierten als im nationalen Rahmen, bezeichnete Konrad den Strukturfonds als ein Instrument auch der Außenpolitik. Dies zeige sich etwa an der Kreation eines Verteilungskriteriums dünner Besiedlung anlässlich des Beitritts von Finnland. Die Integrationshilfen für die Türkei seien ähnlich zu bewerten. Berger forderte vor diesem Hintergrund objektive Kriterien, während Korioth eine strikte Objektivierung auf Grund weiterhin unterschiedlicher Rechtszustände noch nicht für möglich hielt.

Auf die Frage von Frau Flick, ob Europa wirklich so unpopulär sei, machte Issing eine starke, statistisch nachweisbare Strömung »dagegen« aus; Konrad merkte an, dass eine proeuropäische Position einen Garantieschirm an sich ablehnen müsse. Korioth kennzeichnete die gegenwärtige Situation durch ein Defizit öffentlichen Diskurses und bürgerschaftlicher Legitimation der handelnden Organe. Es häuften sich die Fälle, in welchen Gesetze ohne weitere Beratungen erlassen würden, dies geschehe unter Berufung auf angebliche Zeitnot und Alternativlosigkeit. Berger zweifelte, ob Alternativen noch bestünden. Der Euro sei die Krönung des europäischen Integrationsprozesses; sein »Platzen« werde möglicherweise unkontrollierbare politische Reaktionen auslösen, bis hin zum Ende der Gemeinschaft.

Die von Frau Flick angesprochene Option einer »Kerneurozone« hielt Korioth in Hinblick auf den Lissabon-Vertrag für möglich, wenngleich der zwangsweise Ausschluss derzeit nicht geregelt sei, zudem die Chance der Sozialisierung von Nachteilen bestehe. Issing befürchtete Angriffe auf die Unabhängigkeit der Europäischen Zentralbank und sprach sich dafür aus, auch Lösungen zu erwägen, welche eine Änderung der Verträge erforderten. Korioth verwies auf das Einstimmigkeitsprinzip, während Konrad eine Teilgemeinschaft der Vorteilsbegünstigten als mögliche Folge in Betracht zog.

Fragen der Staateninsolvenz standen am Ende des ersten Gesprächs.

Einführend stellte Paulus zunächst fest, dass der Staat von Gesetzes wegen insolvenzunfähig sei und Entsprechendes auch für die übrigen öffentlichen Rechtsträger, insbesondere die Gemeinden, geregelt werden dürfe. Die Länder hätten von dieser Ermächtigung in weitem Umfang Gebrauch gemacht[5]. Dass auf diese Weise eine Liquidation als Folge von Insolvenz ausgeschlossen sei, bedeute nicht, dass eine Überschuldung unter Staaten nicht vorkomme, sondern lediglich, dass darauf mit anderen Instrumenten zu reagieren sei. Ein Schuldenerlass, welcher in der Form des Erlassjahrs bereits im Alten Testament nachzuweisen sei[6], habe im Pariser Club eine Institutionalisierung gefunden, die allerdings in Anbetracht der bei Umschuldungen mitunter gezogenen Verknüpfungen von Freistellung und Bestellung, namentlich bei

Industrieunternehmen verzichtender Staaten, nicht ganz frei von Fragwürdigkeiten sei. Beim Konzept der odious debts, das etwa im Zusammenhang mit dem Sturz des irakischen Machthabers Saddam Hussein Gegenstand der öffentlichen Diskussion gewesen sei, sei zweifelhaft, ob es sich um eine lebende Rechtsfigur handele; in der Gestalt von Selbstbindung sei das Konzept allerdings existent, wie das Beispiel Norwegens zeige, und bewirke so eine Ethisierung des Rechts[7]. Eine Ethisierung ändere aber zugleich die Grundstruktur des Darlehensvertrags, indem sie an die Motive des Schuldners Modifikationen der vereinbarten Rechte und Pflichten anknüpfe. Gewinne das Konzept der odious debts unter Staaten an rechtlicher Verbindlichkeit, dürften sich entsprechende Bewertungen auch in das Privatrecht einschleichen und insbesondere in den Rechtsverhältnissen unter Banken bemerkbar machen. Paulus sprach sich dafür aus, einen rechtlichen Rahmen einer Orientierung für »schlingernde« Staaten zu schaffen und diesen etwa am sogenannten Chapter 9-Verfahren[8] zu orientieren, alternativ lediglich prozedurale Regelungen zu treffen und dabei als zuständige Instanz entweder die Europäische Zentralbank, den Internationalen oder vielleicht auch den Europäischen Gerichtshof zu wählen.

Auf die Frage Issings, ob eine Ethisierung des Rechts auch anderwärts zu beobachten sei, verwies Paulus auf die beständigen Erweiterungen des Verbraucherschutzrechts, Korioth auf die Rechtsprechung zur Bürgschaft durch mittellose Bürgen, Berger auf das Arbeitsrecht.

Ob sich das Problem der Überschuldung eines Staates nicht unabhängig vom Vorhandensein eines verfahrensmäßigen Rahmens zulasten der Gläubiger löse, fragte Korioth. Während Paulus Machtspiele zwischen Gläubigern und Schuldnern für ein Charakteristikum der Insolvenzsituation hielt, fand Berger, dass eine der Liquidation von Unternehmen entsprechende Option des »Besetzens« nicht mehr zur Verfügung stehe und andere Machtfragen in den Vordergrund rückten, etwa, wie der Staat seinen Zugang zum Kapitalmarkt aufrechterhalte oder wiedererlange, wem er schulde, im Schwerpunkt inländischen Gläubigern, insbesondere seinen eigenen Bürgern – wie beispielsweise in Japan –, oder ausländischen Investoren. Die von Paulus vorgestellten Konzepte erleichterten die Kalkulation von Risiken und dienten so der Rechtssicherheit zwischen den Staaten.

Konrad behauptete, dass eine Barwertverbesserung nur dann eintrete, wenn ein Kredit nicht zurückgezahlt werde. Frau Flick überlegte, ob es sinnvoll sei, »Schuldenmacher« durch zeitweisen Ausschluss vom Kapitalmarkt zu bestrafen. Issing erinnerte an den Umgang der früheren Sowjetunion mit den Schulden aus der Zarenzeit. Paulus wollte ökonomische Erkenntnisse im Zusammenhang mit Fairnessspielen[9] auf die Konkurrenz unter Gläubigern übertragen. Dabei seien jeweils kulturspezifische Aufteilungsmaßstäbe zu berücksichtigen. Insolvenzrecht müsse ausschließen, dass ein Gläubiger voll, die übrigen jedoch gar nicht befriedigt würden; dies müsse auch bei Staatsinsolvenzen gelten. Konrad äußerte Zweifel an der Übertragbarkeit, erst recht wenn es sich bei den konkurrierenden Gläubigern ebenfalls um Staaten handele. Frau Flick hingegen stimmte zu und hob den Halbteilungsgrundsatz hervor.

Auf die Frage Koriothś nach den Vor- und Nachteilen eines formalisierten Verfahrens gab Issing zu bedenken, dass die Märkte bei den Renditendifferenzen der Staatsbonds nicht präventiv wirkten und innerhalb kürzester Zeit mit starken Schwankungen reagierten. Notenbanken obliege vor diesem Hintergrund Zurückhaltung, insbesondere was den Auftritt mit Ratings betreffe. Nach Einschätzung Bergers führt nicht jede Umschuldung zu einem lebensfähigen Zustand, wichtig sei auch, das im Wege der Umschuldung Erreichte gegen eine Wiederholung des »Schuldenmachens« abzusichern. Insbesondere die bei einer Unternehmensinsolvenz gängige Auswechslung des Personals bereite im Fall von Staaten wegen der notwendigen demokratischen Legitimation Schwierigkeiten.

Paulus erwog, auch der Staateninsolvenz einen vom Schuldner entworfenen Zahlungsplan zugrunde zu legen, der die Akzeptanz der Gläubiger finden müsse. Er griff nochmals seine Überlegungen zu Fairnessspielen auf. Institutionelle Vorgaben seien notwendig, dabei sei fraglich, ob entsprechende Organe auch innerhalb einer Währungsunion eingerichtet sein dürfen. Issing wandte sich gegen eine Dämonisierung des Internationalen Währungsfonds; bei einem Europäischen Währungsfonds sei das Versprechen strikter Bedingungen Glaubwürdigkeitszweifeln ausgesetzt, im Übrigen bestehe die Gefahr eines moral hazard, wenn für den Krisenfall bereitgestelltes Geld ungenutzt herumliege. Konrad zufolge ist der Stabilitäts- und Wachstumspakt mit einem glaubhaften No-Bailout Grundlage für ein hinreichendes eigenes Interesse der Staaten zum Beispiel an einer Schuldenbremse.

Korioth stellte fest, dass eine Steuerungsschwäche des europäischen Rechts auf ebenfalls steuerungsschwache nationale Vorschriften zur Schuldenbegrenzung treffe wie etwa auf das Gebot grundsätzlich schuldenfreien Ausgleichs der öffentlichen Haushalte[10]. Berger erinnerte daran, dass Staatsschulden auch zu Wirtschaftswachstum führen können, wenn sie für Investitionen verwendet werden. Staatsschulden seien in diesem Fall sehr viel weniger schädlich als bei einer Aufnahme zu Konsumzwecken. Vor diesem Hintergrund hielt Korioth die frühere Fassung der grundgesetzlichen Schuldenbremse[11] für überzeugender, wenngleich der darin verwendete Investitionsbegriff nicht einfach zu handhaben sei. Dieser sei möglichst eng zu fassen, insbesondere seien auch Aufwendungen für Bildung auszuschließen. An der gegenwärtig geltenden Regelung[12] seien die Ausnahmeklauseln bedenklich. Berger sprach sich dafür aus, die Aufnahme von Staatsschulden an eine »Deckung« durch das Wirtschaftswachstum zu binden und eine Verschuldung allein für den Konsum zu verbieten. Mit diesen Erwägungen fand das erste Gespräch seinen Abschluss.

2. Gespräch (Samstag, 19. Juni 2010)

Korioth eröffnete die Gesprächsrunde am Samstagmorgen mit einem Rückblick auf einige am Vortag angesprochene Fragen.

Professor Dr. Dr. h.c. Paul Kirchhof (Heidelberg) wollte die von Paulus geäußerte Befürchtung einer Ethisierung des Rechts nicht teilen. Issing vertrat sogar einen Grundsatz »je unlauterer eine Person, desto lauter ihr Ruf nach ethisch-moralischen Grundlagen«. Berger hingegen sah die Statik des Rechts durch eine zunehmende Ethisierung gefährdet, da der Wandel der entsprechenden Anschauungen schneller vonstatten gehe als der Wandel des Rechts.

In Anknüpfung an die Funktion des Strafrechts, ultima ratio rechtlicher Verhaltenssteuerung zu sein, wies Korioth dem Recht im gesamten Instrumentarium der Verhaltenssteuerung eine entsprechende Funktion zu. Problembehaftet sei die häufig vorkommende symbolische Gesetzgebung, deren Normen nicht ernst gemeint und dadurch in ihrer Verbindlichkeit beeinträchtigt seien. Kirchhof vertrat die Auffassung, dass eine Normenflut die Rechtsordnung letztlich zerstören könne. Rechtssicherheit könne Gefahren für die Individualisierbarkeit von Normbefehlen bergen, so gerieten etwa im Steuerstrafrecht bei festen Wertgrenzen[13] Einzelfallgesichtspunkte leicht außer Acht. Kirchhof sprach sich im Übrigen dafür aus, Verfahren zur Bewältigung staatlicher Zahlungsunfähigkeit auf das Ziel einer Resolvenz auszurichten. Ein in Zusammenhang mit der Staatsverschuldung relevantes Problem stelle die Trennung der Renditechancen von der Verantwortung für den Mitteleinsatz dar.

Auch Issing stand symbolischen Gesetzgebungen kritisch gegenüber, zumal, wenn sie sich mit selektiven Verbindlichkeitsbehauptungen verknüpften. Als gelungenes Beispiel einer Verknüpfung von Renditechancen und Verantwortung für den Mitteleinsatz nannte Issing »grüne« Fonds, die mit ihren einem sozial verantwortlichen Investment verpflichteten Geschäftsmodellen auf die Anforderungen gewisser institutioneller Träger großer Vermögen, wie z. B. zahlreiche US-amerikanische Universitäten, reagiert hätten.

Professor Dr. Dr. h.c. Wolfgang Schön (München) erachtete Kirchhofs Trennungsthese als kennzeichnend für Großbanken und ihre Aktionäre. Werde eine für »systemrelevant« gehaltene Bank zur Begünstigten staatlicher Rettungsbemühungen, komme dies letztlich den Anteilseignern sowie dem Leitungspersonal zugute. Kirchhof rügte, dass die Trennung der Renditechancen von der Verantwortung für den Mitteleinsatz eine Risikoverschiebung zulasten der Steuerzahler bewirke. Paulus hielt die »Systemrelevanz« einzelner Banken nicht für einen unangreifbaren Topos, eher sei die Gesamtheit der Kreditinstitute für die Wirtschaft systemrelevant. Schön erinnerte insofern an die durch das Kartellrecht sichergestellte Diversifizierung des Bankensektors. Berger gab der Beobachtung Ausdruck, dass bei staatlichen Eingriffen gegenüber Banken nicht stets mit demselben Maß gemessen werde. Beispielhaft wies er auf die Fälle von Commerzbank und Hypo Real Estate hin. Issing empfahl, den staatlichen Besteuerungszugriff an den Risiken auszurichten und aus den so gewonnenen Mitteln einen Fonds zu dotieren. Dabei werde auch eine Bremse für das Größenwachstum gewonnen, die anders als das Kartellrecht mittelbar wirke. Eine Insolvenz kleinerer Banken sei gesamtwirtschaftlich unschädlich.

Korioth sah es als eine Aufgabe des Rechts an, Handlung und Verantwortung einander zuzuordnen; in manchen Fällen habe allerdings auch der Staat ein Interesse an Divergenz. Kirchhof erinnerte daran, dass das Recht immer mehr nachgefragt werde, Erwartungshaltung und Ansprüche kontinuierlich stiegen. Eine Norm rechtfertige sich aber als Instrument der »Freiheitspflege«. Abgeordnete verstünden sich zunehmend als Vordenker neuer Staatsleistungen, diese seien aus Steuern, alternativ und die Wahlchancen schonend aber aus weiterer Staatsverschuldung zu finanzieren.

Schön wandte sich der inzwischen eingeführten Schuldenbremse zu, allerdings bestünde keine Aussicht, die erforderlichen Mittel für eine geringere Schuldenaufnahme zu erwirtschaften; möglicherweise sei das Sparpaket bereits eine der letzten Umsteuerungsmöglichkeiten. Stelle sich bei staatlichen Entscheidungen nur noch die Frage, was wirtschaftlich möglich sei, liege darin, so Kirchhof, ein Scheitern des Verfassungsstaats. Issing zweifelte daran, dass in der Politik die Bedeutung der gegenwärtigen Situation als Wendepunkt zutreffend eingeschätzt werde; getroffene Maßnahmen sprächen dagegen. Im Vergleich mit früheren Vorschriften sah Korioth die Schuldenbremse als nur eingeschränkt zweckgerecht an; zudem lege der Aufschub ihres Inkrafttretens (2016 für den Bund, 2020 für die Länder) eine symbolische Gesetzgebung nahe.

Kirchhof erkannte als erforderlich, die Regeln für die Staatsverschuldung zu überdenken. Es sei fragwürdig, wenn Investitionen zu Lasten nachfolgender Generationen beschlossen würden und der Posten »Schuldendienst« im Haushalt beständig wachse. Kirchhof empfahl, an einen Anstieg der Staatsverschuldung normativ ein Absinken bestimmter Staatsleistungen zu knüpfen. Berger sprach sich dagegen aus, Schulden bei einem Staat als per se schlecht anzusehen. Zukünftige Generationen würden nur dann belastet, wenn das Wirtschaftswachstum eine Rückzahlung entsprechender Kredite nicht decke. Im Übrigen kämen diese Schulden einer produktiveren Gesellschaft zugute. Sie seien auch geeignet, Konjunkturzyklen auszugleichen. Allerdings müsse gründlich erwogen werden, in welchem Maß und zu welchem Zweck Schulden aufgenommen würden.

Kirchhof konnten die Ausführungen Bergers nicht überzeugen: Anders als ein Unternehmen sei der Staat nicht produktiv; der behauptete »Ankurbelungseffekt« trete nicht ein. Die Option der Staatsschuld wirke auf Politiker verführerisch. Möglicherweise sei dem Staat die Aufnahme von Schulden überhaupt zu verbieten, er sei auf eine Finanzierung zu verweisen, die allein vom Steuerpotenzial gedeckt sei. Berger wandte ein, dass der Staat im Rahmen seiner Infrastrukturverantwortung, etwa beim Straßenbau, durchaus produktiv tätig werde. Schön erläuterte am Beispiel der Autobahnen, dass der Staat dieselben Projekte gelegentlich mehrfach für die Rechtfertigung von Finanzierungszugriffen heranziehe: die Notwendigkeit, Autobahnen zu bauen, habe zunächst die Mineralölsteuer legitimiert, die neu errichteten Straßen seien sodann als Investitionen deklariert worden, um neue Verschuldung zu rechtfertigen, schließlich würde als Finanzierungsbeitrag der Benutzer eine Autobahnmaut erhoben.

Kirchhof lenkte das Gespräch nochmals auf das Bankenwesen. Die Organisation der Universalbanken bedürfe der Diskussion, ebenso eine Gegenleistung der Banken für staatliche Hilfe. Schön sprach sich für die Ausrichtung einer solchen Gegenleistung an den wirtschaftlichen Grunddaten der Banken aus. Mit Blick auf die großen US-amerikanischen Immobilienfinanzierer wies Issing darauf hin, dass der Staat für Banken dieser Art zwar rechtlich nicht hafte, faktisch jedoch einstehe. Vorgaben für die Kreditvergabe, die auf Grund einer ausgeprägt gleichheitsbezogenen Betrachtung unterschiedliche Risiken bei den Kunden ausblendeten, seien problematisch. Soweit die Europäische Kommission über Kompetenzen in Bezug auf die Sanierung von Kreditinstituten verfüge, sei, so Kirchhof, für den Fall nicht erfolgreicher Sanierungen auch die Kompetenzfrage zu stellen. Berger vermisste einen politischen Ansprechpartner für die Europäische Zentralbank; Issing stimmte dem zu und befürchtete zugleich, dass die Kompetenzen der Kommission eher noch weiter ausgebaut würden. Erkannte Schön eine Verschiebung politischen Einflusses von der Kommission zum Rat, zweifelte Kirchhof in Ansehung eines defizitären politischen Diskurses auf der Ebene der Gemeinschaft, ob die Legitimation durch die Kommission hervorgebrachter Gesetzgebungsakte in einem ausreichenden Maße gewährleistet sei. Issing regte an, einen Europäischen Risikofonds einzurichten und die Kooperation der Finanzaufsichten weiter zu verstärken.

Convoco Forum im Gwandhaus (19. Juni 2010)

Nach einem Grußwort, in dessen Vordergrund Frau Flick den Gedanken einer Europäisierung des Gemeinwohles sowie die Fokussierung staatlichen Handelns auf die Bürger stellte, führte Kirchhof die zahlreich im Gwandhaus erschienenen Gäste des Convoco Forums in das Thema der diesjährigen Veranstaltung ein. Geld sei als ein abstraktes Instrument »Passepartout für beliebige Taten«. Schaffe Geld die Möglichkeit, Freiheit zu gestalten, werde diese durch Schulden beschränkt. Geld vergegenständliche zugleich Vertrauen, nämlich dasjenige in die zukünftige Einlösbarkeit. Dies gelte auch für die folgenden Generationen, insofern bestehe ein Generationenvertrag, dem die Nachfolgenden noch gar nicht hätten zustimmen können. Die Kultur des Maßes sei im Schwinden, seit den sechziger Jahren bedingten mit zunehmender Verbreitung erhobene Forderungen nach einem Mehr an Recht und Rechten höhere Ausgaben. Der Abgeordnete erweise sich dabei als Vordenker neuer Staatsleistungen. Würden diese aus Schulden finanziert, verschiebe sich die Steuerlast auf spätere Generationen. Die Rechtfertigung neuer Staatsverschuldung sei zweifelhaft. Je weiter die Zeiträume reichten, in welchen die Schulden zurückzuzahlen seien, desto problematischer sei deren Aufnahme. Bereits heute litten die Bürger an vergangener Verschuldungspolitik. Gerate ein Staat in Zahlungsschwierigkeiten, sei nicht dessen Insolvenz, sondern eine Resolvenz zu erstreben. Denn die Übernahme von Markt und Kunden durch einen anderen Wettbewerber komme für einen Staat nicht in Betracht. Im Übrigen sei die Freiheitsverheißung des Grundgesetzes in Anbetracht leerer Staatskassen neu zu entdecken.

Vortrag: Lehren aus der Finanzmarktkrise

Issing entwickelte seinen Vortrag über Lehren aus der Finanzmarktkrise in drei Schritten. In einem ersten Schritt wandte er sich den Ursachen zu, analysierte sodann die gegenwärtige Situation, um schließlich einige mögliche Lehren näher zu skizzieren.

Eine Ursache der Krise erblickte Issing in einem hohen Anlagedruck; Renditedifferenzen zwischen den Staatsanleihen einzelner Länder seien geschwunden, die unterschiedlichen Risiken seien nicht mehr in unterschiedlichen Zinssätzen abgebildet gewesen. Der politischen Vorgabe insbesondere in den USA, einer möglichst breiten Schicht von Bürgern den Weg ins Immobilieneigentum zu ebnen, habe eine Illusion permanenter Wertsteigerungen zugrunde gelegen, die der Markt nicht habe einlösen können. Rating-Agenturen seien oftmals nicht frei von eigenen Interessen am Ergebnis ihrer Bewertungen. Schließlich habe der Markt strukturierte Finanzprodukte entwickelt, die selbst für professionelle Teilnehmer nicht mehr verständlich gewesen seien. Diese Gesichtspunkte verwiesen auf Defizite bei der Regulierung sowie der Aufsicht über den Markt. Eine Untersuchung von Finanzmarktkrisen, die über einen Zeitraum von 800 Jahren 66 Länder erfasst habe[14], habe drei Charakteristika herausgearbeitet: eine hohe Verschuldung sowohl des öffentlichen als auch des privaten Sektors, ein strukturelles Ungleichgewicht und eine fatalistische Haltung der Marktteilnehmer dahin, dass »schon alles gut gehen werde«. Auffallend sei im Übrigen, dass zahlreiche Unternehmen eine selbstruinöse Geschäftspolitik betrieben hätten; vorherrschend sei die Auffassung gewesen, die Risiken am Markt seien gleich verteilt. Die Ursachen der Finanzmarktkrise seien insgesamt in einem Zusammenspiel von Staats- und Marktversagen zu suchen.

In der gegenwärtigen Situation seien die Unternehmen optimistisch hinsichtlich neuer Aufträge aus dem Ausland; die Flexibilität am Arbeitsmarkt sei bereits merklich gesteigert worden. Trotz des Einbruchs seien die für den Einzelnen »fühlbaren« Folgen eher unauffällig. Allerdings könnten Überbrückungsmechanismen wie etwa die Kurzarbeit nur über eine bestimmte Zeit eingesetzt werden. Wenngleich die Risiken der Finanzmarktkrise nicht vollständig transparent seien, bestünden Anhaltspunkte dafür, dass sich die Erholung verlangsame. Die USA hätten ihre Staatsverschuldung von 2007 bis 2010 um ungefähr die Hälfte des bisherigen Standes erhöht, in Großbritannien sei es sogar zu einer Verdoppelung gekommen. Aus den USA, Japan, Großbritannien und Europa drängten im Jahr 2010 rund 5,5 Billionen US-Dollar in Form von Staatsanleihen auf den internationalen Finanzmarkt. Das Haushaltsdefizit im Euro-Raum liege noch gut halb so hoch wie in den USA. Im Bereich der Europäischen Währungsunion sei jeweils nach dem Beitritt eines Landes ein Effekt des »Zurücklehnens« zu beobachten; die im Hinblick auf die Stabilitätskriterien unternommenen Anstrengungen ließen nach, wenn das Ziel erreicht sei. So sei in den vergangenen sieben Jahren ein Ansteigen der Lohnstückkosten um 30 Prozent zu verzeichnen, was einer Abwertung des Euro in vergleichbarer Dimension entspreche. Die Lohnpolitik habe sich von den Grunddaten des Arbeitsmarktes entfernt. Für fehlerhafte Investitionen am Immobilienmarkt würden öffentliche Subventionen gewährt. In der nationalen Budgetpolitik bleibe die europäische Verantwortung weitgehend unbeachtet.

Als mögliche Lehren aus der Finanzmarktkrise forderte Issing zunächst Verbesserungen bei Regulierung und Aufsicht. Die Aufsicht müsse um eine systemische Komponente ergänzt werden, um Risiken aus dem Zusammenwirken unterschiedlicher Marktakteure erkennen zu können. Werde der Gedanke des »too big (or: connected) to fail« relativiert, wirke dies auch einem verbreiteten moral hazard entgegen. Hinsichtlich der Verteilung von Risiken sei die Transparenz zu erhöhen. Möglich sei, nationale Instrumente wie eine Schuldenbremse auch mit einem europäischen Zweck zu verwenden; daneben müssten sanktionsbewehrte Kontrollinstrumente treten.

In der auf den Vortrag folgenden Aussprache votierte eine Stimme aus dem Publikum für eine Erhöhung der direkten Steuern; eine – gegenwärtig in der Diskussion befindliche – Anhebung der Mehrwertsteuer zehre das private Konsumpotenzial weiter auf. Berger hielt den gegenwärtig für Stabilisierungsmaßnahmen vorgesehenen Zeitraum von drei Jahren für zu kurz. Issing stimmte dem zu, bezweifelte allerdings auch, dass diese Begrenzung durchgehalten werden könne. Gleichwohl seien Reformanstrengungen zu beobachten, die ohne Finanzmarktkrise nicht vorstellbar gewesen wären. Auf eine Bemerkung aus dem Publikum, systemische Folgerungen, etwa ein Insolvenzrecht für Staaten betreffend, erinnerte Issing daran, dass hierzu eine Änderung der Verträge erforderlich sei, zumindest wenn es um den Ausschluss eines Mitgliedstaates aus der Währungsunion gehe. Hierfür eine Mehrheit zu gewinnen, sei wenig realistisch: Der aufgespannte »Rettungsschirm« biete eine gute Grundlage, Reformen auf nationaler Ebene fortzuführen, etwa auch auf eine Besserung der Steuermoral hinzuwirken. Auf eine abschließende Frage, Sanktionen seitens der Gemeinschaft betreffend, hob Issing hervor, dass ein möglichst automatisch funktionierender Regelungsmechanismus gefunden werden müsse, der politische Entscheidungen über die sachgerechte Reaktion auf nationales »Schuldenmachen« für den Einzelfall weitgehend ausschließe.

Abschlussgespräch

Die Podiumsdiskussion fasste wichtige Thesen und Positionen der vorangegangenen Gespräche für die Gäste des Convoco Forums zusammen. Einführend skizzierte Korioth einige der bisher erörterten Problemkreise. Bezüglich der Wechselwirkung von Markt- und Staatsversagen sei ein Schwerpunkt bei staatlichen Regulierungsfehlern aufgewiesen worden; zu bedenken seien aber auch die Anteile von »Systemfehlern« und individuellem Fehlverhalten. Zwei »Rettungsschirme« seien in der Euro-Zone aufgespannt worden, die Korioth mit Zurückhaltung betrachtete. Er verwies auf die beiden von Konrad beschriebenen Szenarien für die nähere Zukunft, dem wahrscheinlicheren einer europäischen Wirtschaftsregierung, in dem sich die europäische Solidargemeinschaft zu einem Haftungsverbund weiterentwickele, und dem Szenario einer Rückbesinnung auf den Stabilitäts- und Wachstumspakt, die ein glaubhaftes No-Bailout sowie möglicherweise die Einführung eines transparenten Resolvenzverfahrens für Staaten voraussetze. Korioth äußerte Zweifel an der Wirksamkeit der im nationalen Recht reformierten Schuldenbremse und erwähnte das Problem einer Ethisierung von Schulden.

Frau Flick stellte vor diesem Hintergrund die Frage, ob Schulden aus sich heraus schlecht seien, an den Anfang des Gesprächs. Die Antwort Bergers fiel entschieden negierend aus. Schulden könnten dazu dienen, Aktivitäten zu finanzieren; maßgeblich für die Bewertung sei, wieviel Kredit wofür in Anspruch genommen werde. Schulden seien schlecht, wenn das aufgenommene Geld dazu verwendet werde, ein Mehr an Konsum oder Sozialausgaben möglich zu machen. Sie seien gut, wenn die Mittel in Bildung oder Infrastrukturprojekte flössen, auch, wenn sie der Überbrückung vorübergehender konjunktureller Schwierigkeiten dienten. Die Schulden müssten aber stets von Wirtschaftswachstum gedeckt bleiben.

Kirchhof konnte sich dieser Sichtweise nicht anschließen. Er hielt Schulden jedenfalls dann für schlecht, wenn es um den Schuldner »Staat« gehe. Anders als im Unternehmen träfen die Folgen der Verschuldung nicht nur eine andere Politikergeneration, sodass der Verantwortungszusammenhang zwischen Aufnahme und Rückzahlung des Kredits unterbrochen sei, sondern in Anbetracht der bei Staatsschulden längeren Zeiträume letztlich die Kinder der »Schulden machenden« Eltern. Kirchhof forderte eine Verknüpfung der Kreditaufnahme mit einem Verzicht auf bisher gewährte Staatsleistungen und rügte, dass Rating-Agenturen, die nicht nur Unternehmen, sondern auch Staaten bewerten, existentiell erheblichen Einfluss ausübten, ohne über irgendeine demokratische Legitimation zu verfügen.

Schön hob die strukturellen Unterschiede zwischen Inlands- und Auslandsverschuldung hervor und griff sein Autobahn-Beispiel aus dem zweiten Gespräch auf. Zum Votum Bergers äußerte er sich im Grundsatz zustimmend, gab allerdings zu bedenken, dass auch Sondereffekte, wie etwa die Deutsche Einheit, in die Betrachtung einzubeziehen seien; im Übrigen sei Selbstdisziplinierung am Platze, das Sparpaket weise in eine solche Richtung. Korioth erkannte ein Problem weniger bei der Bewertung von Schulden als »gut« oder »schlecht«, sondern beim Maß der Verschuldungsdisziplin. Paulus trat dafür ein, Verhaltensweisen eines moral hazard zu unterbinden, Handeln und Verantwortung wieder enger aufeinander zu beziehen. Ein auf Resolvenz gerichtetes Insolvenzverfahren in Anlehnung an das US-amerikanische Recht könne möglicherweise auch auf die Ebene von Staaten übertragen werden; allerdings sei dies im europäischen Kontext nur bei einer Änderung der Verträge möglich. Kirchhof versprach sich von einem geordneten Verfahren präventive Wirkungen; allerdings könne die Festlegung von Quoten den Zugang des Staates zum Kreditmarkt beeinträchtigen. Berger erachtete eine massive Entschuldung für geboten; neue Regeln seien bereitzustellen, zur Begrenzung von Schulden, zu Restrukturierungen oder – möglichst »automatisch« wirkend – für Sanktionen. Auch die Mitbestimmung der Gläubiger sichernde Regelungen über Resolvenzpläne für Staaten rechneten dazu, ergänzte Paulus.

Auf eine Frage Schöns gab Berger der Einschätzung Ausdruck, dass eine Inflationsgefahr derzeit nicht bestehe. Die Kapazitäten des produzierenden Gewerbes seien nicht ausgelastet. Allerdings könne sich die Lage ändern, wenn die Unabhängigkeit der Europäischen Zentralbank relativiert werde. Der Entschuldungsvorgang sei komplex und werde auch die Bürger ergreifen; daher seien seine sozialen Folgen zu berücksichtigen. Kirchhof fand, dass ein vereinfachtes Steuerrecht Voraussetzungen geschaffen hätte, die Eigenverantwortung zu stärken; im Lissabon-Urteil des Bundesverfassungsgerichts[15] seien Elemente einer Staatsaufgabenlehre entwickelt, mithin auch Grenzen für das Tätigkeitsfeld des Staates gezogen worden. Korioth hielt einen grundsätzlichen Umschwung für nicht wahrscheinlich. Werde eine Aufgabenreduzierung angestrebt, müsse diese auf einer Aufgabenkritik beruhen. Mit Kirchhof stimmte er darin überein, dass sich die Gemeinschaft zumindest hinsichtlich der Währungsunion auch der Frage eines Austrittsrechts werde stellen müssen.

Eine Stimme aus dem Publikum beklagte die »Vollkaskomentalität« der Bürger, auf die um ihre Wiederwahl besorgte Politiker einzugehen hätten, als eine Ursache für falsche

Entscheidungen. Berger forderte politisches Personal, das in bürgerlichen Berufen zuhause sei und daher nicht darauf angewiesen, eingenommene Posten um jeden Preis zu verteidigen. Auf eine weitere Frage bewertete Schön den Spitzensteuersatz bei Gesamtbetrachtung als noch immer sehr hoch. Die aus dem Publikum vorgetragene Empfehlung, Aufgabenkritik, Steuerpolitik und Privatisierungen miteinander zu kombinieren, veranlasste Berger zu dem Hinweis, dass einzelne Sektoren – wie etwa die Wasser- oder Elektrizitätsversorgung – bereits in Deutschland und Frankreich unterschiedlich geordnet seien, was hier zwingend als staatlich angesehen werde, sei dort ebenso selbstverständlich privat. Kirchhof merkte an, dass die Privatisierungseignung bei kommunalen Dienstleistungen differenziert zu betrachten sei. Er bekräftigte im Übrigen seine bereits anlässlich des Convoco Forums 2008 geäußerte Kritik an der Bemessungsgrundlage für die Einkommensteuer. Korioth konnte in Privatisierungen jedenfalls langfristig keine Vorteile erkennen; Staatsausgaben würden lediglich verlagert und Staatsaufgaben neu geschaffen. Schön machte darauf aufmerksam, dass in der neueren Steuergesetzgebung ein Trend zu sehr spezifischer Belastung einzelner Wirtschaftszweige bestehe. Berger versprach sich von einem Mehrheitswahlrecht reformfreudigere Regierungen. Auf eine Frage aus dem Publikum, ob für die Zukunft die Ausgabe von Eurobonds zu erwarten sei, wies Kirchhof auf die rechtlichen Grenzen in den europäischen Verträgen hin; Korioth vermutete, dass eine Intensivierung europäischer Solidaritätsgefühle auf ein solches Szenario hinführen könne.

Mit einem Schlusswort, in dem Corinne Flick einen Appell an die Verantwortung auch der Medien in einer als krisenhaft empfundenen Zeit richtete, fand das Convoco Forum 2010 seinen Ausklang.

Anmerkungen

1 Vgl. etwa G. Franke/J. P. Krahnen/J. Isensee, Ein staatliches Hospital für kranke Banken, FAZ vom 27. 2. 2010, Internet: *http://www.hof.uni-frankfurt.de/images/policy_platform/krahnen_ein_staatliches_hospital_fuer_kranke_banken.pdf.*

2 So auch der Titel des Buchs von K. A. Konrad/H. Zschäpitz, Schulden ohne Sühne? Warum der Absturz der Staatsfinanzen uns alle trifft, 2010.

3 Dazu etwa C. Herrmann, Griechische Tragödie – der währungsverfassungsrechtliche Rahmen für die Rettung, den Austritt oder den Ausschluss von überschuldeten Staaten aus der Eurozone, Europäische Zeitschrift für Wirtschaftsrecht 2010, S. 413 ff.

4 BVerfG, Urteil vom 19. 10. 2006 – 2 BvF 3/03, BVerfGE 116, 327, Internet: *http://www.bverfg.de/entscheidungen/fs20061019_2bvf000303.html.*

5 § 12 Abs. 1 Insolvenzordnung bestimmt: »Unzulässig ist das Insolvenzverfahren über das Vermögen

1. des Bundes oder eines Landes;
2. einer juristischen Person des öffentlichen Rechts, die der Aufsicht eines Landes untersteht, wenn das Landesrecht dies bestimmt.«

Ergänzend regelt etwa das bayerische Landesrecht in Art. 25 Gesetz zur Ausführung des Gerichtsverfassungsgesetzes und von Verfahrensgesetzen des Bundes: »(1) Ein Insolvenzverfahren über das Vermögen juristischer Personen des öffentlichen Rechts, die der

Aufsicht des Freistaates Bayern unterstehen, findet nicht statt. (2) Absatz 1 gilt nicht für die Bayerische Landesbank und die Sparkassen«.

6 3. Mose 25, 8 ff: »Und du sollst zählen sieben Sabbatjahre, siebenmal sieben Jahre, daß die Zeit der sieben Sabbatjahre neunundvierzig Jahre mache. Da sollst du die Posaune blasen lassen durch euer ganzes Land am zehnten Tage des siebenten Monats, an Versöhnungstag. Und ihr sollt das fünfzigste Jahr heiligen und sollt eine Freilassung ausrufen im Lande für alle, die darin wohnen; es soll ein Erlaßjahr für euch sein. Da soll ein jeder bei euch wieder zu seiner Habe und zu seiner Sippe kommen. Als Erlaßjahr soll das fünfzigste Jahr euch gelten. Ihr sollt nicht säen und, was von selber wächst, nicht ernten, auch, was ohne Arbeit wächst, im Weinberg nicht lesen; denn das Erlaßjahr soll euch heilig sein; vom Felde weg dürft ihr essen, was es trägt. Das ist das Erlaßjahr, da jedermann wieder zu dem Seinen kommen soll. Wenn du nun deinem Nächsten etwas verkaufst oder ihm etwas abkaufst, soll keiner seinen Bruder übervorteilen, sondern nach der Zahl der Jahre vom Erlaßjahr an sollst du es von ihm kaufen; danach, wieviel Jahre noch Ertrag bringen, soll er dir's verkaufen. Sind es noch viele Jahre, so darfst du den Kaufpreis steigern; sind es noch wenige Jahre, sollst du den Kaufpreis verringern; denn die Zahl der Ernten verkauft er dir.« (Übersetzung M. Luther).

7 Zum Konzept der odious debts C. Paulus, Stellen »Odious Debts« eine Rechtsfigur dar?, WM 2005, 53 ff.; The Evolution of the »Concept of Odious Debts«, Zeitschrift für ausländisches öffentliches Recht und Völkerrecht 68 (2008), S. 291 ff.; The »Concept of Odious Debts«: A Historical Survey, Norton Annual Review of International Insolvency, 2009, 219 ff., Internet: *http://papers.ssrn.com/sol3/papers.cfm?abstract_id=1077688*.

8 Tit. 11 ch. 9 U. S. Code (Adjustment of Debts of a Municipality), Internet: *http://www.law.cornell.edu/uscode/html/uscode11/usc_sup_01_11_10_9.html*.

9 Dazu etwa G. Gigerenzer, Bauchentscheidungen, 2007, S. 48.

10 Art. 109 Abs. 3 Satz 1 Grundgesetz: »Die Haushalte von Bund und Ländern sind grundsätzlich ohne Einnahmen aus Krediten auszugleichen«.

11 Art. 115 Abs. 1 Grundgesetz (Fassung 1969): »Die Aufnahme von Krediten sowie die Übernahme von Bürgschaften, Garantien oder sonstigen Gewährleistungen, die zu Ausgaben in künftigen Rechnungsjahren führen können, bedürfen einer der Höhe nach bestimmten oder bestimmbaren Ermächtigung durch Bundesgesetz. Die Einnahmen aus Krediten dürfen die Summe der im Haushaltsplan veranschlagten Ausgaben für Investitionen nicht überschreiten; Ausnahmen sind nur zulässig zur Abwehr einer Störung des gesamtwirtschaftlichen Gleichgewichts. Das Nähere wird durch Bundesgesetz geregelt«.

12 Art. 115 Grundgesetz (Fassung 2009): »(1) Die Aufnahme von Krediten sowie die Übernahme von Bürgschaften, Garantien oder sonstigen Gewährleistungen, die zu Ausgaben in künftigen Rechnungsjahren führen können, bedürfen einer der Höhe nach bestimmten oder bestimmbaren Ermächtigung durch Bundesgesetz. (2) Einnahmen und Ausgaben sind grundsätzlich ohne Einnahmen aus Krediten auszugleichen. Diesem Grundsatz ist entsprochen, wenn die Einnahmen aus Krediten 0,35 vom Hundert im Verhältnis zum nominalen Bruttoinlandsprodukt nicht überschreiten. Zusätzlich sind bei einer von der Normallage abweichenden konjunkturellen Entwicklung die Auswirkungen auf den Haushalt im Auf- und Abschwung symmetrisch zu berücksichtigen. Abweichungen der tatsächlichen Kreditaufnahme von der nach den Sätzen 1 bis 3 zulässigen Kreditobergrenze werden auf einem Kontrollkonto erfasst; Belastungen, die den Schwellenwert von 1,5 vom Hundert im Verhältnis zum nominalen Bruttoinlandsprodukt überschreiten, sind konjunkturgerecht zurückzuführen. Näheres, insbesondere die Bereinigung der Einnahmen und Ausgaben um finanzielle Transaktionen und das Verfahren zur Berechnung der Obergrenze der

jährlichen Nettokreditaufnahme unter Berücksichtigung der konjunkturellen Entwicklung auf der Grundlage eines Konjunkturbereinigungsverfahrens sowie die Kontrolle und den Ausgleich von Abweichungen der tatsächlichen Kreditaufnahme von der Regelgrenze, regelt ein Bundesgesetz. Im Falle von Naturkatastrophen oder außergewöhnlichen Notsituationen, die sich der Kontrolle des Staates entziehen und die staatliche Finanzlage erheblich beeinträchtigen, können diese Kreditobergrenzen auf Grund eines Beschlusses der Mehrheit der Mitglieder des Bundestages überschritten werden. Der Beschluss ist mit einem Tilgungsplan zu verbinden. Die Rückführung der nach Satz 6 aufgenommenen Kredite hat binnen eines angemessenen Zeitraumes zu erfolgen«.

[13] Vgl. BGH, Urteil vom 2. 12. 2008 – 1 StR 416/08, BGHSt 53, 71 ff.

[14] C. M. Reinhart/K. S. Rogoff, Dieses Mal ist alles anders. Acht Jahrhunderte Finanzkrisen, 2010.

[15] BVerfG, Urteil vom 30. 6. 2009 – 2 BvE 2/08 pp., BVerfGE 123, 267, Internet: *http://www.bverfg.de/entscheidungen/es20090630_2bve000208.html*.

RESÜMEE

PROF. DR. DR. H.C. MULT. OTMAR ISSING

SYSTEMRISIKEN IM FINANZSYSTEM – ANSÄTZE ZUR REFORM

1. Die Finanzmarktkrise als Katalysator*

Die Finanzmarktkrise wurde durch den Zusammenbruch des Marktes für problematische Hypotheken (»subprime mortgages«) ausgelöst und erfasste schließlich die ganze westliche Welt. Bemerkenswerterweise waren die Schwellenländer davon ausgenommen. Um den Kollaps des ganzen Finanzsystems – ausgelöst durch »systemisches Risiko« – zu verhindern, mussten Staaten wie die USA oder Deutschland eingreifen und eine Reihe von Instituten vor dem Zusammenbruch bewahren.

Systemisches Risiko liegt vor, wenn durch den Zusammenbruch einzelner Institute das ganze Finanzsystem und damit die Versorgung der Märkte mit Krediten und Finanzdienstleistungen gefährdet ist, so dass sich negative realwirtschaftliche Effekte ergeben.

Das Finanzsystem umfasst hierbei nicht nur Banken und Versicherungen, sondern auch das sogenannte Schattenbanksystem – zum Beispiel Hedgefonds, Geldfonds, Zweckgesellschaften etc., welches bisher nicht hinreichend Regulierung und Aufsicht unterlag. Die Institute eines Finanzsystems sind über ein komplexes, oft schwer durch-

* Marcel Bluhm danke ich für die wertvolle Mitarbeit.

schaubares Geflecht gegenseitiger Forderungen und Verbindlichkeiten, zum Beispiel über Kreditbeziehungen und deren Derivate, miteinander verbunden. Zusätzlich mögen Institute in dieselben Produktklassen investiert haben, was das System als Ganzes verwundbarer gegenüber einzelnen Risiken macht.

Beschreibt man das Finanzsystem als ein Netzwerk verflochtener, voneinander abhängiger Finanzinstitute, dann lassen sich die Auslöser systemischen Risikos genauer benennen. Systemisches Risiko ergibt sich, wenn (a) mit der Krise einzelner Institute, (b) und/oder durch gegenseitige Abhängigkeiten ausgelöste Insolvenzen, oder (c) durch hohe Ausfälle in Produktklassen, in die ein Großteil der Finanzinstitute investiert hat, ein signifikanter Teil des Finanzsystems existentiell gefährdet ist. Systemisches Risiko resultiert daher ganz wesentlich aus der finanziellen Verflechtung zwischen Finanzinstitutionen – dies ist gewissermaßen die Kehrseite liquider und globalisierter Finanzmärkte.

Im Verlaufe der gegenwärtigen Krise war systemisches Risiko im Sinne potentieller Schadensereignisse an manchen Tagen förmlich mit den Händen zu greifen. So etwa im Herbst 2008, als Lehman Brothers seine Finanzierungsbasis verlor und schlagartig insbesondere die Märkte für strukturierte Finanzprodukte mit massiven Wertverlusten und Liquiditätsengpässen reagierten. Als wenig später der Versicherungskonzern AIG unter der Last vielfältig eingegangener Kreditabsicherungen in die Knie ging, drohte eine noch größere, weltweite Kettenreaktion die großen Investment- und Kreditbanken zu erfassen. Im Falle eines Konkurses von AIG, die im großen Stil Kreditversicherungen ausgegeben hatte, ohne selber im ausreichenden Umfang abgesichert zu sein, drohte ein Kapitalverlust für weite Teile der Finanzwelt. Aufgrund der Undurchsichtigkeit strukturierter Finanzprodukte, denen die Subprime-Kredite unterlagen, konnte niemand mit Sicherheit sagen, welchen Banken letztendlich hohe Verluste drohten. In der Folge kam es zu einem Vertrauensverlust, der ohne den unverzüglichen Eingriff von Zentralbanken und Regierungen in einem Infarkt der weltweiten Finanzmärkte geendet hätte.

2. Gefährdung der Marktwirtschaft

Die von allen betroffenen Staaten durchgeführten Rettungsmaßnahmen verstärken die Überzeugung, dass es im Fall drohender Insolvenz bedeutender Finanzinstitute keine realistische Alternative zu eben dieser Rettung gibt. Damit sind Finanzinstitute geradezu eingeladen, größer und systemrelevanter zu werden und immer höhere Risiken einzugehen. Schließlich bleiben die Gewinne privat, Verluste im Falle des Scheiterns sind dagegen vom Staat, am Ende also vom Steuerzahler zu tragen. Einen klareren Fall von »Moral Hazard« kann man sich kaum denken.

Eine implizite Bestandsgarantie für systemisch relevante Institute widerspricht jedoch den Prinzipien freier Finanzmärkte, jeder Marktwirtschaft als solcher. In einer Marktwirtschaft können sich die Akteure im Rahmen der Gesetze grundsätzlich frei entfalten, etwas »unternehmen«. Der Anreiz liegt nicht zuletzt darin, im Falle des Erfolgs den Gewinn (nach Steuern) behalten zu dürfen. Zu diesem institutionellen Arrangement gehört aber unverzichtbar auch, privat für Verluste zu haften, bis zum Extrem der Insolvenz. Nur beide Bedingungen zusammen sorgen für das gesellschaftlich richtige Abwägen von Chancen und Risiken. Die Aussicht, im Extremfall Verluste auf den Steuerzahler überwälzen zu können, zerstört diese Balance. Man kann sich durchaus vorstellen, dass eine Wiederholung riesiger Rettungspakete im Falle einer weiteren Krise derartigen – oder sogar größeren – Ausmaßes zur Abschaffung freier Finanzmärkte führen könnte.

Im Rückblick ist kaum zu verstehen, wieso die Staaten diesen Risiken nicht durch entsprechende Auflagen und effiziente Aufsicht Rechnung getragen haben. Ebenso wenig waren hinreichende Vorkehrungen getroffen worden, um im Falle des Zusammenbruchs eines systemisch relevanten Finanzinstitutes den Schaden in Grenzen zu halten, d. h. die Ansteckung des gesamten Finanzsystems zu verhindern bzw. entscheidend zu vermindern.

Die Krise hat nicht nur die Dimension des Problems verdeutlicht, sondern auch eine ganze Reihe von Vorschlägen hervorgebracht, die darauf ausgerichtet sind, dieses Problem so gut wie möglich anzugehen.

Ein direkter Ansatz besteht darin, die Größe und Aktivitäten individueller Finanzinstitutionen zu begrenzen. Es ist jedoch offensichtlich, dass sich dieses Prinzip nur schwerlich auf vernünftige Art und Weise umsetzen ließe. Genauso erscheinen »Narrow Banking« und ähnliche Ansätze wenig überzeugend, da sie zwar eine Bankenpanik im eng abgegrenzten Bankensektor verhindern können, gleichzeitig aber alle risikobehafteten Aktivitäten dem Rest des Finanzsystems überlassen.

Ein überzeugenderer Ansatz sieht vor, die Finanzmittel und die Liquidität systemrelevanter Finanzinstitutionen strikter Regulierung zu unterwerfen. So könnten beispielsweise Liquiditäts- und Eigenkapitalanforderungen mit steigender systemischer Relevanz eines Finanzinstituts anwachsen.

Des Weiteren wird vorgeschlagen, eine Insolvenz systemrelevanter Institute zu vereinfachen, ohne dass dabei Risiken für den Rest des Finanzsystems entstehen. Die Herausforderung derartiger Lösungsansätze für systemrelevante Finanzinstitute besteht darin, Mechanismen zur Verfügung zu stellen, die es großen, komplexen und international stark vernetzten Institutionen ermöglicht, zu fallieren, ohne ein systemisches Kreditereignis hervorzurufen.

Die Expertengruppe für Finanzmarktreformen (»Issing-Kommission«) hat hierfür Vorschläge unterbreitet, die zum einen das Risikoverhalten der Finanzmarktteilnehmer einschränken und zum anderen für den »Fall der Fälle« eine geordnete Insolvenz systemrelevanter Finanzinstitute ermöglichen sollen.[1]

3. Die Vorschläge der Issing-Kommission

Um das Risikoverhalten systemrelevanter Finanzinstitute einzuschränken, schlägt die Expertenkommission eine am systemischen Risiko orientierte Bankenabgabe vor. Die Idee, zusätzlich zu den Kapitalanforderungen nach Basel II und den Einzahlungen zur nationalen Einlagensicherung eine weitere Abgabe für Finanzinstitute einzuführen, findet sich in vielen Vorschlägen aus den USA, Deutschland und des IWF. Der Hauptunterschied zwischen diesen Vorschlägen besteht darin, ob diese Abgabe ex-post oder ex-ante erhoben werden sollte (in Bezug auf eine Finanzkrise). Ein Beispiel für eine ex-post-Abgabe ist die »Financial Crisis Responsibility Fee«[2] (FCR), die von der U.S.-Regierung vorgeschlagen wurde. Im Gegensatz dazu stellt die »Financial Stability Contribution«[3] (FSC), die vom IWF präferiert wird, eine ex-ante-Abgabe dar. In diesem Zusammenhang hat die Expertengruppe für Finanzmarktreformen bereits in ihrem Positionspapier für das G-20-Treffen in Pittsburgh 2009 darauf hingewiesen, dass eine ex-post-Abgabe in Hinblick auf die Verringerung systemischer Risiken kaum zielführend ist.[4]

Im Gegensatz dazu unterstützt die Expertengruppe für Finanzmarktreformen die Einführung einer effektiven ex-ante-Abgabe. Diese umfasst idealerweise zwei Ziele: Erstens ermöglicht sie, die sozialen Kosten, die durch systemische Risiken entstehen, auf der Ebene individueller Finanzinstitute zu internalisieren und zweitens, ausreichend Finanzmittel zu sammeln, damit die Aufsichtsbehörden im Falle von Finanzkrisen Stützungsmaßnahmen durchführen können. Es sei herausgestellt, dass beide Ziele in bisherigen Ansätzen nicht berücksichtigt werden.

Die Details einer am systemischen Risiko orientierten Bankenabgabe sind äußerst wichtig, denn sie entscheiden über Erfolg und Misserfolg der Krisenprävention. Die folgenden Elemente sind für eine effektive systemische Bankenabgabe deshalb von entscheidender Bedeutung:

- Erstens sollte die Abgabe regelmäßig (quartalsweise oder jährlich) erhoben werden, um dauerhafte und deutliche Anreize zur Verminderung des systemischen Risikos zu setzen.
- Zweitens sollte die Abgabe von allen Finanzinstituten erhoben werden, die möglicherweise zum systemischen Risiko beitragen oder von Rettungsoperationen profitieren würden.
- Drittens sollte die Höhe der Abgabe individuell variabel sein und sich nach dem Beitrag eines individuellen Finanzinstituts zum systemischen Risiko bemessen. Da es bei der Einführung einer derartigen Bankenabgabe vermutlich noch keine genauen Maßzahlen für individuelle

Beiträge zum systemischen Risiko gibt, könnte sie anfangs auf der Größe (z. B. alle Verbindlichkeiten ohne Tier-1-Kapital und ohne versicherte Einlagen) sowie einer Kennzahl für die Vernetzung (z. B. das Verhältnis von Interbankverbindlichkeiten zu der Summe aller Aktiva) basieren.

- Viertens sollte das notwendige Gesamtaufkommen, das sich aus den Zahlungen der Banken speist, vom systemischen Gesamtrisiko abhängen; es sollte nicht auf ein festes Niveau gesetzt werden, sondern mit dem systemweiten Risiko variieren, um einen starken Anreiz für eine Verringerung des systemischen Risikos im gesamten Finanzsystem zu bewirken (z. B. indem die Vernetzung zwischen den Instituten, Korrelationen zwischen Portfolios und Fristeninkongruenz verringert werden). Um einen signifikanten Einfluss auf die Entscheidungen des Managements zu haben und somit ein sichereres Bankensystem zu erzeugen, sollte die Abgabe eine Mindesthöhe haben, die wahrscheinlich oberhalb der zeitweise öffentlich diskutierten Summe von 1.2 Milliarden Euro liegen müsste.
- Fünftens sollte die Gesamtsumme der systemischen Bankenabgabe auf ein maximales Niveau begrenzt werden, beispielsweise 5 % des BIP (was in etwa den – vorläufigen – Kosten der Allgemeinheit für die Bankenrettung in den Jahren 2007 bis 2009 entspricht) – vorausgesetzt die Gesamtsumme der systemischen Risikoabgabe kann über einen Zeitraum von mehreren Jahren gesammelt werden, ohne in der Zwischenzeit für eine Bankenrettung herangezogen zu werden.

- Sechstens sollte die Bankenabgabe derart gestaltet sein, dass sie auf die Banken auch eine disziplinierende Wirkung hat, wenn die oben genannte Maximalsumme (z. B. 5 % vom BIP) erreicht ist. Dies könnte beispielsweise dadurch erreicht werden, dass die aus der Bankenabgabe gesammelten Gelder unmittelbar in Form von verzinslichen Anleihen in die zahlenden Institute re-investiert werden. Auf diese Art und Weise hätte die Bankenabgabe keinen liquiditätsmindernden Effekt, da sie Gewinne und Boni zwar schmälert, gleichzeitig aber die offenstehenden Schulden erhöht. Als willkommener Nebeneffekt erhält der Staat zusätzliche Einkünfte in Form der Zinszahlungen auf die Anleihen.

Unter Bezugnahme auf die vorangehenden Punkte ist davon abzuraten, das Aufkommen aus der systemischen Bankenabgabe in einem zentralen Fonds zu sammeln und dort aufzubewahren, um diesen dann bei einer Finanzkrise anzuzapfen. Anstelle dessen bietet sich an, wie bereits vorgeschlagen, das Aufkommen aus der Bankenabgabe unmittelbar in die zahlende Finanzinstitution zu reinvestieren. Der Grund für diesen Vorschlag ist pragmatischer Natur. Durch die unmittelbare Reinvestition der Bankenabgabe wird das Aufkommen auf der Ebene der individuellen Institution aufbewahrt, was das Risiko einer Quersubventionierung zwischen verschiedenen Bankensektoren verhindert.

Des Weiteren besteht nicht die Notwendigkeit, eine angemessene Investitionsstrategie für einen Betrag derartiger

Größenordnung zu entwickeln. Außerdem besteht bei einer unmittelbaren Reinvestition des Aufkommens auch nicht die Gefahr, dass die Gelder für anderweitige Zwecke benutzt werden. Letzteres stellt insbesondere dann ein politisches Risiko dar, wenn der Staatshaushalt angespannt ist und das systemische Risiko (zwischenzeitlich) als gering eingeschätzt wird.

Mit Verweis auf die Pufferfunktion, die mit angesammelten Geldern aus einer Bankenabgabe erreicht werden kann, wurde kürzlich die Verwendung von Wandelschuldverschreibungen (Conditional Convertibles, »Cocos«) diskutiert, insbesondere im Vereinigten Königreich und in den USA. Wandelschuldverschreibungen können eine wertvolle Erweiterung zu den oben genannten Vorschlägen sein und die Stabilisierungsfunktion, die durch eine systemische Bankenabgabe erreicht werden kann, in Krisenzeiten noch verbessern. Allgemein können Wandelschuldverschreibungen in Aktien des emittierenden Unternehmens umgewandelt werden. Das Recht, die Umwandlung der Schuldverschreibung in eine Aktie auszulösen, wird bei der Emission bestimmt und sollte im Falle von Wandelschuldverschreibungen, die zur Stabilisierung mit Geldern aus der am systemischen Risiko orientierten Bankenabgabe finanziert werden, entweder dem Europäischen Ausschuss für Systemrisiken (European Systemic Risk Board, ESRB) oder der nationalen Aufsicht übertragen werden.

Insgesamt gibt es viele gute Gründe, eine ex-ante-Bankenabgabe, wie im obigen Abschnitt beschrieben, ins Leben zu rufen. Demgegenüber gibt es, abgesehen von der Möglichkeit, Einkommen für den Staat zu generieren, keine überzeugenden Argumente, die für eine ex-post-orientierte Bankenabgabe, wie z. B. die »Financial Crisis Responsibility Fee« der U.S.-Regierung, sprechen, da diese bei der Verminderung systemischer Risiken wenig hilfreich ist und die Widerstandskraft des Finanzsystems schwächen kann.

Ein System zur geordneten Abwicklung systemrelevanter Banken

Die Glaubwürdigkeit systemischer Risikoprävention ist von entscheidender Bedeutung. »Glaubwürdigkeit« bedeutet, dass sowohl Aktien- als auch Anleihenbesitzer davon überzeugt sind, im Fall einer Finanzkrise – sei diese systemisch oder nicht – nicht vom Steuerzahler gerettet zu werden. Es muss klar sein, welche Parteien im Falle einer Finanzkrise entsprechend ihrer Vorrangigkeit zuerst bedient werden und welche Parteien Verluste realisieren müssen. Die Erwartung über den tatsächlichen Ablauf von Bankenrettungen ist nicht nur von entscheidender Wichtigkeit für das Verhalten aller beteiligten Parteien, Anleihebesitzer, Aktionäre und Management, sondern auch eine Vorbedingung dafür, dass sich Ausfallrisiken angemessen in Marktpreisen und Finanzratings widerspiegeln.

Ein durchführbarer Ansatz sollte die folgenden Eigenschaften aufweisen: Zuerst muss eine Rechtsgrundlage zur schnellen Abwicklung eines in finanzielle Schieflage geratenen Instituts geschaffen werden. Für Deutschland bedeutet dies wahrscheinlich eher eine Änderung im Kreditwesengesetz als in der Insolvenzordnung. In dieser Hinsicht sollten Aktionäre nicht die Möglichkeit haben, eine schnelle Abwicklung zu verhindern, die eine »Verwässerung« ihrer Anteilsscheine implizieren würde.

Des Weiteren muss ein Prozess zur Bankenabwicklung zwischen dem Verhindern sowohl von Ansteckungsrisiken im Finanzsystem als auch von Rettungsaktionen (»Bail-outs«) für Anleihebesitzer abwägen. Beides sind sinnvolle Ziele, hängen jedoch eng miteinander zusammen. Tatsächlich verhindert eine Rettungsaktion für Gläubiger zwar kurzfristig das Risiko von Ansteckungseffekten im Finanzsystem, führt aber wegen des »Moral Hazards«, der daraus erwächst, langfristig zu einem höheren Niveau systemischen Risikos. Um den Teufelskreis aus Rettungsaktionen und ansteigenden systemischen Risiken zu durchbrechen, schlägt die Expertengruppe für Finanzmarktreformen vor, die Gläubigerhaftung zu verstärken. Gläubiger müssen ex-ante verstehen, dass Fremdkapital, welches von Investoren außerhalb des (»systemrelevanten«) Finanzsystems gehalten wird, im Fall einer Finanzkrise verloren ist. Dieses führt dazu, dass Risikoaufschläge für derartige Bankenanleihen bei sich abzeichnenden krisenhaften Entwicklungen bereits frühzeitig ansteigen. Auf der anderen Seite des Spektrums sind die Bankenverbindlichkeiten, die von anderen Finanzinstituten (innerhalb des »systemrelevanten Finanzsystems«) gehalten werden und im Falle einer Finanzkrise in den Genuss von Rettungsaktionen kommen, damit Ansteckungsrisiken im Finanzsystem verhindert werden.

Weiterhin muss ein derartiges Abwicklungsregime, um glaubwürdig zu sein, an eine Minimalanforderung bezüglich des Anteils an Anleihen, die außerhalb des Finanzsystems gehalten werden, gekoppelt sein. Falls dies nicht der Fall ist, könnte das Fremdkapital von insolvenzbedrohten Banken an systemrelevante Banken weitergereicht werden, da diese bereit wären, hierfür den höchsten Preis zu zahlen.

Abschließend gibt es – zusätzlich zur Notwendigkeit, das Risikoverhalten der Finanzmarktteilnehmer einzuschränken und ein System zur geordneten Abwicklung von systemrelevanten Banken zu etablieren – weitere notwendige Reformschritte, beispielsweise um das Ansteckungsrisiko durch schwebende Derivatkontrakte, insbesondere Optionen und Kreditausfallversicherungen zu bewältigen. Die meisten diesbezüglichen Bedenken sollten sich durch zentrale Abwicklungssysteme sowie durch angemessene Hinterlegungssummen ausräumen lassen.

4. Ausblick

Die Finanzmarktkrise hat – im Gegensatz zum wirtschaftlichen Krieg aller gegen alle in den Jahren nach 1929 – die Überzeugung gebracht, dass gute und dauerhafte Lösungen nur gemeinsam gefunden werden können. Zu diesem Zweck haben sich erstmals in der Geschichte die Staats- und Regierungschefs der 20 wichtigsten Länder zunächst in Washington (2008) auf ein abgestimmtes Vorgehen geeinigt. Auch wenn es bisher noch keineswegs einen umfassenden Durchbruch gegeben hat, so sind doch auf wichtigen Feldern Fortschritte zu verzeichnen. Dies gilt beispielsweise für die Arbeit des Basler Ausschusses für Bankenaufsicht zur Stärkung der Eigenkapitalbasis.

Nicht zuletzt weil die Implementierung dieser Vorschriften noch lange Zeit beanspruchen wird, sollten die Vorschläge zu einer am systemischen Risiko orientierten Bankenabgabe und die Einrichtung eines Restrukturierungssystems unbedingt weiter verfolgt werden.

Anmerkungen

1 Issing, O., J. P. Krahnen, K. Regling, W. White (2010): Criteria for a Workable Approach Towards Bank Levies and Bank Restructuring, CFS White Paper No. IV. Für weitere Analysen der Expertengruppe siehe die Whitepaper Serie des Center for Financial Studies unter: www.ifk-cfs.de/index.php?id=1563. Zugang am 30. Juli 2010.

[2] Für eine kurze Übersicht über diese Bankenabgabe siehe z. B. http://www.whitehouse.gov/sites/default/files/financial_responsibility_fee_fact_sheet.pdf, Zugang am 30. Juli 2010.

[3] Siehe: IWF, A Fair and Substantial Contribution by the Financial Sector, Financial Report for the G-20, 2010.

[4] Der Grund hierfür ist, dass eine ex-post-Abgabe nicht genau zwischen Verursachern und Leidtragenden systemischer Risiken unterscheiden kann und aus diesem Grund Finanzinstituten keinen Anreiz bietet, ihren Beitrag zum systemischen Risiko zu verhindern. Es kann jedoch nicht geleugnet werden, dass eine derartige Abgabe den Vorteil hätte, Staatseinnahmen zu generieren. Siehe auch: Issing-Commission (2009). Preparatory Comments for the G-20 Meeting in Pittsburgh, memo.

PROF. DR. DR. H.C. MULT. PAUL KIRCHHOF

FREIHEIT IN DER KRISE

Wenn der staatliche Rettungsschirm gefährdete Unternehmen rettet, ihre Konkurrenten aber im Regen stehen lässt und die Steuerzahler in die Traufe bringt, so werden diese Rechtsfolgen nicht in der Kompetenz und Transparenz des Gesetzgebers entschieden[1], sondern zwischen Regierung und Unternehmen, Insolvenzverwaltern und Kreditgebern, Staaten und weltweit tätigen Unternehmen verhandelt. Bei diesen Gesprächen wird der Begünstigte bewusst, meist aber nicht öffentlich ersichtlich gemacht. Die Rettung gilt den Unternehmen, schützt aber ebenso kreditgebende Institute vor einem Forderungsausfall und vor Verlusten. Diese Kreditinstitute aber sind vielfach auch Kreditgeber des Staates, gewinnen dadurch Einfluss auf staatliche Entscheidungen, verhandeln also für sich und beeinflussen den Verhandlungspartner Staat, belasten den unbeteiligten Steuerzahler, bei einer kreditfinanzierten Zuwendung oder Garantiezusage den heute noch wehrlosen zukünftigen Steuerzahler.

Verbundgeschäfte zu Lasten Dritter

Diese Verbundgeschäfte zu Lasten Dritter werden in ihrer Paradoxie[2] erkennbar, wenn wir die Beteiligten – grob vereinfachend – in Staat und Finanzmarkt einander gegenüberstellen. Der Finanzmarkt beansprucht vom Staat Finanzzuweisungen, weil er den Kreditbedarf der Privatwirtschaft nicht befriedigen könne. Der Staat verweist auf seine überhöhte Verschuldung, die ihm weitere Finanzhilfen nicht erlaube. Der Finanzmarkt bietet deshalb dem Staat verzinsliche Kredite an, die der Staat entgegennimmt, um die Kreditsumme dem Finanzmarkt zu geben. Der Finanzmarkt sucht sich für die so gewonnenen Finanzmittel einen möglichst verlässlichen Schuldner mit hohem unbefriedigtem Finanzbedarf, bietet das Geld deshalb dem Staat als Kredit an. Der Staat nimmt dieses Angebot an und zahlt erneut Zinsen. Getilgt wird nicht. Dadurch steigen die Staatsschuld und die Bemessungsgrundlage für zukünftige Zinsen.

Überforderung, Abhängigkeit, verengter Handlungsraum

Diese Rettungsschirme kombinieren in einer modernen Art der Feudalherrschaft Wirkungen der Freiheitsrechte und der Sozialisierung. Geldeigentümer überlassen ihr Eigentum dem Staat zinspflichtig zu Lehen, gewinnt mit diesem Kapital die Herrschaft über Staat und Wirtschaft, auch über konkurrierende kleinere Unternehmen, festigt dieses hierarchische System durch Abhängigkeits- und Treueverhältnisse. Aus dem Benefiz folgen Gegenleistungspflichten oder Gegenleistungszwänge bis hin zu gesetzlichen Rettungsschirmen[3]. Die Rettungsschirme geben den gefährdeten Unternehmen und Kreditinstituten tatsächliche Grundlagen ihrer Freiheit, nehmen zukünftige Produktionsmittel – die steuerbare, finanzielle Leistungsfähigkeit, das Kapital der nächsten Generation – in der Verschuldung vorweg, setzen diesen Vorgriff auf zukünftige Steuererträge für gegenwärtige Vorhaben ein, ohne dass die zukünftigen Träger dieser Last sich heute wehren könnten. Der Finanzstaat ist überfordert und gerät in Abhängigkeit von weltweit tätigen Finanzinstituten und Ratingagenturen. Kaufmännische Vorsicht und privatwirtschaftliche Leistungsanreize werden geschwächt. Auch die Verwendung zukünftiger Steuerkraft in der Gegenwart verengt den Handlungsraum der nachfolgenden Staatsorgane.

Beantwortung der Krise durch Freiheitsgewähr

Das Grundgesetz antwortet 1949 auf die damalige politische, moralische und wirtschaftliche Krise durch die Gewährleistung der Freiheit. Nach der Kapitulation[4] waren Wohnungen und Produktionsstätten zerstört, die Rechts- und Wirtschaftsstrukturen verworren, viele Menschen getötet oder in Gefangenschaft. Die Ministerpräsidenten stellten die Frage, »Wie kommen wir durch den nächsten Winter?«[5] 1948 fürchtete man einen dritten Weltkrieg[6]. In dieser dramatischen Krise setzt der Verfassunggeber gänzlich auf das Prinzip der Freiheit, wirft den einzelnen auf sein Selbstbewusstsein, seine Tatkraft und Entscheidungsfreude zurück, stützt sich auf den Willen und die Kraft aller, Gesellschaft, Wirtschaft und Staat grundlegend besser zu gestalten.

Freiheit – ein Erfolgskonzept

Das Ergebnis dieser freiheitlichen Selbsthilfe – die Staatskassen waren leer, staatliche »Rettungsschirme« nicht möglich – waren ein unerwartet schneller, langfristig anhaltender wirtschaftlicher Aufschwung (»Wirtschaftswunder«)[7], das Entstehen eines bald gefestigten Verfassungsstaates[8], die Westintegration, die Entwicklung der Europäischen Wirtschaftsgemeinschaft und später der Europäischen Union mit Deutschland als einem der Gründerstaaten[9], die Wehrverfassung als erster Eintritt in ein System kollektiver Sicherheit[10], das Entstehen eines verlässlichen, grundrechtsgeprägten, demokratischen Verfassungsstaates mit sozialen und insbesondere auch technisch-industriellen Sicherungsaufgaben[11]. Die Freiheit vom Staat ist die Grundlage moderner Staatlichkeit. Die Gegenwart eines freiheitsgewährleistenden Staates wird von steigenden Freiheitserwartungen an den Staat bestimmt. Diese Erwartungen drängen auf Veränderung unserer Entscheidungsmaßstäbe. Freiheit berechtigt nicht zu Zahlungen aus der Staatskasse, sondern Freiheit meint Handeln auf eigene Chance und eigenes Risiko.

Anmerkungen

1 Vgl. den Gesetzesvorbehalt mit Junktimklausel ausdrücklich für Enteignung und Sozialisierung in Art. 14 Abs. 3 Satz 2, Art. 15 Satz 1 GG.

[2] Zum Begriff der Paradoxie (sprachliches Verwirrspiel) vgl. Otfried Höffe, Paradoxie, Dialog, Abhandlung, Aphorismus: Die vier Kardinalsprachen der Philosophie, in: Paul Kirchhof (Hg.), Wissenschaft und Gesellschaft, Ihre Begegnung in Sprache, Symposion zur Hundertjahrfeier der Heidelberger Akademie der Wissenschaften, 2010.

[3] Vgl. Finanzmarktstabilisierungsgesetz (FMStG) vom 17. Oktober 2008 (BGBl. 2008 I, S. 1982).

[4] Dazu Michael Stolleis, Besatzungsherrschaft und Wiederaufbau deutscher Staatlichkeit 1945–1949, HStR I, 3. Aufl., 2003, § 7, Rn. 23 f.; Reinhard Mußgnug, Zustandekommen des Grundgesetzes und Entstehen der Bundesrepublik Deutschland, daselbst § 8, Rn. 2.

[5] So das Thema der Münchener Ministerpräsidentenkonferenz vom 6. Juni 1947, Mußgnug, a. a. O., Rn. 11.

[6] Konrad Adenauer, Sitzung des Parlamentarischen Rates vom 15. 9. 1948, Sitzungsprotokolle der Unionsfraktion, eingeleitet und bearbeitet von Rainer Salzmann, Forschungen und Quellen zur Zeitgeschichte, Bd. 2, 1981, S. 1 B, S. 9; Manfred Görtemaker, Geschichte der Bundesrepublik Deutschland, von der Gründung bis zur Gegenwart, 1999, S. 47.

[7] W. Focke, Über das Wirtschaftswunder, 1953.

[8] Hasso Hofmann, Die Entwicklung des Grundgesetzes von 1949 bis 1990, HStR I, ^{3}2003, § 9, Rn. 1 f., 62 f.

[9] Hasso Hofmann, a. a. O., Rn. 39 f.

[10] Hasso Hofmann, a. a. O., Rn. 44 f.

[11] Dieter Grimm, Ursprung und Wandel der Verfassung, HStR I, 3. Aufl., 2003, § 1 Rn. 66 ff.

PROF. DR. KAI A. KONRAD

DIE ZUKUNFT DER EUROZONE

Mit einem Bürgschaftsrahmen von 750 Milliarden Euro hat die Europäische Union im Mai 2010 in Verbindung mit dem Internationalen Währungsfonds den unmittelbar drohenden Staatsbankrott Griechenlands und möglicherweise weiterer Mitglieder der Eurozone 2010 zunächst abgewendet. Die Politik in Europa hat sich damit einige Jahre Zeit erkauft. Gleichzeitig hat dieses Ereignis zu einem Reparaturbetrieb auf europäischer Ebene geführt, bei dem die EU unter Führung der Europäischen Kommission einerseits und van Rompuys Task Force andererseits eine Überarbeitung der Europäischen Finanzverfassung vorbereitet. Diese politischen Veränderungen werden die Verfassung der Staatsfinanzen in Europa, das Verhältnis der Länder zueinander und die Machtkonstellation zwischen Europäischer Kommission, Rat und den Einzelstaaten grundlegend verändern.

Diese derzeit diskutierten Reformen sind zwar radikal. Sie sind aber wenig geeignet, die Europäische Staatsschuldenkrise langfristig zu überwinden. Das Versagen des Stabilitäts- und Wachstumspakts in Europa hat seine Ursachen nicht in den Regeln des Pakts selbst. Die Ursachen liegen vielmehr im wirtschaftlichen und politischen Umfeld und insbesondere in Schwächen des privaten Finanzmarktsystems begründet. Deshalb muss eine erfolgversprechende Therapie dort, und nicht bei einer Reform der europäischen Haushaltsregeln, ansetzen.

Das Entstehen der Staatsschuldenkrise

Der Staatsschuldenkrise sind zwei andere Krisen vorausgegangen, die auch inhaltlich mit der Staatsschuldenkrise in Verbindung stehen. Zunächst wurde in der Finanzmarktkrise eine »Kernschmelze« des Finanzsystems durch Bürgschaften, Staatshilfen und eine einzigartige Flutung der Finanzmärkte mit Liquidität vermieden. Durch die konsequente staatliche Rettung großer Finanzinstitute und durch die Flutung der Märkte mit Liquidität wurde in dieser Krise allen Akteuren sehr deutlich gemacht, dass im Falle eines drohenden Kollapses der Staat und damit der Steuerzahler einspringt und hilft; die Verlustrisiken für die Investoren und Akteure an den Finanzmärkten sind und bleiben begrenzt.

In der auf die Finanzkrise folgenden Wirtschaftskrise wurden rekordverdächtige Konjunkturprogramme auf Kredit beschlossen. Die Neuverschuldung stieg somit 2009 und 2010 in vielen Staaten in die Höhe. Im Zuge der Weltwirtschaftskrise wurde in Deutschland ein Staatsfonds aufgelegt, dessen Zweck die Rettung finanziell gefährdeter Unternehmen war. Ein anderes Beispiel aus den USA ist die Rettung von General Motors, also eines Unternehmens in einer Branche, der Experten Überkapazitäten bescheinigen und für die sie eine Marktbereinigung als sinnvoll betrachten.

Auf Finanzkrise und Weltwirtschaftskrise folgte die Europäische Staatsschuldenkrise. Für das Entstehen der Krise dürften die Finanzkrise und die Weltwirtschaftskrise als Auslöser eine Rolle gespielt haben. Im Zuge dieser Krise haben die Mitgliedsstaaten der Europäischen Union in Verbindung mit dem IWF mit einem 750 Milliarden Euro umfassenden Bürgschaftsrahmen für Mitgliedsstaaten bewusst und für jeden erkennbar eine der wichtigsten Vorkehrungen der Europäischen Finanzverfassung außer Kraft gesetzt: die No-Bail-out-Klausel.

Diese im Artikel 125 des Lissabonner Vertrags festgeschriebene Klausel besagt, dass Mitgliedsstaaten der Eurozone im Fall einer Schieflage ihrer Haushaltsfinanzen keine Hilfe seitens der übrigen Mitgliedsstaaten erwarten können. Im Grunde sollte dieses gegenseitige Nichthilfeversprechen die Selbstverantwortung der Mitgliedsstaaten stärken und einzelstaatliche Anreize für eine nachhaltige Finanzpolitik setzen. Ein in sehr ernsthafte Zahlungsschwierigkeiten geratener Mitgliedsstaat sollte, so die Idee, seine Finanzen durch eine Umschuldung in Ordnung bringen müssen, mit entsprechenden Abschreibungen von Forderungen seitens der Kreditgeber. Diese drohenden Verluste in der Folge einer Umschuldung sollten die Kreditgeber bei ihrer Kreditvergabe wachsam und vorsichtig machen und so ein wichtiges Regulativ für Schuldenstaaten in Gang setzen: Das mit der Schuldenlast eines Staats wachsende Risiko einer Umschuldung mit nachfolgenden Forderungsabschreibungen der Kreditgeber sollte dazu führen, dass höher verschuldete Staaten höhere Zinsen zahlen, bzw. ab einem gewissen Punkt gar keinen weiteren Kredit mehr erhalten. So sollte der Kreditmarkt eine disziplinierende Funktion ausüben.

Die No-Bail-out-Klausel war zudem als Automatismus ausgestaltet: Die Nicht-Hilfe sollte automatisch erfolgen, nicht als Ergebnis eines Ratsbeschlusses. Sie sollte nicht von der Frage des Zustandekommens einer politischen Mehrheit innerhalb der Eurozone abhängen. Im Ergebnis haben die Eurostaaten im Mai 2010 dann aber den Automatismus durch einen politischen Beschluss außer Kraft gesetzt.

Damit haben die Eurostaaten die Glaubwürdigkeit der No-Bail-out-Klausel nachhaltig beschädigt. Staaten und Kreditgeber hatten vielleicht auch zuvor bereits an der Glaubwürdigkeit der No-Bail-out-Klausel gezweifelt und möglichen Kredithilfen zumindest eine positive Wahrscheinlichkeit eingeräumt. Sie können nach den Erfahrungen des Frühjahrs 2010 nun mit wesentlich höherer Wahrscheinlichkeit darauf vertrauen, dass in Zahlungsschwierigkeiten geratenen Staaten von den anderen Mitgliedsstaaten geholfen wird. Dieser weitere Glaubwürdigkeitsverlust zerstört eine wichtige europäische Institution und verkörpert die Hauptkosten des ohnehin schon teuren Rettungsschirms. Das Vertrauen der Bürger in langfristig stabile Staatsfinanzen ist empfindlich gestört. Ängste grassieren nun, wonach es mit nachhaltiger europäischer Haushaltspolitik dauerhaft vorbei ist.

Automatismen und Haushaltskontrolle auf EU-Ebene nützen wenig

Auf europäischer Ebene ist durch diese Ereignisse ein Reformprozess in Gang gekommen, der eine erstaunliche Dynamik entwickelt. Schon im Verlauf der Europäischen Staatsschuldenkrise wurden von verschiedenen Seiten Reformvorschläge eingebracht. Besondere Beachtung verdienen dabei die Vorschläge, die unter der Bezeichnung »Reform des Stabilitäts- und Wachstumspakts« diskutiert werden. Zu den prominentesten Vorschlägen gehört die Schaffung erweiterter Haushaltskontrollkompetenzen für die Europäische Kommission und andere europäische überstaatliche Entscheidungsgremien.

Solche Bestrebungen bzw. aktuelle Reformen werden damit begründet, dass eine frühzeitige Kontrolle der Einzelhaushalte die Finanzmisere Griechenlands eher ans Licht gebracht hätte. Man hätte dann, so das Argument, Griechenland schon weit früher auf einen finanzpolitisch nachhaltigeren Kurs bringen können.

Zudem sollen mögliche Sanktionen für Staaten mit zu hohen Schuldenständen oder Defiziten nicht mehr diskretionär vom Europäischen Rat beschlossen werden, sondern automatisch greifen. Diskutiert werden von verschiedenen Seiten die Kürzung oder Einbehaltung von Strukturfondsmitteln, Strafzahlungen und Stimmrechtsentzug. Die Sanktionen sollen innerhalb einer kurzen Zeitspanne durch

Mehrheitsbeschluss aber ausgesetzt werden können. Begründet werden derlei Korrekturen des Regelwerks damit, dass in der Vergangenheit »Defizitsünder über Sanktionen für andere Defizitsünder« entscheiden mussten, und eben deshalb keinen ausreichenden Anreiz gehabt hätten, solche Sanktionen zu beschließen.

So plausibel die Begründungen für solche Reformen zunächst auch scheinen mögen: zwei Arten von Fakten lassen den Erfolg solcher Reformen als fraglich erscheinen.

Fehlende Information über mangelnde Nachhaltigkeit in der Haushaltspolitik einzelner Mitgliedsländer war wohl nicht das Problem, das zur Europäischen Staatsschuldenkrise geführt hat. Dafür gibt es jedenfalls einige Indizien. Griechenland beispielsweise hat seit seinem Beitritt zur Eurozone in neun von zehn Jahren den Referenzwert von drei Prozent Nettoneuverschuldung überschritten. Auffällig dabei ist auch: In allen Jahren war der revidierte (ex-post) Wert des Defizits höher als der ursprünglich avisierte (ex-ante) Wert. Man darf wohl erwarten, dass es einem Einzelstaat in der Eurozone auch weiterhin gelingen dürfte, in der mittleren Finanzvorschau einen Weg scheinbarer Nachhaltigkeit in der Finanzpolitik aufzuzeichnen und parallel dazu weiter in die Verschuldung zu laufen. Ist die Regierung eines Staats entschlossen, weitere Schulden zu machen, und wird sie dabei von breiten Teilen der eigenen Bevölkerung unterstützt, wird sie hierfür Wege finden, die auch ein engmaschiges Regelwerk unterlaufen. Und diese Sorte Schulden ist meist teurer als eine offene Staatsverschuldung.Fälle von Bilanzkosmetik dieser Art hat es auch in der Vergangenheit gegeben. Aus der Literatur sind Beispiele aus der Phase bekannt, in der die Einhaltung der Referenzwerte für den möglichen Eintritt in die Währungsunion ausschlaggebend war. Der Phantasie waren und sind damals wie heute nur wenige Grenzen gesetzt. Der Verkauf von öffentlichen Gebäuden zu hohen Preisen in Verbindung mit überhöhten Pachtzinsen (»sell and lease back«) oder die Schuldenaufnahme über Kredite von öffentlichen Unternehmen, für die eine staatliche Bürgschaft besteht, sind nur zwei Beispiele für eine ganze Klasse von mehr oder weniger verdeckten Kreditverträgen, mit denen ein Staat sich an seinem offiziellen Haushalt vorbei zu Lasten der Zukunft in der Gegenwart mehr Zahlungskraft verschaffen kann.

Eine penible und umfassende Kontrolle der einzelstaatlichen Haushalte durch die Europäische Kommission in Verbindung mit einer entsprechenden einzelstaatlichen Energie, die Referenzkriterien zu umgehen, hat dabei eine vielleicht überraschende Nebenwirkung. Kommt es nämlich angesichts einer solchen Überwachung und einer Einschränkung der einzelstaatlichen Entscheidungsautonomie dennoch zu einer extremen Haushaltsnotlage in einem Mitgliedsstaat, kann dieses Mitglied mit gutem Grund auf Hilfen seitens der Europäischen Gemeinschaft pochen: wer nicht durch autonome Entscheidungen in Not gerät, dem kann man auch keine Eigenverantwortung für das Handlungsergebnis abverlangen.

Man darf auch bezweifeln, dass sich die Glaubwürdigkeit von Sanktionen entscheidend erhöht, wenn man von diskretionär zu beschließenden Sanktionen zu Sanktionen übergeht, die automatisch von der EU-Kommission verhängt werden sollen, wenn bestimmte Situationen eingetreten sind. Der Stabilitätspakt ist in seiner derzeitigen Ausgestaltung bereits durch eine Reihe von Automatismen gekennzeichnet. Und interessanterweise sind gerade diese Automatismen in der Vergangenheit durch Mehrheitsbeschluss außer Kraft gesetzt worden. Zu den prominentesten Beispielen hierfür gehört die politische Intervention der Bundesregierung, mit der sie versucht hat, dass die EU-Kommission ein eigentlich völlig automatisch einsetzendes Mahnverfahren eben doch nicht einleitet. Die Verhinderung des sogenannten »blauen Briefs« für das Budgetjahr 2002 hat zu einer »Neuinterpretation« des Stabilitäts- und Wachstumspakts geführt. Sie zeigt zugleich, dass auch automatische Regeln relativ leicht unterlaufen werden können. Das noch wesentlich dramatischere Beispiel für das Versagen automatischer Regeln ist der große Rettungsschirm: Die Nicht-Hilfe ist als ein Automatismus konzipiert, hat die Eurostaaten aber nicht davon abgehalten, sich politisch über diese Regel hinwegzusetzen.

Trotz solcher Bedenken nimmt der Prozess der Reform des Stabilitäts- und Wachstumspakts zunehmend an Fahrt auf. Ein wichtiger Faktor zur Erklärung dieser Entwicklung ist die politische Interessenlage der zentralen Handlungsträger. Eine bekannte bürokratietheoretische Hypothese geht davon aus, dass Bürokraten ihre eigene Behörde gern vergrößern und stärken. Die Entstehung einer europäischen Finanzaufsicht und die Befassung der europäischen Ebene mit der jährlichen Budgetplanung und der mittleren Haushaltsvorausschau der Mitgliedsstaaten oder mit der Prüfung möglicher makroökonomischer Ungleichgewichte zwischen den Mitgliedsstaaten sind theoriekonform, was das Interessenprofil eines »Chefbürokraten« bei der Europäischen Kommission angeht.

Aber auch weitergehende Reformen der europäischen Verfassung der öffentlichen Haushalte sind derzeit denkbar. Zu diesen gehören Spielräume und Rechte für eine öffentliche Verschuldung auf europäischer Ebene. Sie lassen sich vordergründig mit den möglichen Kommissionsaufgaben bei der Rettung systemrelevanter Finanzinstitute oder von Mitgliedsstaaten am Rande der Zahlungsunfähigkeit begründen. Im September 2010 deuten sich entsprechende Bestrebungen mit dem Ziel eines systematischen Ausbaus und einer Perpetuierung der mit dem Rettungsschirm begründeten Einrichtungen bereits an. Hinzu treten könnten automatische Sanktionsrechte der Europäischen Kommission gegenüber Defizitsündern bei der Umsetzung der Überwachung der Haushalte der Mitgliedsstaaten. Automatische Kontrollmechanismen dieser Art würden das europäische Machtgleichgewicht verändern und den Einfluss der Kommission weiter stärken.

Der Übergang zu automatischen Sanktionsmechanismen wird anscheinend auch im Ministerrat zumindest von einigen Mitgliedern wohlwollend betrachtet. Das mag ganz unterschiedliche Gründe haben. Vielleicht ist das Vertrauen in die Glaubwürdigkeit automatischer Sanktionen noch weit verbreitet. Vielleicht geht es auch darum, Handlungs- und Problemlösungsfähigkeit zu demonstrieren. Einige Mitgliedsstaaten mögen solche Reformen als Zugeständnisse an die Staaten mit stabileren öffentlichen Haushalten betrachten. Oder sie sehen darin die Chance für einen zügigen Ausbau bestehender zwischenstaatlicher europäischer Transferinstitutionen wie dem Kohäsionsfonds.

Die zu beobachtenden Trends sind bürokratietheoriekonforme Entwicklungen. Und da die Europäische Kommission bei der Entwicklung von Reformvorschlägen für die europäische Finanzverfassung an entscheidender Stelle mitwirkt, würde man sich nicht wundern, wenn sie diesen Auftrag für eine Ausweitung der Handlungsspielräume entlang dieser Überlegungen nutzt.

Das Samariterdilemma

Es gibt unterschiedliche Spekulationen darüber, weshalb die Europäische Union im Mai 2010 mit dem 750 Milliarden Euro schweren Rettungsschirm einen zwischenstaatlichen Hilfsmechanismus – zunächst auf Zeit – installiert hat. Gelegentlich hört man, dass die Europäische Kommission ein erhebliches Eigeninteresse am Zustandekommen des Rettungsschirms und an einer Weiterentwicklung und Stärkung europäischer Institutionen im Bereich der staatlichen Haushaltspolitik hatte und schon deshalb an einer Umschuldung von Mitgliedsländern der Eurozone weniger interessiert war.

Eine prominentere und nicht notwendig damit konkurrierende Erklärung basiert auf Hypothesen über die wirtschaftlichen Folgen eines Verzichts auf eine solche Rettungsmaßnahme innerhalb Europas. Neben Griechenland drohten weitere Staaten der Eurozone in eine Situation zu gelangen, in der eine Anschlussfinanzierung ihrer Staatsschulden auf dem Kapitalmarkt entweder gar nicht oder nur noch mit enormen Risikoaufschlägen möglich gewesen wäre. Die drohende Umschuldung dieser Staaten hätte angesichts der Situation auf den Finanzmärkten zu erheblichen Verwerfungen auf diesen Märkten geführt, mit der möglichen Folge einer drohenden Insolvenz großer privater Kreditinstitute, einem erneut aufkeimenden Misstrauen der Banken untereinander bis hin zu einer Kernschmelze des gesamten Systems. Den in Schwierigkeiten geratenen Staaten nicht zu helfen, hätte insofern nachhaltig negative Konsequenzen gehabt, und zwar auch für die Staaten, deren Haushaltslage von den Finanzmärkten als solide eingeschätzt wurde. Wegen dieser negativen Konsequenzen befand sich Europa in einer Situation, die als »Samariterdilemma« bekannt ist.

Das Samariterdilemma, das von James Buchanan in die ökonomische Theorie eingebracht wurde, beschreiben Konrad und Zschäpitz in ihrem Buch »Schulden ohne Sühne?« am Beispiel des Verhältnisses eines Vaters zu seinem spielsüchtigen Sohn (S. 175):

Was macht ein Vater nur mit seinem Sohn, der ein leidenschaftlicher Spieler ist, oder auf andere Art viel Geld ausgibt, und dann Schuldscheine bei Kredithaien unterschreibt? Schaut der Vater zu, wie dem Sohn vom Geldeintreiber die Knochen gebrochen werden? Oder zahlt er lieber die Rechnung? Er zahlt. Und wenn er die aktuellen Schulden bezahlt hat, schwört er sich selbst und seinem Sohn: das war das letzte Mal! Nie wieder wird er für den Sohn zahlen. Das soll sich der Filius gefälligst hinter die Ohren schreiben. Wenn er das nächste Mal bei einer Runde Poker sitzt, wird ihm niemand mehr helfen.
Glaubhaft ist dieser Schwur natürlich nicht. Es ist eine leere Drohung. Und beide wissen das, Vater und Sohn. Auch das nächste Mal, wenn dem Sohn der Knochenbrecher droht, wird der Vater schwach werden und helfen. Glaubhaft ist die Drohung deshalb nicht, weil der Vater den Sohn nicht leiden sehen kann, ohne selbst zu leiden. Beide sind durch ein Band miteinander verbunden, das das Wohlbefinden des Einen an das Wohlbefinden des Anderen koppelt.

Im Verhältnis der Europäischen Staaten zueinander ist es dabei nicht ein tiefes Band der Zuneigung oder des Altruismus, was die solventeren Staaten veranlasst, den weniger solventen Staaten zu helfen. Es ist das nackte Eigeninteresse, durch die Hilfen die für das eigene Land negativen Folgen einer Umschuldung eines Mitglieds der Eurozone abzuwenden.

Das eigentliche Dilemma entwickelt sich über die Zeit, weil die zu erwartende Hilfsleistung am Rande der Insolvenz oder mögliche dauerhafte Transferleistungen über die Zeit ihre eigenen schädlichen Anreize entfalten. Am unmittelbarsten sind die Anreize für Staaten, die die Konsequenzen ihrer unsoliden Haushaltspolitik nicht zu tragen haben, weil andere Staaten im Zweifel helfen. Diese Staaten haben geradezu einen Anreiz, sich weiter zu überschulden, weil sie so Transfers der anderen Staaten erhalten können.

Anreize gibt es auch für die Staaten, denen die Rolle des immer wiederkehrenden Retters zugedacht ist. Sie könnten versuchen, die Retterrolle abzulegen, indem sie sich selbst hoch verschulden. Denn wer selbst nichts hat, kann anderen nicht helfen. Und im Zweifel ist es wohl angenehmer, das vorhandene eigene Vermögen selbst zu verprassen, als dadurch arm zu werden, dass man das Vermögen anderen schenkt.

Auch auf den Finanzmärkten entwickeln solche Hilfen massive Fehlanreize. Wenn die Kreditgeber darauf vertrauen können, dass die solventeren Staaten der Eurozone die weniger solventen Staaten im Zweifel vor dem Staatsbankrott retten, dann müssen sie zwischen Krediten an Staaten mit maroden Finanzen und Krediten an Staaten mit gesunden Finanzen nicht unterscheiden: die Rückzahlung beider Arten von Krediten erfolgt mit der gleichen Wahrscheinlichkeit; beide Kreditarten haben die gleiche Bonität. Für das Eintreten dieses Zustands ist es unerheblich, welche Sanktionen den weniger solventen Mitgliedsstaaten im Vorfeld einer Rettung oder im Zusammenhang mit einer Rettung auferlegt werden. Für den Anleger sind solche Sanktionen nicht wirklich relevant: für ihn zählt nicht, wer seine Kredite bedient, sondern ob seine Kredite bedient werden. Kreditgeber verlieren in dieser Situation den Anreiz, die Bonität einzelner Staaten zu prüfen und auf eine Verschlechterung der Bonität eines Mitgliedsstaats mit Zurückhaltung bei einer weiteren Kreditvergabe zu reagieren.

Die Haftungsgemeinschaft, in der sich die Mitgliedsstaaten der Eurozone durch ein gegenseitiges Rettungsversprechen oder eine entsprechende Bürgschaftsinstitution begeben, hat auch eine Wirkung auf die Kreditkosten zusätzlich aufgenommener Schulden. Nimmt ein Staat zusätzliche Kredite auf, verschlechtert er die Bonität der Haftungsgemeinschaft insgesamt. Die Refinanzierungskosten der Haftungsgemeinschaft als Ganzes steigen. Ein einzelnes, zumal ein kleines Mitgliedsland trägt damit nur einen Bruchteil der Bonitätskosten, die seine eigenen zusätzlichen Schulden verursachen. Der größere Teil der Bonitätskosten wird auf die anderen Mitgliedsstaaten abgewälzt. Da der Einzelstaat also nicht die vollen Kosten zusätzlicher Kredite zahlt, üben prinzipiell alle Mitgliedsstaaten eine zu hohe Kreditnachfrage aus, mit entsprechenden Folgen für die gemeinschaftliche Bonität.

Wichtiger noch als die Wirkung auf den Kreditmärkten für Staatsschuldtitel und für die Haushaltspolitik der Mitgliedsstaaten könnten die politischen Wirkungen des Samariterdilemmas für das »Projekt Europa« sein. Wiederholte Hilfszahlungen oder umfangreiche Transfers von den reicheren zu den ärmeren Mitgliedern, die sich über viele Jahre erstrecken, dürften auf Dauer zu politischen Spannungen zwischen Geber- und Nehmerstaaten führen.

Das Frühjahr 2010 hat uns einen Vorgeschmack auf solche Spannungen gegeben. Im Zusammenhang mit der Diskussion um eine Rettung des griechischen Staatshaushalts gab es in Deutschland verbreitet eine Diskussion über die Mentalität »der Griechen«. Klischees über Griechen als faule Steuerbetrüger machten sich breit. Dass man in Deutschland den Gürtel enger schnallen solle, um Geld nach Griechenland zu schicken, war nicht sonderlich gut vermittelbar. Reportagen beherrschten die Diskussion, in denen Personen erklärten, für welche Zwecke man Geld lieber in Deutschland einsetzen solle, anstatt es nach Griechenland zu überweisen. In Griechenland wurden zur gleichen Zeit mögliche deutsche Reparationszahlungen im Zusammenhang mit dem Zweiten Weltkrieg diskutiert, auch wenn die offizielle Politik sich diese erst einmal nicht zu eigen machte. Ein anhaltendes Samariterdilemma hat große Sprengkraft und kann zu einer politischen Zerreißprobe der Europäischen Union werden. Es zeichnet sich in Europa eine Trennlinie ab zwischen den Staaten mit solideren Staatsfinanzen und solchen mit weniger soliden Staatsfinanzen. Angesichts der Geschichte Europas ist es unwahrscheinlich, dass Deutschland den ersten Schritt in Richtung auf einen Austritt tut. Vorstellbar ist aber, dass einige Länder im Norden Europas Konsequenzen ziehen und beispielsweise über eine Nordeuropaunion nachdenken.

Neben den internationalen Spannungen, die sich aus zwischenstaatlichen Transfers entwickeln können, trägt eine europäische Transferunion auch den Keim möglicher Radikalisierung in einzelnen Staaten in sich. Slogans wie »Sparen für die Griechen? Nein Danke!« könnten populistischen Strömungen vom rechten wie vom linken politischen Spektrum Auftrieb verleihen. Wenn Geld mehr oder weniger regelmäßig aus dem eigenen Land abgesaugt und über die Europäische Union an andere Mitglieder mit chronischen extremen Haushaltsnotlagen gepumpt wird, lässt sich das gut in politische Münze prägen. Schon in den vergangenen Jahren waren die Positionen der Mitglieder der EU als Nettozahler Thema vieler politischer Debatten und spielten auch innenpolitisch eine Rolle. Dabei waren diese Zahlungsströme klein im Verhältnis zu den möglichen Strömen, die sich in einer europäischen Transferunion entwickeln könnten. Sollten in einzelnen Mitgliedsstaaten radikale Populisten mit diesem Thema Regierungsverantwortung erlangen, könnte das zum Auslöser für mögliche Spaltungsprozesse innerhalb der Europäischen Union werden.

Die teuer erkaufte Zeit richtig nutzen!

In der Politik gibt es eine Tendenz, zu Gunsten der Gegenwart und zu Lasten der Zukunft zu handeln. Probleme werden gern in die Zukunft verlagert. Die Politik reagiert auf unmittelbaren Handlungsdruck; die Lösung sich langfristig andeutender Probleme wird eher vertagt. Mit dem europäischen Rettungsschirm hat der unmittelbar erkennbare Handlungsdruck erst einmal nachgelassen. Die Welt geht in diesem Jahr nicht unter, auch wenn Reformen unterbleiben. Die eigentlichen Probleme sind indes nicht gelöst. Das ist eine ohnehin schon wenig erfreuliche Ausgangslage. Schlimmer noch: die Akteure, die mit der Systemreform betraut sind, haben Interessen, die einer sinnvollen und nachhaltigen Ordnung der europäischen Finanzverfassung jedenfalls nicht gleichgerichtet sind.

Aber was wäre denn ein richtiges Konzept? Eine Antwort hierauf hat jüngst der Wissenschaftliche Beirat beim Bundesministerium der Finanzen in einem Brief an den Minister skizziert. Im Kern fordert der Beirat, die Europäische Finanzverfassung formal unangetastet zu lassen. Mit einer unabhängigen Zentralbank, einem Haushaltsüberwachungsverfahren (Artikel 126) und vor allem einem Nicht-Hilfe-Gebot, also der No-Bail-out-Klausel des Artikels 125 sind gute Regeln vorhanden. Diese Regeln sind, würden sie eingehalten, ausreichend für Preisniveaustabilität und nachhaltige Haushaltspolitik. Das Problem seien also nicht die Regeln an sich, sondern ihre konsequente und glaubwürdige Anwendung.

Dass die Regeln nicht konsequent angewendet werden, bzw. sogar Automatismen wie die No-Bail-out-Klausel diskretionär außer Kraft gesetzt werden, dafür sind weniger die Regeln selbst verantwortlich als der institutionelle Kontext, in dem die Entscheidungen über die Anwendung der Regeln getroffen werden. Nicht die Regeln selbst sind reformbedürftig. Vielmehr muss ein Entscheidungsrahmen geschaffen werden, der die bestehenden Regeln glaubwürdig macht.

Man muss also zunächst fragen, welche Faktoren im institutionellen Umfeld dafür verantwortlich waren, dass z. B. ein Automatismus wie die No-Bail-out-Klausel außer Kraft gesetzt wurde. Dann muss man fragen, wie sich diese Faktoren verändern lassen.

Drei prominente Faktoren lassen sich identifizieren. Ein möglicher Grund bestand darin, dass im Mai verschiedene Banken und andere Finanzinstitute in Deutschland, Frankreich und anderen Mitgliedsstaaten erhebliche Bestände an Anleihen von Griechenland in ihren Anlagebeständen hatten. Eine Nicht-Hilfe mit anschließender Umschuldung hätte zu Abschreibungen in den betreffenden Instituten geführt. Soweit diese Institute als systemrelevant eingestuft sind, hätten diese Mitgliedsstaaten statt Griechenland dann diese Institute »retten« müssen.

Im Mai 2010 sind ferner die Befürchtungen groß gewesen, dass eine Staateninsolvenz mit nachfolgender Umschuldung eines oder mehrerer Mitgliedsstaaten der Eurozone dramatische Auswirkungen auf den Finanzmärkten gehabt hätte. Die mit einer Umschuldung einhergehende Abwertung der Staatsschuldtitel hätte mutmaßlich einige Banken in den Ruin getrieben, bzw. hätte die betreffenden Staaten gezwungen, diese Institutionen zu retten, um größere Finanzmarktturbulenzen ähnlich derer nach der Lehman-Pleite zu vermeiden.

Will man diese beiden Gründe im Falle zukünftiger Schieflagen von Eurostaaten ausschalten, kann das nur durch Reformen auf den Finanzmärkten erfolgen, und nicht durch eine Reform des Stabilitäts- und Wachstumspakts. Die Veränderung auf den Finanzmärkten muss einen Zustand herbeiführen, in dem ein Mitgliedsstaat der Eurozone nicht mehr »systemrelevant« ist. Eine Umschuldung eines Eurostaats ist in keinem Fall ein angenehmes Ereignis für die Finanzmärkte. Aber ein hinreichend robustes Bankensystem kann die Abschreibungen im Zuge einer Umschuldung eines Eurostaats relativ unbeschadet überstehen. Für diese Robustheit muss das Bankensystem reichlich mit

Eigenkapital ausgestattet sein. Die Anreize müssen so gesetzt sein, dass große Banken keine einseitigen großen Positionen an Schuldtiteln eines einzelnen Staats aufbauen, sondern ihre Anlagen ausgewogen auf unterschiedliche Länder und Anlageformen verteilen, Eigenkapitalstarke Banken mit einer hinreichend konservativen Anlagestrategie können solche Abschreibungen verkraften, ohne dadurch selbst in eine Schieflage zu gelangen.

Ein so robuster Zustand der Banken- und Finanzmärkte ist dabei keine Utopie, sondern eine im Grunde stabile Situation: In einer Finanzwelt, in der alle Banken und Finanzinstitute gut mit Eigenkapital ausgestattet sind und eine konservative Anlagestrategie verfolgen, hat das einzelne Institut kaum einen Anreiz, von einer solchen Strategie abzuweichen: es könnte mit einem gewaltigen Kredithebel durchaus riesige einseitige Positionen aufbauen. Das wäre für das Institut aber sehr gefährlich. Denn angesichts der Robustheit aller anderen Institute und des Systems überhaupt würde das Institut einfach untergehen, wenn es sich verspekuliert hat: der Staat könnte auf eine Rettung des Instituts verzichten, denn in einer robusten Finanzwelt wäre dieses einzelne Institut nicht systemrelevant.

Wie man aus der »Welt des Finanzmarktcasinos« in eine solche robuste Finanzwelt gelangt, ist kein triviales, aber auch kein unlösbares Problem. Und der Übergang ist ganz sicher auch mit Kosten verbunden. Am Beginn der Lösung des Problems steht indes die Einsicht, dass in der Lösung dieses Problems auch der Schlüssel zur Lösung des Glaubwürdigkeitsproblems des Stabilitäts- und Wachstumspakts liegt.

Dieser Beitrag macht Anleihen bei verschiedenen meiner früheren Veröffentlichungen. Im Kern folgt die Argumentation K. A. Konrad und Holger Zschäpitz (2010): *Schulden ohne Sühne? Warum der Absturz der Staatsfinanzen uns alle trifft*, C.H. Beck Verlag.

PROF. DR. STEFAN KORIOTH

ALTERNATIVLOSIGKEIT ODER SÜNDENFALL? DIE RETTUNGSPAKETE DER EURO-STAATEN VOM MAI 2010

I. Grundsätze der Währungsunion

Wer verstehen möchte, was gegenwärtig zur »Rettung« oder letzten Endes vielleicht zum Schaden oder sogar zum Verderben des Euro geschieht, sollte an die Anfänge der Europäischen Union zurückgehen. Ein wesentlicher Gegenstand des 1992 geschlossenen und 1993 in Kraft getretenen Vertrages über die Europäische Union (Vertrag von Maastricht) war die Begründung einer in mehreren Stufen zu verwirklichenden Europäischen Währungsunion, in der schließlich die Währungspolitik in einem Europäischen System der Zentralbanken vergemeinschaftet werden sollte. Dies ist zwischenzeitlich erreicht. Die dritte Stufe der Währungsunion hat den Euro als einheitliche Währung im Jahre 2002 eingeführt. Die Mitglieder der Europäischen Union verständigten sich 1992 darauf, die Währungsunion als Stabilitätsunion zu gestalten. Die gemeinsame Euro-Währung, darauf legten vor allem deutsche Politiker größten Wert, sollte (mindestens) so stabil wie die D-Mark werden. Zahlreiche deutsche Stimmen bekräftigten sogar, nur unter dieser Voraussetzung bereit zu sein, die D-Mark zugunsten des Euro aufzugeben und die deutsche Mitgliedschaft in der Währungsunion voranzutreiben.

Zur Sicherung des Stabilitätszieles sehen die Rechtsgrundlagen der Währungsunion – seit dem Vertrag von Lissabon

(2007/2009) enthält der Vertrag über die Arbeitsweise der Europäischen Union (AEUV) die primärrechtlichen Regelungen – drei Elemente vor. Das erste Element sind die Begrenzungen der Neu- und der Gesamtverschuldung der öffentlichen Gesamthaushalte der Mitgliedstaaten anhand von in Haushaltskennzahlen gefassten Größen; die Aufnahme von EU-Mitgliedern in die Euro-Zone hängt von der Erfüllung entsprechender Konvergenzkriterien ab (vgl. Art. 126, 136 AEUV). Der Stabilitäts- und Wachstumspakt von 1997 sieht im Interesse der Stabilität des Euro eine jährliche Neuverschuldung von maximal drei Prozent des Bruttoinlandsprodukts und einen Schuldenstand von maximal 60 % des BIP vor. Diese Kriterien sind bei und seit der Euro-Einführung von der Union eher nachlässig gehandhabt worden. Beim Start der Währungsunion (1999) hätte nach den Konvergenzkriterien jedenfalls Griechenland nicht zur Euro-Zone zugelassen werden dürfen. In den ersten Jahren nach der vollen Einführung des Euro (2002) verstießen insbesondere Frankreich und Deutschland gegen die Stabilitätskriterien. Das zweite Element der Stabilitätsunion ist die Europäische Zentralbank (EZB). Sie ist institutionell politischem Einfluss entzogen und vorrangig der Wahrung der Preisstabilität verpflichtet (Art. 130 AEUV). Das dritte Element bilden die Haftungsausschlüsse (Art. 125 Abs. 1 AEUV): »Die Union haftet nicht für die Verbindlichkeiten der Zentralregierungen, der regionalen oder lokalen Gebietskörperschaften oder anderer öffentlich-rechtlicher Körperschaften, sonstiger Einrichtungen des öffentlichen Rechts oder öffentlicher Unternehmen von Mitgliedstaaten und tritt nicht für derartige Verbindlichkeiten ein; dies gilt unbeschadet der finanziellen Garantien für die gemeinsame Durchführung eines bestimmten Vorhabens. Ein Mitgliedstaat haftet nicht für die Verbindlichkeiten der Zentalregierungen, der regionalen oder lokalen Gebietskörperschaften oder anderen öffentlich-rechtlichen Körperschaften, sonstiger Einrichtungen des öffentlichen Rechts oder öffentlicher Unternehmen eines anderen Mitgliedstaates, und tritt nicht für derartige Verbindlichkeiten ein; dies gilt unbeschadet der gegenseitigen finanziellen Garantien für die gemeinsame Durchführung eines bestimmten Vorhabens.« Art. 123 AEUV verbietet der EZB die Kreditgewährung an die Union und die Mitgliedstaaten.

Der Haftungsausschluss und der Ausschluss finanzieller Ausgleichsmechanismen (»No-Bail-Out«) ist für das Stabilitätsverständnis in der Währungsunion von zentraler Bedeutung. Dies folgt daraus, dass die Währungsunion von Beginn an nicht durch eine politische und (vollständige) wirtschaftliche Union begleitet und unterlegt wurde und wird. Nach wie vor gibt es keine Vereinheitlichung der jeweiligen nationalen Wirtschafts-, Finanz-, Haushalts- und Sozialpolitik, insbesondere gab es und gibt es keine Konvergenz im Sozialleistungsbereich und bei den Löhnen. Nur ansatzweise unterliegt die Wirtschaftspolitik der Koordinierung (vgl. Art. 121 AEUV). Ansonsten fallen die genannten Politikbereiche nach wie vor in die volle Zuständigkeit der Mitgliedstaaten. Unterschiedliche Ausgangspunkte und

Entwicklungen in diesen Bereichen, die durchaus zu Konflikten führen können, beantwortet die Stabilitätsunion mit einer knappen und klaren Auskunft: Alle Mitglieder der Euro-Zone sind verpflichtet, die Stabilitätsvorgaben des Vertrages zu beachten, insbesondere übermäßige Defizite zu vermeiden. Das No-Bail-out des Art. 125 AEUV verdeutlicht, dass jeder Mitgliedstaat seine finanzrelevanten Entscheidungen selbständig und in eigener Verantwortung trifft. Die Folgen unsolider Haushaltspolitik treffen jeden Mitgliedstaat und können nicht externalisiert werden. Eine europäische Transferunion mit wechselseitigen, vom Gedanken finanzieller Solidarität getragenen Ausgleichsbeziehungen gibt es nicht. Das unterscheidet den europäischen Staatenverbund vom Bundesstaat. Dieser kann auf finanzielle Ausgleichsmechanismen zwischen Bund und Ländern nicht verzichten. Allerdings können diese sehr unterschiedlich ausgestaltet sein. Zwischen Verschiedenheit und Ausgleich der Länderfinanzen, also zwischen Autonomie und Solidarität, gibt es auch im Bundesstaat eine große Spannweite von Lösungen. Jedenfalls im deutschen Bundesstaat gilt zudem, dass es keine wechselseitige Haftung von Bund und Ländern für Schulden gibt.

Das historisch und rechtsvergleichend einzigartige Vorhaben einer Währungsunion ohne politische Union wirft die Frage auf, ob es auf halbem Wege stehen bleibt: Kann es auf Dauer einen stabilen Währungsverbund ohne Ausgleichsmechanismen zwischen den Mitgliedstaaten geben? Diese Frage sei zunächst zurückgestellt. Die Befürworter des Euro hielten dies jedenfalls bei seiner Einführung für unproblematisch, weil die Nationalstaaten über gemeinschaftliche Handlungsparameter im Währungsbereich größeren Einfluss im Rahmen der Globalisierung erreichen könnten und finanzielle Disparitäten in der Euro-Zone gerade wegen der gemeinsamen Währung sich verringern würden. Jedenfalls die letztere Annahme erwies sich als folgenschwerer Irrtum.

II. Die Rettungsschirme

1. Griechenland ist seit 2001 Mitglied der Euro-Gruppe, die 16 von 27 Mitgliedstaaten der Europäischen Union umfasst. Im Jahre 2009 mussten die Angaben zum Umfang des griechischen Haushaltsdefizits von 5 % auf knapp 13 % des BIP korrigiert werden. Für 2010 rechnet Griechenland mit einem Anstieg der Staatsverschuldung auf 125 % des BIP, also mehr als das Doppelte des Referenzwertes von 60 %. Damit wurde zugleich offenbar, dass die griechischen Angaben zu den Vorjahren nicht der tatsächlichen Lage entsprochen hatten.

Im Februar 2010 beriet der Europäische Rat der Staats- und Regierungschefs über Maßnahmen zur Wahrung der Euro-Stabilität. Zugleich verlangte der Rat für Wirtschaft und Finanzen (ECOFIN-Rat) von Griechenland, das Haushaltsdefizit bis 2012 auf 3 % des BIP zurückzuführen. Angesichts zunehmender Unruhe der Finanzmärkte bekundeten die Staaten der Euro-Zone Ende März 2010 ihre Bereitschaft, Griechenland zusätzlich zu Finanzhilfen des Internationalen Währungsfonds (IWF) mit bilateralen Darlehen zu unterstützen. Nachdem dies keine Beruhigung der Märkte bewirkt hatte – die Ratingagentur Fitch setzte Anfang April 2010 ihr Rating für Griechenland auf BBB– herab –, beschlossen die Euro-Finanzminister am 11. April 2010 Einzelheiten der Darlehen. Um Griechenland den Weg der Rückkehr zur Marktfinanzierung zu ermöglichen, wurde die Zinsberechnungsformel des IWF als grundsätzliche Bezugsgröße für die Bedingungen der bilateralen Kredite herangezogen. Die Kommission verhandelte auf dieser Basis mit dem IWF und Griechenland. Die Unterstützung sollte in dem Zeitpunkt aktiviert werden können, zu dem sie tatsächlich benötigt wurde.

Am 23. April 2010 beantragte Griechenland Finanzhilfen der EU und des IWF. Die Staaten der Euro-Gruppe erklärten sich am 2. Mai 2010 bereit, im Rahmen eines dreijährigen Rettungsprogramms im Zusammenwirken mit dem IWF bis zu 80 Mrd. Euro in Form koordinierter bilateraler Kredite bereitzustellen. Der Anteil der einzelnen Staaten richtet sich nach dem jeweiligen Anteil am Kapitalmarkt der EZB. Der Anteil Deutschlands beläuft sich danach auf 27,92 %, also rund 22,4 Mrd. Euro, davon 8,4 Mrd. Euro im ersten Jahr. Der IWF übernimmt einen Anteil von 30 Mrd. Euro.

Den Finanzhilfen der Euro-Staaten liegen zwei Vereinbarungen zugrunde. Die erste, mit Griechenland geschlossene, sieht strenge Auflagen zur Haushaltssanierung als Voraussetzung der Kreditauszahlung vor. Eine Vereinbarung der Geberländer untereinander regelt einen internen Zins- und Zahlungsausgleich für Geberländer in wirtschaftlichen Schwierigkeiten.

Die im nationalen Recht notwendigen Schritte zur Umsetzung dieses Rettungspaketes traf der deutsche Gesetzgeber an nur einem Tag, dem 7. Mai 2010. Um 12.00 Uhr verabschiedete der Deutsche Bundestag das »Gesetz zur Übernahme von Gewährleistungen zum Erhalt der für die Finanzstabilität in der Währungsunion erforderlichen Zahlungsfähigkeit der Hellenischen Republik« (Währungsunion-Finanzstabilitätsgesetz – WFStG, BGBl. I S. 537), um 14.30 Uhr stimmte der Bundesrat zu. Nach Unterzeichnung und Ausfertigung durch den Bundespräsidenten trat das Gesetz am 8. Mai 2010 in Kraft. Bereits zwischen der Verabschiedung des Gesetzes im Bundestag und der Zustimmung durch den Bundesrat gingen beim Bundesverfassungsgericht Verfassungsbeschwerden gegen das Gesetz ein, verbunden mit Anträgen auf Gewährung einstweiligen Rechtsschutzes. Letztere wies das Gericht am 7. Mai 2010 zurück (2 BvR 987/10). Entscheidungen zur Hauptsache stehen noch aus.

2. Die Rettungsmaßnahmen zugunsten Griechenlands erwiesen sich schnell als nur erster Schritt umfassender Euro-

Rettungsmaßnahmen. Am 7. Mai 2010 forderten die Staats- und Regierungschefs der Euro-Zone, alle nötigen Mittel einzusetzen, um die Stabilität des Euro-Währungsgebietes zu bewahren. Sie vereinbarten, dass die Kommission einen europäischen Stabilitätsmechanismus (Euro-»Rettungsschirm«) vorschlagen solle. Daraus entstand die Verordnung (EU) Nr. 407/2010 vom 11. Mai 2010 zur Einführung eines europäischen Finanzstabilisierungsmechanismus (EFSM). Sie stützt sich auf Art. 122 Abs. 2 AEUV. Danach kann einem Mitgliedstaat, der aufgrund außergewöhnlicher Ereignisse, die sich seiner Kontrolle entziehen, von Schwierigkeiten betroffen ist, finanzieller Beistand der EU gewährt werden. Der Rat war der Ansicht, die außergewöhnliche Situation liege darin, dass die weltweite Finanzkrise für mehrere Mitgliedstaaten der Euro-Zone zu einer tiefgreifenden Verschlechterung der Kreditkondition geführt habe, die sich allein durch wirtschaftliche Fundamentaldaten nicht erklären lassen. Über das Gesamtvolumen des Stabilisierungsmechanismus äußert sich die Verordnung ebenso wenig wie über die Laufzeit. Die öffentlichen Verlautbarungen, das Gesamtvolumen sei auf 60 Mrd. Euro begrenzt und der Mechanismus gelte für drei Jahre, ist also politischer Wille.

Neben dem EFSM verpflichteten sich die Staaten der Euro-Gruppe, über eine Zweckgesellschaft (»European Financial Stability Facility«, EFSF) Hilfe zu leisten. Für die Zweckgesellschaft bürgen die Mitgliedstaaten entsprechend ihrem Anteil an eingezahltem Kapital der EZB. Die Zweckgesellschaft wurde nach luxemburgischem Recht gegründet. Ihr Zweck ist die Emission von Anleihen sowie die Darlehensgewährung an Mitgliedstaaten in Schwierigkeiten. Die Garantiehöhe beträgt insgesamt 440 Mrd. Euro. Der deutsche Anteil am Garantievolumen beläuft sich auf 123 Mrd. Euro. Auch für dieses gigantische Paket – dieses ist rechtlich auf drei Jahre begrenzt – waren nationale Rechtssetzungsakte erforderlich. Am 21. Mai 2010 verabschiedete der Deutsche Bundestag das »Gesetz zur Übernahme von Gewährleistungen im Rahmen eines europäischen Stabilisierungsmechanismus« (StabMechG, BGBl. I S. 627), das vom Bundesrat wiederum am gleichen Tag gebilligt und am 22. Mai 2010 ausgefertigt und verkündet wurde. Am 23. Mai 2010 trat es in Kraft. Auch gegen dieses Gesetz wurde am 21. Mai 2010 Verfassungsbeschwerde eingelegt und der Erlass einer einstweiligen Anordnung beantragt. Den letzteren Antrag hat das Bundesverfassungsgericht am 9. Juni 2010 zurückgewiesen (2 BvR 1099/10).

Abschließend gehört zum Euro-Rettungsschirm, dass der Internationale Währungsfonds (IWF) bis zu 250 Mrd. Euro zur Verfügung stellt, um Euro-Staaten mit Finanzierungsschwierigkeiten zu unterstützen. Insgesamt hat der Rettungsschirm damit ein Volumen von bis zu 750 Mrd. Euro.

Die geschilderte Chronologie ist mehr als nur staunenswert: Innerhalb weniger Wochen garantieren die Union und die Staaten der Euro-Zone, flankiert vom IWF, mehr als 700 Mrd. Euro. Holen diese Maßnahmen konkret und in der Krise nach, was vor der Einführung des Euro an der Währungsunion abstrakt nicht genügend durchdacht war? Handelt es sich um Rettungsschirme letztlich zugunsten der Banken und Versicherungen, die durch die drohende Zahlungsunfähigkeit von Euro-Staaten in den Abgrund gerissen zu werden drohen? Zahlt der nationale Steuerzahler nur oder profitiert er auch? Alle diese Fragen dürften wirklich seriös noch nicht zu beantworten sein. Deshalb sei eine einfachere Frage gestellt: Sind die Euro-Rettungsschirme eigentlich rechtmäßig?

III. Vereinbarkeit der Rettungsschirme mit europäischem Recht?

Es gibt eine ganze Reihe von Argumenten dafür, dass die Rettungsschirme mit dem geltenden europäischen Primärrecht nicht vereinbar sind.

1. Die Bail-out-Maßnahme zugunsten Griechenlands

Das gilt zunächst für die Unterstützung Griechenlands. Art. 125 AEUV verbietet jedem Mitgliedstaat die Haftung oder das Eintreten für die Verbindlichkeiten eines anderen Mitgliedstaates. Ein Bail-out durch Kredite ist daher unzulässig. Art. 125 AEUV umfasst nicht nur die erzwungene Haftung, sondern auch die freiwillige Übernahme von Verbindlichkeiten. Die Kreditvergabe durch die Kreditanstalt für Wiederaufbau (KfW), die § 1 Abs. 1 S. 2 WFStG vorsieht, unterliegt den Begrenzungen des Art. 124 AEUV. Danach darf die KfW Griechenland-Kredite nur zu marktüblichen Bedingungen ausgeben, nicht aber zu politisch festgelegten.

Sollte Griechenland auf dem Markt keine Kredite mehr aufnehmen können, dann ist jede Kreditvergabe durch die KfW untersagt. Es ist ausgeschlossen, dass ein Griechenland gewährter Kredit, obwohl sich das Land am Finanzmarkt nicht refinanzieren kann, zu marktüblichen Konditionen vergeben werden könnte. In diesem Fall würde, in der Sprache der Ökonomen, der Marktzins unendlich. Die Ausnahme vom Verbot eines Bail-out und Art. 122 AEUV dürfte kaum einschlägig sein. Griechenland hat durch unsolide Finanzpolitik, insbesondere überhöhte Verschuldung, selbst und in eigener Verantwortung die maßgebliche Ursache für seine Hilfsbedürftigkeit gesetzt. Das ist keine unvorhergesehene Notsituation, die sich der Kontrolle Griechenlands entzöge.

2. Das Euro-Rettungssystem

Die genannten Einwände treffen auch das umfassende Euro-Rettungssystem. Sowohl die Finanzierungen von EU-Anleihen als auch bilaterale Garantien rechtfertigen sich nicht unter Berufung auf Art. 122 AEUV. Die Lage der jetzt oder zukünftig von Finanzierungsschwierigkeiten am Kapitalmarkt betroffenen Staaten ist selbstverschuldet. Die Notstandsklausel des Art. 122 Abs. 2 AEUV passt schon deshalb nicht, weil »außergewöhnliche« Ereignisse im Sinne dieser Vorschrift nur solche sein können, die von außen einwirken und nicht auf eine nationalstaatliche Finanzpolitik zurückzuführen sind, die mit den Anforderungen der Stabilitätskriterien unvereinbar ist. Erfasst von der Ausnahme sind etwa Fälle schwerer Naturkatastrophen oder so ungewöhnliche Ereignisse wie die deutsche Einheit. Wollte man die Klausel anders verstehen, dann würde dies bedeuten, die bewusst herbeigeführte höchste Verschuldung in der Eurozone auch noch durch solidarische Hilfe zu prämieren. In jedem Fall ermächtigt Art. 122 AEUV nur zu Hilfen im Einzelfall – ein Euro-Stabilitätsmechanismus, der auf eine unbestimmte Zahl von Finanzkrisen Anwendung finden kann, ist dadurch nicht gedeckt. Schließlich ermächtigt Art. 122 Abs. 2 AEUV nur die Union, nicht dagegen die Mitgliedstaaten, die ausnahmslos an Art. 125 Abs. 1 AEUV gebunden sind.

IV. Folgerungen: Solidar- oder Stabilitätsgemeinschaft?

Es sprechen also gewichtige Gründe für eine Nichtvereinbarkeit der Rettungsschirme mit dem Unionsrecht. Ein ungeschriebener Notstandsvorbehalt, den offenbar manche Stellungnahmen aus der Politik zur Rechtfertigung heranziehen wollen, ist dem Unionsrecht außerhalb des Art. 122

Abs. 2 AEUV schon wegen des Grundsatzes der begrenzten Einzelermächtigung der Union (Art. 2 AEUV) fremd. Dennoch wird die rechtliche Fragwürdigkeit vermutlich folgenlos bleiben. Der Gerichtshof der Union kann in der vorliegenden Konstellation nicht von einzelnen Bürgern angerufen werden. Nationale Verfassungsgerichte werden sich schwertun, die Wand der europäischen politischen Einmütigkeit unter Heranziehung des nationalen Verfassungsrechts zu überwinden, obwohl es – in der Terminologie des Bundesverfassungsgerichts – nahe läge, die Kategorie des ausbrechenden europäischen Hoheitsaktes zu bemühen – mit der Besonderheit allerdings, dass in diesem Fall nicht nur die Union, sondern auch die Mitgliedstaaten im Zusammenwirken die Rechtsgrundlage der Stabilitätsunion sehr frei, vielleicht über die Belastungsgrenzen hinaus, handhaben. Mit Recht hat der frühere Verfassungsrichter Ernst-Wolfgang Böckenförde das Hilfspaket für Griechenland und den Europäischen Finanzierungsmechanismus als »abenteuerlich« bezeichnet: »Gezielt wird das Bail-out-Verbot außer Kraft gesetzt [...] und die Veränderung der Währungsunion in Richtung einer Transferunion angebahnt. Dafür gibt es im Vertragsrecht der EU weder eine Ermächtigung noch eine andere Rechtfertigung.« (in: NZZ vom 21. Juni 2010).

Natürlich hat die politische Einmütigkeit, die bisher hochgehaltene Stabilitätspolitik einfach über Bord zu werfen, Gründe. Kurzfristig geht es darum, Beruhigung zu schaffen. Langfristig wird zu entscheiden sein, ob aus der Stabilitätsunion mit ihren ursprünglichen Prinzipien eine solidarische Union wird. Das Bundesverfassungsgericht hat in seinem Urteil zum Vertrag von Maastricht von 1993 diese Möglichkeit vorhergesehen und jedenfalls das Verlassen des Stabilitätspfades auch mit den damals wie heute geltenden Verpflichtungen des Vertrages unvereinbar angesehen: »Sollte die Währungsunion die bei Eintritt in die dritte Stufe vorhandene Stabilität nicht kontinuierlich im Sinne des vereinbarten Stabilitätsauftrags fortentwickeln können, so würde sie die vertragliche Konzeption verlassen« (BVerfGE 89, 155, 205). Gemessen am nationalen Recht, hat das Bundesverfassungsgericht für diesen Fall die demokratische Legitimation der Befugnisübertragung von der Bundesbank auf die EZB für fragwürdig angesehen: »Die mit Blick auf die Europäische Union vorgenommene Ergänzung des Art. 88 GG gestattet eine Übertragung von Befugnissen der Bundesbank auf eine Europäische Zentralbank, wenn diese den ›strengen Kriterien des Maastrichter Vertrages und der Satzung des Europäischen Systems der Zentralbanken hinsichtlich der Unabhängigkeit der Zentralbank und der Priorität der Geldwertstabilität‹ entspricht [...]. Der Wille des verfassungsändernden Gesetzgebers zielt also ersichtlich darauf, für die im Unions-Vertrag vorgesehene Währungsunion eine verfassungsrechtliche Grundlage zu schaffen, die Einräumung der damit verbundenen [...] Befugnisse und Institutionen jedoch auch auf diesen Fall zu begrenzen. Diese Modifikation des Demokratieprinzips im Dienste der Sicherung des in eine Währung gesetzten Einlösungsvertrauens ist vertretbar, weil es der – in der deutschen Rechtsordnung erprobten und, auch aus wissenschaftlicher Sicht, bewährten – Besonderheit Rechnung trägt, dass eine unabhängige Zentralbank den Geldwert und damit die allgemeine ökonomische Grundlage für die staatliche Haushaltspolitik und für private Planungen und Dispositionen bei der Wahrnehmung wirtschaftlicher Freiheitsrechte eher sichert als Hoheitsorgane, die ihrerseits in ihren Handlungsmöglichkeiten und Handlungsmitteln wesentlich von Geldmenge und Geldwert abhängen und auf die kurzfristige Zustimmung politischer Kräfte angewiesen sind« (BVerfGE 89, 155, 208 f.).

Diese auf die Befugnisse der Europäischen Zentralbank zielenden Feststellungen lassen sich auf die Rettungsschirme übertragen: Sie sind nicht von der verfassungsrechtlich gebilligten Übertragung von Hoheitsrechten, wie sie in den geltenden Verträgen niedergelegt ist, umfasst. Es findet mit ihnen eine gravierende Umbildung der Verträge ohne Vertragsänderung, ohne politische Diskussion des Für und Wider, ohne ökonomisch rationale Abwägung der Folgen statt. Der Weg in die Transferunion ist vorgezeichnet, wenn nicht doch die Rückkehr zur ursprünglichen Stabilitätskonstruktion mit No-Bail-out beschlossen werden sollte. Jetzt rächt sich, dass bei der nationalen Debatte über die Einführung des Euro im Jahre 1998 viele Fragen der Stabilitätsunion ohne politische Union offen blieben. Die damaligen Befürworter des Euro machten insbesondere geltend, der Euro werde Reformprogramme in allen

Mitgliedstaaten vorantreiben. Der luxemburgische Ministerpräsident Juncker spottete sogar, dass Transferleistungen zwischen den Euro-Ländern so unwahrscheinlich seien »wie eine Hungersnot in Bayern«. Schon damals hätte aber klar sein können, dass ein dauerhaftes Fehlen von Konvergenz im Sozialleistungsbereich und in der Lohn- und Abgabenpolitik die Währungsunion unter Druck setzen müsste, der entweder den sozialen Frieden in den schwächeren oder die Haushaltsstabilität in den stärkeren Staaten bedrohen müsste. In der Debatte des Deutschen Bundestages am 23. April 1998 (Plenarprotokoll 13/230) hat die Abgeordnete Hartenstein (SPD) ein jetzt Realität werdendes Szenario vorhergesehen: »Was geschähe denn, wenn unter dem Druck steigender Arbeitslosigkeit und schwindender Staatseinnahmen sowie einsturzgefährdeter Sozialsysteme neue Schuldenaufnahmen getätigt würden – und das nicht nur in einem Land, sondern in mehreren Ländern gleichzeitig. Dann gibt es doch mit hoher Wahrscheinlichkeit nur zwei Möglichkeiten: entweder wackere Transfers von den stärkeren in die schwächeren Länder oder aber eine Aufweichung des Euro. […] Damit käme ein fatales Roulette ins Rollen: Inflation und Kaufkraftverluste, Flucht der Kapitalanleger, höhere Zinsen, sinkender Außenwert.«

Bei der dringend notwendigen Diskussion, wie es mit der Europäischen Union am jetzigen Scheideweg weitergehen soll, sollten die deutschen Erfahrungen mit Finanzkrisen einzelner Länder im bundesstaatlichen System berücksichtigt werden. Die Situation ist mit den europäischen Rettungsschirmen zwar insofern nicht vergleichbar, als es sich um die Frage des Ranges finanzieller Solidarität im Bundesstaat handelt und die bisherigen innerstaatlichen Krisen keine nachhaltige Beunruhigung der Finanzmärkte bis hin zu drastisch verschlechterten Kreditbedingungen einzelner Länder verursachten. Vergleichbar aber ist die Frage nach den Möglichkeiten und Chancen externer Sanierung eines Haushalts. Hier sind die deutschen Erfahrungen negativ. Das Bundesverfassungsgericht hatte im Jahre 1992 den Ländern Bremen und Saarland eine extreme Haushaltsnotlage bescheinigt, aus der sich die Länder aus eigener Kraft nicht befreien könnten und deshalb der finanziellen Hilfe des Bundes bedürften (BVerfGE 86, 148). Der Bund unterstützte beide Länder zwischen 1994 und 2004 durch Gewährung von jeweils ca. 8 Mrd. Euro an Sanierungsmitteln. Der Erfolg blieb aus. Eine nachhaltige Verbesserung der finanziellen Situation beider Länder gelang nicht. Im Fall Bremens ließ sich sogar feststellen, dass das Land die erhaltenen Mittel nicht zur Schuldentilgung eingesetzt hatte. Das Bundesverfassungsgericht zog aus dieser Erfahrung die Folgen. Als es 2006 über die Finanzkrise des Landes Berlin zu entscheiden hatte, verweigerte es diesem Land, das zeitweise die höchste Pro-Kopf-Verschuldung aller Länder in Deutschland aufwies, Sanierungsanspruch gegen den Bund. Ein Anspruch auf Rettung eines hochverschuldeten Landes durch andere Länder und den Bund könne nur im Falle eines »bundesstaatlichen Notstands« bestehen – eine Situation, die das Gericht bewusst ohne nähere Umschreibung ließ, um zu verdeutlichen, dass sie bei der Finanzkrise einzelner Länder jedenfalls nicht vorliege (BVerfGE 116, 327). Aus der bundesstaatlichen Erfahrung lässt sich lernen: Nachhaltige Haushaltssanierung ist Sache interner Disziplin und selbstverantworteter Entscheidung, sie kann dagegen nicht von außen durch Finanzhilfe bewirkt werden. Das legt die Vermutung nahe, dass europäische und bilaterale Kredite an Griechenland und andere schwache Staaten der Euro-Zone die maroden Staatsfinanzen nicht sanieren werden und sogar zu einer weiteren Schwächung dieser Länder beitragen können. Mittelfristig könnte der Euro dauerhaft an Wert verlieren, die Stabilitätsgemeinschaft könnte sich in eine Schuldengemeinschaft verwandeln. Demgegenüber ist an die Zielsetzung des Art. 119 Abs. 3 AEUV zu erinnern: Die »Tätigkeit der Mitgliedstaaten und der Union setzt die Einhaltung der folgenden richtungweisenden Grundsätze voraus: stabile Preise, gesunde öffentliche Finanzen und monetäre Rahmenbedingungen sowie dauerhaft finanzierbare Zahlungsbilanzen.«

PROF. DR. CHRISTOPH G. PAULUS

HAUSHALTS-DISZIPLINIERUNG DURCH EIN RESOLVENZRECHT

Insolvenzrecht als Sanierungsrecht

Die jüngste Finanz- und Wirtschaftskrise hat das Thema »Insolvenz« in den Vordergrund der allgemeinen, öffentlichen Diskussion geschwemmt wie schon lange kein Ereignis zuvor in Deutschland. Dieser seit buchstäblich Jahrtausenden mit einem massiven sozialen Stigma behaftete Begriff wird allmählich auch hierzulande – nach etwa den USA und Großbritannien – um eine Konnotationsnuance bereichert, die das Makelbehaftete durch nichts Geringeres als eine Chance ersetzt. Denn in der Tat hält das moderne Insolvenzrecht die Option bereit, statt allein marktbereinigender Liquidation die Restrukturierung des Schuldners herbeizuführen und somit die Marktfähigkeit gerade wiederherzustellen. Damit hat das Insolvenzrecht, historisch gesehen, einen weiten Weg zurückgelegt – von der ursprünglich allein angesagten physischen Vernichtung des Schuldners über die Versilberung des gesamten schuldnerischen Vermögens hin zur jetzt ermöglichten Rettung des Schuldners, damit er wieder markttauglich wird.

Vorbild für diesen weltweiten Gestaltungswandel des Insolvenzrechts ist das berühmte Chapter 11-Verfahren des US-amerikanischen Bankruptcy Code, das auch für das sogenannte Planverfahren der Insolvenzordnung Pate gestanden hat. Die Implikationen, die mit diesem Wandel einhergehen, sind von enormer Tragweite – ermöglicht doch die sanierende Rettung eines bankrotten Schuldners nunmehr auch die Anwendung des Insolvenzrechts auf zahlungsunfähige bzw. überschuldete Einheiten, die bisher aus diesem Kontext teils implizit, teils explizit ausgenommen waren.

Was die implizite Ausnahme anbelangt, so hat sie unter dem Terminus »too big to fail« unselige Berühmtheit erlangt. Wie es nämlich Issing in seinem Beitrag treffend zum Ausdruck bringt, können grundsätzlich insolvenzfähige juristische Einheiten dadurch dem Insolvenzrisiko – und damit einem der Grundprinzipien eines jeden Marktverhaltens – entkommen, dass sie eine solche Größe erlangen, die ihnen den politischen Entscheidungsträgern gegenüber gewissermaßen ein Erpressungspotential an die Hand gibt, aus systemischen Gründen die Rettung finanzieren zu müssen. Mit den Worten Issings: »(D)ie Gewinne (bleiben) privat, Verluste im Falle des Scheiterns sind dagegen vom Staat, am Ende also vom Steuerzahler zu tragen.« Das gilt freilich nicht nur für die von ihm allein adressierten Banken, sondern auch für Unternehmen wie Opel oder (früher schon) die Philipp Holzmann AG.

Die explizite Ausnahme der Insolvenzfähigkeit betrifft Staaten. Von Souveränen sagt der Gesetzgeber unbeschadet einer Jahrhunderte, womöglich aber auch hier wieder Jahrtausende zurückreichenden Geschichte von Zahlungsunfähigkeiten und Überschuldungen, dass sie nicht pleite gehen könnten. Als Erklärung wird gerne angeführt, dass ihnen doch insbesondere die Möglichkeit verbleibe, die Notenpresse anzukurbeln und auf diese Weise ihre Schulden »wegzuinflationieren«, oder könnten sie doch die Steuerschraube anziehen. Letzteres ist ein besonders zynisches Argument, wenn man sich die zwischenzeitlich seit Jahrzehnten währende Notlage der Bevölkerung der armen und ärmsten Länder auf diesem Globus ansieht.

Die Sanierungs- oder Restrukturierungsoption des modernen Insolvenzrechts eröffnet in beiden Fällen, dem der bisherigen impliziten wie expliziten Ausnahme, die Anwendbarkeit seines Wirkungsmechanismus. Im Falle des »too big to fail« liegt der große Vorteil sogar gerade darin, dass die Politik durch das Planverfahren von ihrer Verantwortlichkeit recht eigentlich entlastet wird – kann sie doch auf dieses jüngst erst eingeführte (1999) Verfahren verweisen und die Verantwortlichkeit damit den betroffenen Akteuren zuweisen. Denn es ist gerade die Besonderheit des Planverfahrens, dass Schuldner und Gläubiger zusammen an einen Tisch gesetzt werden, um dort privatautonom das alle gemeinsam (aber an sich auch nur sie) betreffende Problem des Schuldners zu lösen.

Im Falle der Zahlungsunfähigkeit und Überschuldung von Souveränen ist die Übertragbarkeit der Sanierungsoption bislang allerdings noch weniger bekannt als in jenen Fällen. Doch dass sie funktionieren kann, zeigt mit wünschenswerter Deutlichkeit das US-amerikanische Chapter 9-Verfahren, das nichts anderes als eine auf die speziellen Belange von »municipalities«, also Körperschaften des öffentlichen Rechts, zugeschnittene Variante des Chapter 11-Verfahrens ist. Der besondere Zuschnitt resultiert daraus, dass es einzig und allein um die Restrukturierungs-, nicht aber auch um die Liquidationsvariante geht, und dass der Unantastbarkeit all der für die Ausübung hoheitlicher Rechte und Pflichten unerlässlichen Gegenstände Rechnung getragen werden muss. Das hat in den vergangenen Dekaden dutzende von Malen zu erfolgreichen Sanierungen geführt und lässt sich somit als Vorbild für Staateninsolvenzen verwenden, wenn auch hierbei natürlich wieder weitere Anpassungen vorgenommen werden müssen.

Die Sanierungsoption für Staaten in Europa

Das Frühjahr 2010 hat innerhalb Europas insofern ein Umdenken gebracht, als die Überprüfung der Insolvenzfähigkeit von Staaten auf die politische Agenda gesetzt worden ist. Das war im Falle Argentiniens 2001 noch nicht so sehr der Fall; da hatte sich hauptsächlich der Internationale Währungsfonds (IWF) um eine insolvenzrechtliche Lösung bemüht, bis ihm 2003 ein wohl politisch motiviertes Veto dabei Einhalt gebot. Nun aber hat die Griechenlandkrise dazu geführt, dass über ein Insolvenzverfahren für Staaten nicht nur nachgedacht, sondern in seiner konkreten Ausgestaltung diskutiert wird. Ermöglicht wurde das natürlich nur dadurch, dass es jetzt eben die zuvor angesprochene ausschließliche Sanierungsoption gibt. Sie – und nur sie allein – ist Gegenstand aller diesbezüglicher Überlegungen.

Das verdient deswegen besonders hervorgehoben zu werden, weil die Vorbehalte gegen das Phänomen »Insolvenz« unbeschadet der einleitend beschriebenen jüngsten Entwicklung nach wie vor sehr negativ besetzt sind. Aus diesem Grund erscheint es auch angezeigt, eine terminologische Abgrenzung vorzunehmen und – einen Vorschlag Kirchhofs aufgreifend – im Zusammenhang mit Staaten allein von »Resolvenzverfahren« zu sprechen. Wie der im englischsprachigen Rechtskreis übliche Sprachgebrauch »turnaround« bringt Resolvenz die Umkehr wieder hin zur Solvenz trefflich zum Ausdruck und kennzeichnet damit das maßgebliche Wesensmerkmal dieses Verfahrenstyps.

Losgelöst von derartigen sprachlichen Überlegungen ist aber natürlich vorrangig die Frage zu beantworten, warum es denn überhaupt wünschenswert sein sollte, ein Resolvenzverfahren für Staaten zu etablieren. Denn natürlich bedeutet dessen Einführung nicht die Lösung aller Probleme auf einen Schlag – so als wäre mit der Schaffung eines solchen Verfahrens allein das Thema der Staateninsolvenz ein für allemal ad acta gelegt. Das ist zweifelsfrei nicht der Fall – was allerdings mit Einführung eines Resolvenzverfahrens in jedem Fall schon einmal bestünde, wäre ein mehr oder minder klar vorgegebenes Verfahren, bei dem alle Betroffenen wüssten, welcher Schritt jetzt und als nächstes vorgenommen werden muss. Vergegenwärtigt man sich noch einmal die durch die große Unsicherheit geprägte Zeitspanne im Frühjahr 2010, als die griechische Krise offenkundig geworden war, die Mitglieder des Stabilitäts- und Währungspakts aber noch nicht wussten, wie sie reagieren sollten, und dadurch das Ausmaß der Krise immer größeren Umfang annahm, wird einem der Wert eines die nächsten Handlungsschritte festlegenden Verfahrens unmittelbar einsichtig.

Aber das ist natürlich nicht der einzige Vorzug, der Überlegungen wie die hier angestellten rechtfertigen würde. Die Einführung eines wie auch immer ausgestalteten Resolvenzverfahrens brächte vielmehr weitere, ganz entscheidende Vorteile mit sich:

- Zum einen die aus dem zivilrechtlichen Insolvenzrecht her bekannte Disziplinierungsfunktion allen beteiligten Akteuren gegenüber. Wenn es ein Insolvenzrisiko gibt, müssen und werden Schuldner wie Gläubiger bei der Begründung neuer Verbindlichkeiten vorsichtiger sein. Denn im ärgsten Fall sind sie es, die den Verlust zu tragen haben.
- Soweit das Resolvenzverfahren insolvenzrechtlich ausgeprägt ist, hat es den – juristisch gesehen – unschätzbaren Vorteil, aus der Gesamtheit der Betroffenen (also Schuldner und sämtliche Gläubiger) eine Zwangsgemeinschaft zu bilden, die es dem Gesetzgeber gestattet, von dem üblichen, im allgemeinen Wirtschaftsleben anzu-

wendenden Einstimmigkeitserfordernis abzuweichen und statt dessen eine Mehrheitsentscheidung für die Begründung und Abänderung von Vereinbarungen genügen zu lassen. Um also beispielsweise zu einem Schuldenerlass von 30 % zu kommen, ist nicht mehr die Zustimmung eines jeden einzelnen Gläubigers erforderlich, sondern es mag reichen, dass nur 75 % aller Gläubiger damit einverstanden sind. Es dürfte unmittelbar einleuchten, dass dadurch Vereinbarungen deutlich leichter zustande kommen.

- Und schließlich: Indem das erwähnte Stigma vermutlich zumindest partiell auch einem Resolvenzverfahren anhaften dürfte, erhöht sich die vorgenannte Disziplinierungsfunktion. Wie bei dem aus früherer politischer Diskussion vertrauten Slogan »Friede durch Abschreckung« ist ein Resolvenzverfahren gerade dann besonders erfolgreich, wenn es selten oder gar nicht angewendet werden muss. Immerhin muss zu einem gegebenen Zeitpunkt der verantwortliche Politiker vor die Fernsehkameras treten und seinem Volk verkünden, dass das Resolvenzverfahren beantragt werden muss. Um diesen Vorteil jedoch richtig zum Tragen kommen zu lassen, müssen dem Resolvenzverfahren effektive Warnungen vorgeschaltet werden; Beispiele dieser Art finden sich bereits jetzt schon in Art. 126 II AEUV [Vertrag über die Arbeitsweise der Europäischen Union] (sie sind bislang allerdings nicht ernst genommen und wirklich angewendet worden).

Es zeigt sich mithin, dass die Etablierung eines Resolvenzverfahrens ganz erhebliche Vorteile mit sich brächte, deren größter wohl darin liegen dürfte, dass eine größere Haushaltsdisziplin erreicht würde.

Eine mögliche Verfahrensausgestaltung

Damit stellt sich die Folgefrage, wie denn ein entsprechendes Verfahren aussehen könnte. Es wurde zuvor schon wiederholt darauf hingewiesen, dass es keinesfalls angeht, ohne Modifikationen ein bereits existierendes Modell zu übernehmen und auf gut Glück dessen Erfolg herbeizuwünschen. Es dürfte aber überdies auch ausgeschlossen sein, die bereits anlässlich der Argentinienkrise vorgelegten Modelle zu kopieren: Nicht nur, dass sie gewissermaßen politisch »verbrannt« sind; sie waren wohl auch insgesamt allzu ambitioniert. Was infolgedessen angezeigt ist, ist eine Selbstbeschränkung, die den Vorschlag eines realistischen und realisierbaren Verfahrens unterbreitet.

An dieser Stelle eröffnet sich eine aufschlussreiche Parallele zu einer Entwicklung, die etwa Mitte der sechziger Jahre des letzten Jahrhunderts zu großen Eklats und intensiver Diskussion geführt hatte. Zu diesem Zeitpunkt nämlich kulminierten die gegensätzlichen Ansichten von Investoren und Empfängerländern darüber, wie die jeweiligen Investitionen zu schützen seien. Die Weltbank beschränkte sich in dieser kritischen Situation darauf, eine Schiedsgerichtsinstitution zu gründen und zu diesem Zweck ein bloßes Verfahren zur Verfügung zu stellen. Dieses International Centre for the Settlement of Investment Disputes (ICSID) hat durch seine Entscheidungen zwischenzeitlich ganz erheblich dazu beigetragen, dass es heutzutage ein ausdifferenziertes Völkerinvestitionsrecht gibt.

Eine vergleichbare Entwicklung könnte sich hinsichtlich des Staatenresolvenzrechts ergeben. Was dafür benötigt wird, ist die Schaffung einer gerichtsgleichen Institution, etwa eines Sovereign Debt Tribunals (SDT), für welches eine Verfahrensordnung erlassen werden muss. Diese muss den folgenden Ablauf der Geschehnisse widerspiegeln:

Den Beginn macht die Präsentation eines Planes durch den allein zur Antragstellung berechtigten Schuldnerstaat, in dem minutiös aufgeschlüsselt ist, wie die Resolvenz herbeigeführt werden soll und welche Beiträge Schuldner wie Gläubiger hierzu zu leisten haben. Dieser Entwurf, der im Verlauf der nachfolgenden Erörterung mit den Gläubigern natürlich noch vielfältigen Änderungen ausgesetzt sein kann, dient gewissermaßen als Einlasskontrolle in das Verfahren; denn das SDT wird seine Fundiertheit und Realisierbarkeit überprüfen.

Die Gläubiger werden in Gruppen eingeteilt, die selbstverständlich sachlichen Einordnungskriterien genügen müssen. Diese Komprimierung ist allein schon deswegen unausweichlich, weil die schiere Anzahl der Gläubiger anderenfalls die größten logistischen Probleme auslösen würde. Diese Gruppenbildung ist von außerordentlicher Bedeutung, weil die schließliche Abstimmung über den Plan der Zustimmung durch eben diese Gruppen bedarf. Auch wenn die Zustimmung jeder einzelnen Gruppe benötigt werden sollte, impliziert das, dass nicht etwa jeder einzelne Gläubiger sein Plazet erteilen muss, sondern es genügt die (wie auch immer zu normierende, also entweder einfache oder qualifizierte, d. h. etwa 66 % oder 75 % oder 80 %) Mehrheit der gruppengebundenen Gläubiger. Sollte also für die gruppeninterne Abstimmung die einfache Mehrheit vorgesehen sein, genügt für ein ›Ja‹ die Zustimmung von 50 % + x der Gläubiger dieser Gruppe.

Bis es aber zu dieser Abstimmung kommt, werden Schuldner und Gläubiger gemeinsam an einen Tisch gebracht, an dem sie den vorgelegten Plan diskutieren. Zur weiteren Reduzierung der Massen von Gläubigern könnte man daran denken, spezielle Gläubigervertreter als handelnde und verhandelnde Akteure vorzusehen, wie sie etwa auch nach dem neuen Schuldverschreibungsgesetz, § 7, möglich sind. Bei diesen Verhandlungen wird es naturgemäß darum gehen, den eigenen Individualinteressen zum Durchbruch zu verhelfen. Das Gesetz tut aber gut daran, an dieser Stelle keinerlei substantielle Vorgaben zu machen; es sollte auf das Kräfteverhältnis der Verhandlungen vertraut werden.

Es ist nicht zwingend erforderlich, dass diese Verhandlungen mit denjenigen verknüpft werden, die der Schuldnerstaat wohl auch zu dieser Zeit wird führen müssen – nämlich die Zurverfügungstellung neuer Finanzmittel. Ob diese mit dem IWF geführt werden oder mit sonstigen potentiellen Geldgebern (je nach Planausgestaltung und seine öffentlich verkündete Akzeptanzfähigkeit erscheint zumindest nicht von vornherein ausgeschlossen, dass die Suche nach frischem Geld auch über Anleihen erfolgen kann), mag dahinstehen. Doch ist nicht auszuschließen, dass der potentielle Neugläubiger an den Planverhandlungen teilnehmen will. Das dürfte dann zu einem zusätzlichen Disziplinierungseffekt des Schuldners führen.

Zu einem bestimmten Zeitpunkt muss der Plan sodann zur Abstimmung gestellt werden. Aus dem Zustimmungserfordernis ergibt sich der Druck für den Schuldner, die Gläubigerbelange hinreichend zu berücksichtigen. Denn ohne den Plan verändert sich die Rechtslage und damit Höhe wie Fälligkeiten der Forderungen nicht. Diese Abhängigkeit von den Gläubigern ist die Kompensation für das aus politischen wie praktischen Gründen allein dem Schuldner zu verleihende Recht, das Verfahren in Gang zu setzen. Allerdings kann diese Abhängigkeit dadurch gemildert werden, dass man das Einstimmigkeitserfordernis der Gruppen (nicht: innerhalb der Gruppen!) reduziert. Vorbild dafür könnte die sogenannte ›cram-down-rule‹ des § 245 InsO sein, die unter bestimmten Voraussetzungen eine einfache Gruppenmehrheit genügen lässt. Wird der Plan auf diese Weise angenommen, muss ihn das Gericht bestätigen und zu diesem Zweck den Verfahrensablauf noch einmal auf seine Rechtmäßigkeit hin überprüfen. Aus diesem Grunde sollte während der Verhandlungen stets zumindest einer der Richter zugegen sein; sinnvollerweise leitet er diese. Die eigentliche Umsetzung des Planes erfolgt erst im Anschluss daran. Um den Schuldner auch in dieser Zeit zur Einhaltung seiner durch den Plan übernommenen Verpflichtungen anzuhalten, könnte vorgesehen werden, dass bei einem substantiellen Verstoß die ursprünglichen Rechtspositionen sämtlicher Gläubiger wieder aufleben und die mit dem Plan erzielten Vorteile mithin verloren sind.

Wenn der Plan allerdings die erforderliche Mehrheit nicht erzielen kann, sollte es zumindest die einmalige Chance zur Nachbesserung, d. h. zur Nachverhandlung geben. Wenn aber auch diese scheitert, so bietet die Währungsunion (anders als bei sonstigen überschuldeten Staaten) die Möglichkeit, eine ganze Palette von Sanktionen vorzusehen, die auch den Ausschluss aus dem Stabilitäts- und Währungspakt umfassen könnten. Dies stellt sicherlich die härteste Sanktion gegenüber dem Schuldnerstaat dar; das Scheitern könnte aber auch in den Verantwortungsbereich eines oder mehrerer Gläubiger fallen, die einen sogenannten ›holdout‹ versuchen. Ihnen gegenüber könnte das Gericht das Stimmrecht entziehen oder aber ihr Votum in jedem Fall als ein ›Ja‹ werten. Auf diese Weise könnten beide Seiten diszipliniert werden.

Resümee

Die Vorteile eines insolvenzähnlichen Verfahrens für Staaten sind mit Händen zu greifen. Die weltweite Entwicklung allein des letzten Jahrzehnts mit so prominenten Vertretern wie Argentinien, Island, Griechenland sowie einer ganzen Reihe weiterer so genannter Transitionsländer zeigt darüber hinaus, dass dafür ein echter Bedarf besteht. Und schließlich lassen die Überlegungen zur konkreten Ausgestaltung eines derartigen Verfahrens die Zeit dafür reif erscheinen, ein solches Verfahren auch tatsächlich einzurichten. Europa könnte dafür ein Vorreiter sein, dem alsbald das globale Dorf folgen würde.

Weiterführende Literatur:

Buckley, The Bankruptcy of Nations: An Idea Whose Time Has Come, 43 The International Lawyer, S. 1189 ff. (2009);

Hagan, A Legal Framework to Rescue Sovereign Debt, 36 Georgetown Journal of International Law, S. 299 ff. (2005);

Paulus, Ein Regelungssystem zur Schaffung eines Internationalen Insolvenzrechts für Staaten, Zeitschrift für Gesetzgebung 2010;

Paulus, Die Eurozone als Probefahrt für ein Resolvenzrecht für Staaten, Recht der internationalen Wirtschaft (RIW) 9/2010, S. I (Editorial).

PROF. DR. BURKHARD SCHWENKER

MEHR WACHSTUM, MEHR OPTIMISMUS: EUROPAS WERTE, EUROPAS ZUKUNFT

Folgt man dem aktuellen Mainstream, ist Europa augenscheinlich am Ende. »Kleinmacht Europa« stand Ende September 2010 in der *Financial Times Deutschland*, »Europa ohne Schwung«, das war kurz zuvor in der *Süddeutschen Zeitung* zu lesen: Der Aufschwung sei blutleer, der Zustand der EU miserabel. Und Starökonom Nouriel Roubini rechnete im *Handelsblatt* mit dem Auseinanderbrechen der Euro-Zone.

Mich erinnert dieser Pessimismus fatal an den Jahresbeginn 2009: Die Wachstumsprognosen wurden mit besorgniserregender Geschwindigkeit nach unten korrigiert, die meisten Beobachter rechneten für die konjunkturelle Entwicklung mit einer U- oder gar L-Kurve, vielfach war die Rede vom wirtschaftlichen Kollaps, kaum jemand glaubte noch an Auftriebskräfte. Das ist alles nicht so gekommen, aber anstatt nun selbstbewusst und optimistisch den Wachstumspfad zu stabilisieren, werden schon wieder die nächsten Untergangsszenarien beschworen. Für mich gilt damals wie heute: In komplexen Situationen versagen Prognosen, spielt Spekulation eine große Rolle und die Finanzmärkte verlieren ihre Leitfunktion. Deswegen lohnt sich ein Blick auf fundamentale Entwicklungen. Mir sind fünf Punkte wichtig:

Erstens: Unabhängig von den Spekulationen gegen den Euro und den finanzwirtschaftlichen Problemen vieler europäischer Staaten bleibt eine Erkenntnis aus der Finanz- und Wirtschaftskrise richtig und wichtig: Am Ende zählt die industrielle Kompetenz, weil die Realwirtschaft – Industrie, Handel, hochwertige Dienstleistungen – die entscheidende Rolle spielt, wenn es um Wachstum, Beschäftigung und Wettbewerbsvorteile geht. Wir sind über viele Jahre hinweg dafür belächelt worden, dass unsere Industrie einen so hohen Anteil an unserer Wertschöpfung hat. In der Euphorie der sogenannten Wissensgesellschaft galten wir als Ökonomien der Vergangenheit. Heute beneiden uns viele darum, denn wir sind mit Blick auf die Zukunft besser aufgestellt als andere: In Kontinentaleuropa liegt der Anteil der Industrie bei fast 19 %, in Deutschland sogar bei 24 %, während er in Amerika nur 12 % und in England sogar nur 10 % beträgt.

Die überlegene industrielle Kompetenz der (kontinental-) europäischen Volkswirtschaften zeigt sich auch in den Reports des World Economic Forum zur wirtschaftlichen Wettbewerbsfähigkeit der großen Wirtschaftsnationen, gerade auch in der aktuellen Ausgabe 2010/11:

- Europäische Länder liegen auf 8 der 10 Top-Ten-Plätze, was die »Einzigartigkeit des Wettbewerbsvorteils« betrifft. Übersetzt heißt das: Wir können uns mit unseren Produkten und Dienstleistungen international offensichtlich am besten differenzieren.
- Es sind ebenfalls europäische Länder auf 8 der 10 Top-

Ten-Plätze, wo es um die »Intelligenz und Qualität der Produktionsprozesse« geht. Anders gesagt: Hochwertige Industrie ist unsere Stärke.

An dieser Stelle lohnt sich ein genauerer Blick auf Deutschland. Platz 1 bei der Innovationskapazität: Forschung und Entwicklung sind hervorragend positioniert; Platz 3 bei der Qualität der lokalen Zulieferer: Es gelingt uns besser als vielen anderen, verlässliche Zulieferverbünde zu schaffen und zu managen; Platz 1 bei der Tiefe der Wertschöpfung unserer Exportunternehmen. Das ist die Basis, auf der sich zuletzt ein dynamisches Wachstum von mehr als 3 % entwickelt hat!

Solche Platzierungen erreicht man nicht über Nacht, sie sind auch kein Zufallsprodukt. Sie zeigen, dass deutsche und europäische Unternehmen ganz offensichtlich die europäischen Stärken und die Vielfalt, die Europa bietet, genutzt und in Wettbewerbsvorteile umgesetzt haben. Deswegen verschiebt sich das unternehmerische Kräfteverhältnis auch zunehmend nach Europa, denn 23 der größten Unternehmen dieser Welt haben inzwischen ihren Sitz hier, während die Zahl der amerikanischen Unternehmen in dieser Spitzenliga ständig schrumpft und nur noch bei 16 liegt – 25 waren es noch vor ein paar Jahren. Warum das wichtig ist? Weil sich die Stärke einer Volkswirtschaft vor allem an der Wettbewerbsfähigkeit ihrer Unternehmen zeigt.

Zweitens: Es ist nicht allein das Gewicht der Industrie, das Europa stark machen wird, es ist perspektivisch vor allem unsere Fähigkeit, Industrie und Dienstleistungen intelligent zu neuen Lösungen zu verbinden. Denn wir können heute feststellen, dass sich eine weitere Grundannahme der Wissensgesellschaft nicht verwirklicht hat: Hochwertige Dienstleistungen siedeln sich nicht irgendwo auf der Welt an, sondern entwickeln sich am besten um industrielle Kerne herum, weil die räumliche Nähe bessere Möglichkeiten schafft, Vertrauen für eine enge Zusammenarbeit in Entwicklung und Fertigung aufzubauen. Hier schließt sich auch der Kreis zu den Top-Positionierungen in den Rankings, denn die Fähigkeit zu differenzieren oder verlässliche Zulieferverbünde aufzubauen, schafft dafür genau die richtigen Voraussetzungen – und damit für Wachstumspotentiale.

Diese Kompetenzen sind noch aus einer anderen Überlegung heraus wichtig: Sie bieten eine Grundlage für nachhaltiges Wachstum. Der amerikanische Präsident Barack Obama hat gesagt: »Frieden ist mehr als die Abwesenheit einer Krise.« In Anlehnung daran gilt, dass Wachstum mehr ist als die Abwesenheit einer Wirtschaftskrise. Zukunftsfähiges, anhaltendes Wachstum werden wir nur erreichen können, wenn es gelingt, die großen Probleme der Welt wie Klimawandel oder Demografie, den Umgang mit knappen Ressourcen, mit mehr Produktivität zu verbinden. Green Tech ist eine zukunftsweisende Antwort, die europäische Industrie ist exzellent positioniert. Green Tech stellt einen intelligenten Querschnitt aus Maschinen- und Anlagenbau, Elektrotechnik und technischen Dienstleistungen dar, das entspricht unseren Stärken. Ähnliches gilt für den demografischen Wandel. Wir können ihn als Bedrohung sehen, aber auch als industrielle Chance. Denn abnehmende Erwerbstätigkeit ist nur durch beschleunigtes Produktivitätswachstum zu kompensieren – und schafft damit ganz neue Märkte für hochwertige industrielle Lösungen.

Drittens: Exzellente Unternehmensführung ist nötig, damit wir industrielle Kompetenz kapitalisieren können. Wir haben uns die Frage nach einem spezifischen »European way of management« zu lange nicht gestellt, bis heute haben Amerikaner die Art der Führung weltweit massiv beeinflusst. Dafür gibt es eine Reihe von Gründen, die sich gegenseitig verstärkt haben:

- Die Wirtschaftswissenschaft ist über Jahrzehnte hinweg amerikanisch geprägt worden – von Managementtheoretikern wie Peter Drucker, Philip Kotler und Michael Porter oder von Volkswirten wie Samuelson und Friedman, die Schulen begründet und weltweit wissenschaftliche wie unternehmenspraktische Debatten beeinflusst haben;
- fast alle Managementansätze der letzten 20 Jahre haben einen amerikanischen Ursprung, ob es die Erfahrungskurve ist, Portfoliomanagement, Shareholder Value oder Corporate Finance;
- wichtige internationale Organisationen wie der IWF oder die Weltbank oder die WTO sitzen in den USA – und werden direkt und indirekt von amerikanischer Managementphilosophie beeinflusst;

- hinzu kommt, dass es die USA bestens verstanden haben, von Rechnungslegung bis Rating ihre Standards zu setzen.

Es gibt noch einen weiteren Grund für die amerikanische Vorherrschaft: Wenn wir ehrlich sind, steckt unsere Generation voller heimlicher Bewunderung für amerikanische Unternehmen. Auf die Frage, welche Unternehmen wirklich global sind, wird mit hoher Wahrscheinlichkeit ein amerikanisches genannt. Nicht VW, nicht Siemens, und ganz sicher nicht die vielen mittelständischen Unternehmen, die in ihren Segmenten weltweit führend sind. Nüchtern betrachtet überrascht damit die amerikanische Dominanz nicht. Doch hat die Krise deutlich gezeigt, dass das amerikanische Managementmodell in weiten Teilen gescheitert ist – mit seiner Kurzfristigkeit, der Fixierung auf Kapitalmärkte, einer viel zu starken Finanzorientierung, der »Hire-and-fire«-Mentalität, einem missverständlichen Shareholder-Value-Denken. Ausgerechnet Jack Welch, der ehemalige CEO von General Electric, einer der bekanntesten Verfechter der Shareholder-Value-Philosophie, hat in einem Interview mit der *Financial Times* gesagt: »Shareholder value is the dumbest idea in the world. Shareholder value is a result, not a strategy (...). The main pillars are your employees, your customers and your products.«

Diese Aussage ist deswegen bemerkenswert, weil wir das in Europa schon immer gewusst haben – aber wir haben uns nicht getraut, selbstbewusst einen europäischen Gegenentwurf zu vermarkten. Doch mit Auslösern und Folgen der Finanz- und Wirtschaftskrise vor Augen ist jetzt die Zeit dafür gekommen. Wir Europäer sind fundamental besser gerüstet

- mit unserer langfristigen Orientierung, gerade auch, was Beschäftigung betrifft,
- mit einer stärkeren Verankerung unserer Unternehmen in der Gesellschaft,
- mit einem breiteren Verständnis von Unternehmenserfolg – das Vorsichtsprinzip des HGB war (und ist) die bessere Lösung,
- mit unserer humanistischen Bildung, deren Breite und Interdisziplinarität die Voraussetzung für Urteilsfähigkeit in komplexen Situationen schafft.

Das Konzept europäischer Unternehmensführung hat auch eine empirische Grundlage. Wir haben die Daten der 3.000 größten Unternehmen der Welt von 1998 bis 2008 analysiert, mit beeindruckenden Ergebnissen:

- 32 % dieser größten Unternehmen sind europäisch;
- sie stehen für 42 % der Gesamtgewinne, die noch dazu schneller gewachsen sind: mit durchschnittlich 13,1 %. Für die nordamerikanischen und japanischen Unternehmen haben wir nur ca. 7 % ermittelt;
- und schließlich machen Europas Unternehmen etwa 40 % ihrer Umsätze außerhalb des europäischen Heimatmarktes, mehr als Amerikaner oder Japaner, die nur bei knapp 30 % liegen: Europas Unternehmen sind die wahren »Global Players«.

Ein letzter Punkt: Europas Unternehmen halten sich länger am Markt – oder sind nachhaltiger erfolgreich als ihre

Wettbewerber, denn fast 80 % der Europäer haben es geschafft, über den gesamten Zehnjahreszeitraum zur Spitzengruppe zu gehören, aber nur 76 % der Amerikaner und nur 56 % der Japaner. Die Leistungsfähigkeit der europäischen Unternehmen absolut und vor allem im Vergleich zu ihren amerikanischen Wettbewerbern rechtfertigt also das Postulat eines europäischen Managementmodells, zumal sich – bei allen Schwierigkeiten, aus individuellen Strategien Muster abzuleiten – einige Gemeinsamkeiten zeigen. Zum Beispiel:

- Europäer sehen ein Geschäft strategisch und langfristig – und halten Strategien auch durch.
- Europäern geht es um die langfristige Differenzierung, sie denken in Produkten und Technologien und nicht primär an den Kapitalmarkt.
- Europäer sind dezentraler aufgestellt, sie lassen Managern in den regionalen Märkten mehr Entscheidungsspielraum und unternehmerische Freiheiten.

Wir können daraus eine klare Abgrenzung zum amerikanischen Managementstil ableiten, eine Basis für eine erfolgreichere Art europäischer Unternehmensführung. Gerade dieses gehört zu den fundamentalen Entwicklungen, die mit Blick auf Europa wichtig sind.

Viertens: Zu diesen fundamentalen Entwicklungen gehört auch, dass es völlig untergeht, schon während der Wirtschaftskrise, leider aber auch in der aktuellen Diskussion und Bewertung, dass Europa seit dem Jahr 2000 viel erreicht hat. Die Lissabon Agenda war kein Flop, denn sie hat

18 Millionen zusätzliche Jobs geschaffen, den Pro-Kopf-Wohlstand um 13,5 % gesteigert und den Innovationsabstand zu Amerika signifikant verringert. Und vor allem: Sie war ambitioniert und hatte auf Aufbruch gesetzt – Europa als wettbewerbsstärkste Region der Welt! Dass wir die Ziele (natürlich) nicht vollständig erreicht haben, spielt keine entscheidende Rolle. Wichtiger ist, dass wir Mobilisierung und Begeisterung erzeugen konnten.

Zu den Erfolgen gehört auch die Osterweiterung der EU. Weil sie für die mehr als 100 Millionen Menschen in den neuen Ländern zu neuen Chancen auf Wohlstand und für uns alle zu mehr Sicherheit geführt hat. Europa ist in den vergangenen zehn Jahren groß geworden, aus 15 Mitgliedsstaaten sind 27 geworden, aus 370 Millionen Einwohnern 500 Millionen – die Größe, die wir brauchen, um im Wettbewerb mit den anderen großen Regionen dieser Welt überhaupt eine Rolle zu spielen.

Und schließlich gehört zur richtigen Einordnung der Erfolge auch, dass ausgerechnet das am höchsten verschuldete Land der Welt – die USA – immer wieder und mit Nachdruck die »europäische Schwäche« anprangert. Jedenfalls relativiert ein Vergleich mit dem Dollar die Währungsschwankungen des Euro deutlich, denn auch der Dollar hatte seine Höhen und Tiefen, schwankte beispielsweise in der Dekade vor der Euroeinführung zwischen 1,60 DM und 3,50 DM. Hysterie über den Auf- und Abschwung des Euro war nie gerechtfertigt; am Ende überwiegen die Vorteile: ein Währungsraum mit einigen starken Volkswirtschaften und gutem Zukunftspotential.

Fünftens: Leider stehen die europäischen Volkswirtschaften in einer Krise. Im Augenblick ist es nur Deutschland, das mit einer außerordentlich dynamischen Wirtschaftsentwicklung und einer Wachstumsprognose von zuletzt 3,5 % (Herbstgutachten der führenden Wirtschaftsforscher) dafür sorgt, dass die Eurozone doch noch auf eine Wachstumsrate von 1,7 % kommen kann. Wenn alles gut läuft! Frankreich, England und Italien fallen als Wachstumstreiber aus; Spaniens Wirtschaft wird aller Voraussicht nach sogar weiter leicht schrumpfen.

Über allem schwebt zudem die extrem hohe Schuldenlast. Die öffentlichen Hilfen haben die Defizite auf den höchsten Stand seit dem Zweiten Weltkrieg katapultiert. In Europa gilt das in geringstem Maße noch für Deutschland (nach 3,3 % 2009 werden 3,7 % 2010 erwartet, für 2011 aber nur noch 2,5 %), alle anderen Länder sind in schwieriger Lage. Nach den Prognosen des IWF erhöht sich das Verhältnis von Schulden zur Wirtschaftsleistung (gemessen am Bruttoinlandsprodukt) in den entwickelten Ländern sprunghaft: Lag die Quote vor der Krise 2006 im Schnitt bei 78 %, erreicht sie in diesem Jahr vermutlich schon 106 %, 2014 könnte sie auf 114 % steigen. Kenneth Rogoff und seine Kollegin Carmen Reinhart kommen zu dem Schluss, dass die öffentliche Kreditlast Wachstum zu kosten beginnt, wenn das Defizit 90 % der jährlichen Wirtschaftsleistung übersteigt. Griechenland und Italien haben schon mehr als 100 % erreicht. Das ist eine der schlimmsten Hypotheken für unsere Zukunft.

Was können wir tun, wie geht es weiter? Das Bild ist diffus; wir haben auf der einen Seite ausgesprochene europäische Stärken – unsere industrielle Kompetenz, die Vielfalt in Europa, die zu kreativen Lösungen führt, einen spezifischen Weg einer überlegenen europäischen Unternehmensführung. Auf der anderen Seite volkswirtschaftliche Ungleichgewichte, eine erdrückende Schuldenlast – und keine überzeugende europäische Politik.

Die Antwort kann nur heißen: Stärken verstärken, auf Wachstum setzen und Begeisterung für Europa schaffen. Wir brauchen ein neues Europaprojekt, das die Menschen überzeugt und handfeste wirtschaftliche Vorteile in den Vordergrund stellt, anstatt komplexe Verfassungsfragen, die die regionale und nationale Identität in Frage stellen. Dazu gehört ein klares Bekenntnis zur europäischen Vielfalt und mehr Werbung für unsere industriellen Stärken. Es geht in die richtige Richtung, wenn die Stoßrichtung der Regierung in London heißt: »Weniger City, mehr Industrie«. Dazu gehört auch eine schnelle und vollständige Integration des europäischen Binnenmarktes über alle nationalen Egoismen und Grenzen hinweg, denn nur so kann es gelingen, für unsere Unternehmen einen ausreichend großen Heimatmarkt zu schaffen – 500 Millionen Europäer machen einen Unterschied, 80 Millionen Deutsche oder

64 Millionen Franzosen nicht. Außerdem müssen wir unsere europäische Wirtschaftspolitik besser koordinieren, bis hin zu einem Europäischen Wirtschaftsfonds und einer Ratingagentur, um Stärke und Selbstbewusstsein zu zeigen und die Amerikanisierung zu reduzieren.

Selbstverständlich gehört auch ein kluges Sparen dazu, denn es liegt im Interesse von uns allen, dass die öffentlichen Haushalte saniert werden. Aber nicht durch politisch korrekte proportionale Kürzungen, sondern durch massive Einsparungen in überfälligen Bereichen wie Bürokratie und Subventionen bei gleichzeitigen Investitionen in Wachstum: Forschung und Entwicklung, Bildung, Private Public Partnerships, grüne Technologien, Absicherung unserer Energieversorgung. Ansatzpunkte für überzeugende Europaprojekte gäbe es genug!

Was uns gelingen muss, ist eine innovative Kombination aus Sparen und Wachstumsinvestitionen. Hier weist der Ratschlag des IWF in die richtige Richtung: Es geht um einen ausgewogenen Mix; die Konjunkturprogramme sollten auslaufen, Pro-Kopf-Ausgaben eingefroren und das Steueraufkommen durch das Stopfen von Schlupflöchern und Ausnahmen erhöht werden. Gleichzeitig braucht es neue Regeln für den Umgang mit der Staatsverschuldung, genauso wie es Regeln braucht, um das Funktionieren der Finanzmärkte zu gewährleisten. Die Euro-Rettungspakete sollten in keinem Fall verlängert werden; sie waren gut und richtig, um den Euro zu stabilisieren, aber sie dürfen nicht zu einer (ausnutzbaren) dauerhaften Solidarhaftung der finanziell soliden Länder für die sorgloseren unter den EU-Staaten führen. Denn die Rettungsschirme refinanzieren sich nicht am Kapitalmarkt und wir müssen deswegen gewährleisten, dass die disziplinierende Wirkung der Märkte nicht dauerhaft ausgeschaltet wird.

Außerdem brauchen wir klare Regelwerke, wie die Staatsverschuldung zurückgeführt und restrukturiert wird. Die aktuelle Diskussion, beispielsweise über die Umkehrung des Abstimmungsverfahrens – nach Vorschlägen der EU-Kommission braucht es eine Zwei-Drittel-Mehrheit gegen Sanktionen und nicht mehr für ein Defizitverfahren – schafft dafür eine gute Grundlage. Genauso wichtig ist es, dass wir nie wieder Länder aufnehmen, die wirtschaftlich nicht genügend leistungsfähig sind. Eine Arabeske in diesem Zusammenhang – und gleichzeitig ein Schlaglicht auf die Finanzkrise – ist, dass im Falle Griechenlands auch eine Investmentbank bei der kreativen Zahlengestaltung behilflich war. Aber: Mehr Regeln heißt nicht mehr Staat – stark und schlank ist kein Gegensatz! Der Staat, oder in diesem Fall Europa, muss Regeln setzen und durchsetzen, und ansonsten viel Freiraum für Privatinitiativen lassen.

Ist das chancenlos? Es gibt eine interessante Untersuchung von Ulrike Reisach, Professorin für Intercultural Management, Betriebswirtschaftslehre und Unternehmenskommunikation an der Hochschule Neu-Ulm, über kulturelle Unterschiede zwischen Amerika und Europa, in der sie zu dem Ergebnis kommt, dass Amerika für eine Kaufmannskultur steht, also schneller Profit und persönlicher Reichtum eine große Rolle spielen, während Europa durch eine Handwerkskultur geprägt ist mit dem Wunsch, etwas Dauerhaftes, Bleibendes zu schaffen. Genau aus diesem Unterschied werden wir unsere Stärke für die nächste Dekade ziehen – mit Selbstbewusstsein und Gelassenheit.

DR. CORINNE MICHAELA FLICK
UND DIE AUTOREN

NEUN THESEN ZUR STAATS- UND WIRTSCHAFTS-FINANZIERUNG

Roland Berger

Die Eurozone braucht eine koordinierte Wirtschafts- und Fiskalpolitik und einen neu gefassten Stabilitätspakt – das »Window of Opportunity« für letzteres besteht bis Ende 2010.

Sir Howard Davies

There is a lengthy agenda of change ahead in EMU, to refurbish it in the light of the crisis. If the overhaul is not completed, some of the passengers may choose to man the lifeboats.

Um die EWU im Angesicht der Krise zu erneuern, steht ihr ein langwieriges Programm mit vielen Veränderungen bevor. Wenn diese Überholung nicht zu Ende gebracht wird, werden es einige Passagiere vorziehen, die Rettungsboote zu besteigen.

Corinne Michaela Flick

Die Globalisierung ist unsere größte Herausforderung. In einer globalisierten Welt müssen alle lernen, die Perspektive der Anderen mit einzubeziehen. Das *bonum commune* Ciceros und Cäsars ist auch für das Zusammenleben von Staaten unabdingbar. Zum eigenen Leistungsstreben muss die Verantwortung für die Gemeinschaft – auch für die Staatengemeinschaft – kommen, damit Glück und Gemeinwohl entstehen.

Otmar Issing
Es sollte eine am systemischen Risiko orientierte ex-ante-Bankenabgabe eingerichtet werden und ein Restrukturierungssystem für in Schieflage geratene Banken geschaffen werden.

Paul Kirchhof
Die Freiheit vom Staat ist die Grundlage moderner Staatlichkeit. Die Gegenwart eines freiheitsgewährleistenden Staates wird von steigenden Freiheitserwartungen an den Staat bestimmt. Diese Erwartungen drängen auf Veränderung unserer Entscheidungsmaßstäbe. Freiheit berechtigt nicht zu Zahlungen aus der Staatskasse, sondern Freiheit meint Handeln auf eigene Chance und eigenes Risiko.

Kai A. Konrad
Die auf europäischer Ebene derzeit diskutierten Reformen der Finanzverfassung der EU sind zwar radikal. Sie sind aber ungeeignet, die europäische Staatsschuldenkrise langfristig zu überwinden. Das Versagen des Stabilitäts- und Wachstumspakts in Europa hat seine Ursachen nicht in den Regeln des Pakts selbst. Die Ursachen liegen vielmehr im wirtschaftlichen und politischen Umfeld und insbesondere in Schwächen des privaten Finanzmarktsystems begründet. Deshalb muss eine erfolgversprechende Therapie dort und nicht bei einer Reform der europäischen Haushaltsregeln ansetzen.

Stefan Korioth

Die Rettungsmaßnahmen für Griechenland und den Euro, die von der Europäischen Union und den Mitgliedstaaten im Frühjahr 2010 in aller Eile getroffen wurden, waren unionsrechtlich fragwürdig, politisch aber verständlich. Sie haben noch einmal gezeigt, welches Wagnis es ist, eine Währungsunion ohne politische Union in Gang zu setzen und aufrechtzuerhalten. Die gemeinsame Währung ohne gemeinsamen Finanzminister wird auch in Zukunft Probleme bereiten. Hier muss sich die Union weiterentwickeln.

Christoph G. Paulus

Das moderne Insolvenzrecht hält die Option bereit, statt allein marktbereinigender Liquidation die Restrukturierung des Schuldners herbeizuführen. Im Falle der Zahlungsunfähigkeit von Souveränen geht es allein um die Restrukturierungsvariante. Die Vorteile eines solchen Resolvenzrechts für Staaten sind eindeutig: ein klar vorgegebenes Verfahren und dadurch eine größere Haushaltsdisziplin. Die Zeit dafür ist reif. Europa könnte ein Vorreiter sein.

Burkhard Schwenker

Unabhängig von Spekulationen gegen den Euro und finanzwirtschaftlichen Problemen vieler EU-Staaten bleibt eine Erkenntnis aus der Finanz- und Wirtschaftskrise richtig: Die industrielle Kompetenz Europas wird eine entscheidende Rolle spielen, wenn es um Wachstum, Beschäftigung und Wettbewerbsvorteile geht. Und über noch etwas sollten wir selbstbewusst reden: Unsere Unternehmen werden geführt von einem Management, das einen besonders erfolgreichen, spezifisch europäischen Weg eingeschlagen hat. Schuldenabbau und Wachstumsinvestitionen, beides kann uns gelingen, wenn wir die richtigen Rahmenbedingungen schaffen.

AUTOREN UND TEIL-NEHMER CONVOCO 2010

Prof. Dr. h.c. Roland Berger ist Gründer und Vorsitzender des Aufsichtsrats von Roland Berger Strategy Consultants, München. Studium der Betriebswirtschaftslehre in München und Hamburg. 1971–1972 Lehrbeauftragter für Marketing und Werbung an der Technischen Universität München. Seit 1996 Gastprofessor, seit 2000 Honorarprofessor für Betriebswirtschaft und Unternehmensberatung an der Brandenburgischen Technischen Universität Cottbus. Mitglied der Hochschulräte der Ludwig-Maximilians-Universität und der Hochschule für Musik und Theater, München, des Kuratoriums des ifo Instituts für Wirtschaftsforschung an der Universität München und des Boards der Business School INSEAD. Er gehört verschiedenen internationalen Beiräten und Aufsichtsräten an. Seit 2008 Vorsitzender des Kuratoriums der Roland Berger Stiftung.

Sir Howard Davies ist Direktor der London School of Economics and Political Science. 1997–2003 Chairman der Financial Services Authority. Drei Jahre lang Generaldirektor der Confederation of British Industry, zwei Jahre stellvertretender Direktor der Bank von England. 1987–1992 Controller in der Audit Commission, 1982–1987 bei McKinsey & Company, London. 1985–1986 Sonderberater des Schatzkanzlers. Davor beim Treasury und beim Foreign and Commonwealth Office. Zwei Jahre Privatsekretär des britischen Botschafters in Paris. Studium am Merton College, Oxford. MA in Geschichte und Neueren Sprachen, 1980 MSc in Management Sciences an der Stanford Graduate School of Business, California. 2002–2010 Trustee der Tate, Mitglied des Aufsichtsgremiums der Royal Academy of Music, 2004 Honorary Fellowship am Merton College, seit 2004 u. a. im Board von Morgan Stanley. Publikationen u. a.: »The Chancellors' Tales« (2006), »Global Financial Regulation: The Essential Guide« (2008).

Dr. Kai Engelbrecht, Studium der Rechtswissenschaft und Referendariat in Berlin; Promotion zum Dr. jur. 2009. Von 2003 bis 2008 Wissenschaftlicher Assistent am Lehrstuhl für Öffentliches Recht und Kirchenrecht der Universität München; derzeit Rechtsrat bei der Stadt Bad Reichenhall. Veröffentlichungen zum Staats- und Verwaltungsrecht, u. a. »Die Kollisionsregel im föderalen Ordnungsverbund« (2010). Dem Convoco Forum seit 2004 als Protokollführer verbunden.

Dr. Corinne Michaela Flick, Doppelstudium der Rechtswissenschaft und der Literaturwissenschaft mit Nebenfach Amerikanistik. Promotion zum Dr. phil. 1989. Rechtsanwältin bei der Bertelsmann Buch AG und bei Amazon.com. Seit 1998 auch Gesellschafterin der Vivil GmbH und Co. KG, Offenburg. Mitbegründerin des Freundeskreises der Bayerischen Staatsbibliothek München, Kuratoriumsmitglied der TU München und Mitglied des International

Councils der Tate Gallery, London. Gründerin und Vorstand der Convoco gemeinnützige Stiftungs-GmbH.

Prof. Dr. Dr. h.c. mult. Otmar Issing ist u. a. Vorsitzender des Kuratoriums des House of Finance, Universität Frankfurt (2007), Präsident des Center for Financial Studies (2006), International Advisor bei Goldman Sachs Int. (2006) und Mitglied des Advisory Board of Globalization and Monetary Policy Institute an der Federal Reserve Bank von Dallas. 1998–2006 Mitglied des Direktoriums der EZB, zuständig für die Generaldirektionen Volkswirtschaft und Volkswirtschaftliche Forschung. 1990–1998 Mitglied des Direktoriums und des Zentralbankrates der Deutschen Bundesbank. 1988–1990 Mitglied des Sachverständigenrates zur Begutachtung der gesamtwirtschaftlichen Entwicklung. 2008 Leitung der Issing-Kommission. 2008–2009 Mitglied der De Larosière Kommission. Honorarprofessor in Frankfurt (2007) und Würzburg (1991). Professor für VWL in Würzburg (1973–1990) und Erlangen-Nürnberg (1967–1973). Träger des Großen Bundesverdienstkreuzes. Ehrendoktorwürden der Universitäten Frankfurt, Konstanz und Bayreuth. Ordentliches Mitglied der Akademie der Wissenschaften und der Literatur sowie der Academia Scientiarum et Artium Europaea.

Prof. Dr. Dr. h.c. mult. Paul Kirchhof, Promotion zum Dr. jur. 1968, Habilitation 1974, ord. Professor für Öffentliches Recht und Steuerrecht in Münster 1975–1981, seit 1981 in Heidelberg. Richter des Bundesverfassungsgerichts 1987–1999, Veröffentlichungen im Staats-, Verwaltungs- und Steuerrecht, u. a. »Besteuerungsgewalt und Grundgesetz« (1973), »Verwalten durch mittelbares Einwirken« (1976), »Die kulturellen Voraussetzungen der Freiheit« (1995), »Der sanfte Verlust der Freiheit. Für ein neues Steuerrecht« (2004), »Das Gesetz der Hydra« (2006), »Das Maß der Gerechtigkeit – Bringt unser Land wieder ins Gleichgewicht!« (2009).

Prof. Dr. Kai A. Konrad, Promotion (1990) und Habilitation (1993) an der Universität München. Er hat an den Universitäten München, Bonn, Bergen (Norwegen) und an der University of California in Irvine geforscht und unterrichtet. 1994–2009 Universitätsprofessor im Fachbereich Wirtschaftswissenschaft an der Freien Universität Berlin und 2001–2009 Direktor am Wissenschaftszentrum Berlin für Sozialforschung. Seit 2009 Direktor am Max-Planck-Institut für Geistiges Eigentum, Wettbewerbs- und Steuerrecht, München. Co-Editor des »Journal of Public Economics« und im Herausgebergremium einer Anzahl weiterer internationaler Fachzeitschriften. Mitglied des Wissenschaftlichen Beirats beim Bundesministerium der Finanzen und seit 2007 dessen Stellvertretender Vorsitzender.

Prof. Dr. Stefan Korioth, Promotion zum Dr. jur. 1990, Habilitation für Öffentliches Recht und Verfassungsgeschichte, ord. Professor für Öffentliches Recht 1996–2000, Verfassungsgeschichte und Staatslehre in Greifswald, seit

2000 Leiter des Lehrstuhls Öffentliches Recht und Kirchenrecht an der Ludwig-Maximilians-Universität München; Veröffentlichungen u. a.: »Integration und Bundesstaat« (1990), »Der Finanzausgleich zwischen Bund und Ländern« (1997), »Grundzüge des Staatskirchenrechts« (mit B. Jean d'Heur, 2000), »Das Bundesverfassungsgericht« (zusammen mit Klaus Schlaich, 7. Auflage 2007).

Prof. Dr. Christoph G. Paulus, LL.M. (Berkeley), Studium der Rechte in München, Promotion zum Dr. jur. 1980, Habilitation im Bürgerlichen und Zivilprozessrecht sowie im Römischen Recht 1991, Auszeichnung der Habilschrift mit der Medaille der Universität Paris II, 1989–1990 Feodor Lynen-Stipendiat der Humboldt-Stiftung in Berkeley. Ord. Professor in Augsburg 1992–1993, seit 1994 an der Juristischen Fakultät der Humboldt-Universität zu Berlin, 2008–2010 Dekan ebd. Seit 2009 Leiter des Instituts für Interdisziplinäre Restrukturierung e.V., Berater des Internationalen Währungsfonds, Mitglied des International Insolvency Institute, des American College of Bankruptcy, Fachgutachter des DAAD, Berater der Weltbank. Herausgeber der Zeitschrift »Computer und Recht«, Mitarbeiter der »EWiR«, Mitherausgeber der Internetzeitschrift »Forum historiae iuris«, Herausgeberbeirat der Zeitschriften »Multimedia und Recht« und »ZIP«, Mitredakteur des Technical Paper zum World Bank Insolvency Project.

Prof. Dr. Dr. h.c. Wolfgang Schön, Promotion zum Dr. jur. 1985, Habilitation im Bürgerlichen Recht, Handels-,

Wirtschafts- und Steuerrecht 1992, ord. Professor in Bielefeld 1992–1996, Bonn 1996–2002, Direktor am Max-Planck-Institut für Geistiges Eigentum, Wettbewerbs- und Steuerrecht in München seit 2002, Honorarprofessor an der Ludwig-Maximilians-Universität München, Mitglied des Wissenschaftlichen Beirats beim Bundesministerium der Finanzen (2003–2006), Vizepräsident der Max-Planck-Gesellschaft seit 2008. Zahlreiche Veröffentlichungen zum deutschen und europäischen Gesellschafts-, Bilanz- und Steuerrecht.

Prof. Dr. Burkhard Schwenker, seit 1. 8. 2010 Vorsitzender des Aufsichtsrats von Roland Berger Strategy Consultants. Zuvor seit 1998 Mitglied der Geschäftsführung und seit 2003 Vorsitzender des Global Executive Committees der Strategieberatung. Seit 1. 9. 2010 Vorsitzender des Vorstands der Roland Berger Stiftung. Nach Studium der Betriebswirtschaftslehre (Dipl. Kfm.) und Mathematik eine erste berufliche Station bei den PWA Papierwerken Waldhof-Aschaffenburg und Promotion. Seit 1989 bei Roland Berger Strategy Consultants, seit 1992 Partner. Beratungsschwerpunkte Strategie, Organisation und Unternehmenstransformation. Professor für strategisches Management an der Handelshochschule Leipzig, Vorstand der Stiftung der EBS, im Hochschulrat der TU Bergakademie Freiberg, Mitglied der Wissenschaftlichen Gesellschaft für Marketing und Unternehmensführung, der Gesellschaft für Unternehmensgeschichte und der Deutschen Gesellschaft für Auswärtige Politik. Visiting Fellow an der

Saïd Business School der Universität Oxford. Unter anderem stellvertretender Vorsitzender der Atlantik-Brücke e.V. sowie in den Kuratorien des WWF, der Stiftung Deutsche Sporthilfe, der Wertekommission e.V. und des Stifterverbands für die Deutsche Wissenschaft. Zudem Stiftungsrat der Roland Berger Stiftung für europäische Unternehmensführung.